# The
# Void

By
## Brett J. Talley

JournalStone
San Francisco

JournalStone books may be ordered through booksellers or by contacting:

JournalStone
199 State Street
San Mateo, CA 94401
www.journalstone.com

The views expressed in this work are solely those of the authors and do not necessarily reflect the views of the publisher, and the publisher hereby disclaims any responsibility for them.

ISBN:   978-1-936564-43-9     (sc)
ISBN:   978-1-936564-44-6     (hc)
ISBN:   978-1-936564-45-3     (ebook)

Library of Congress Control Number:     2012935828

Printed in the United States of America
JournalStone rev. date: July 13, 2012


Cover Design:   Denise Daniel
Cover Art:       Philip Renne

Edited By: Elizabeth Reuter

# INTRODUCTION

"What Dreams May Come": An Introduction to Brett Talley's *The Void*.

By

## Dr. Michael R. Collings,

Author of *The Slab, The House Beyond the Hill,* and other tales of wonder and fear.

When I was first approached to write an introduction to Brett Talley's new novel, *The Void,* I had two reactions.

First, I felt an immediate sense of… well, of *inevitability*. After all, a little over two years ago, I had published *In the Void: Poems of Science Fiction, Myth and Fantasy, & Horror* (Wildside, 2009), and here was a new opportunity to explore the mysteries of that fascinating, that frightening place. Since my expedition had been by way of poetry, surely Talley's prose would introduce new possibilities… and perhaps new terrors.

Second, I had already met Talley's work through the mediation of his first novel, the Bram Stoker Award-nominated *That Which Should Not Be* (JournalStone, 2011), a more-than-creditable H. P. Lovecraft *pastiche* that brought new life to conventions long considered stale and passé. The book had not only captured the essence of the Lovecraftian Chtulhu mythos in its quartet of tales-within-a-tale but did so with sufficient ease to allow loving sidelong glances not only at Lovecraft's typical people, places, and things but also at suggestions of Bram Stoker, H. G. Wells, and other fantasists. Reading it had been, in fact, a delight.

So, of course, I agreed. Who could pass up an opportunity to enter the unknown with an author who had already demonstrated not only his capacity as a writer but his mastery of his craft?

Then I read the first line of *The Void*: June 18, 2159.

What's this? The *future*? Where is the darkness, the mystery, the horror?

This sounds like *Science-fiction*, which, though I enjoy and appreciate it, is not what I anticipated from Talley.

But I had agreed, so I continued reading.
Wise choice.

*The Void* **is** science-fictional. It takes place in the near-future, in a universe in which star travel has become possible through the invention of a warp drive that, triggered near the outer reaches of the Solar System, enables ships to move almost instantly to distant stars, systems, and quadrants. Earth's entire economy—and, of course, the economies of all of the colony worlds—has become dependent upon the new technology. As a result, star flight has become so commonplace as to become almost mundane.

Almost….

Because there is one, small—infinitesimally small, actually—problem. To pass through the warp and remain sane, passengers and crew must all submit to a stasis-sleep… and in that sleep, come the Dreams.

Everyone has them, without exception. For each individual the Dream is always the same, no matter how often the dreamer enters stasis. More than that, the Dream remains with the dreamer, upon waking, haunting, pervasive, foreshadowing images that must inevitably recur the next time, on the next flight.

Even more than that, the Dreams *terrify*. And occasionally, they drive certain dreamers to madness. Or to death.

Ahhh, here it comes, the *horror*. Talley plays his cards close to the chest, so the reader is well immersed in an ostensible science-fictional narrative before—word by word, phrase by phrase, image by image—he reveals the darkness beneath the technology, the threat that presents itself first through the Dreams and then by its determination to intrude into *this* world.

His language occasionally feels Lovecraftian, but his version of the Great Old Ones, Lovecraft's survivors from a previous, highly advanced stage of the universe, is not; his terrors are his own. There are no *eldritch* horrors in *The Void*; no monolithic buildings employing skewed, crazed architecture; no tentacled fungoid monstrosities waiting for some misled magician to chant arcane passages from the *Necronomicon* and invite them again into our world.

The shadows in the Dreams are far worse, because in part, they reside within each of the Dreamers.

Talley reveals the truth with masterful pacing and precision. At times he rivets us in this reality through his use of hard-edged, solid, scientifically-oriented prose. At other times, he urges us to see beyond this reality by lengthy passages that are poetic in their fluidity, their movement, their ability to conjure images of time and space and possibility. Yet throughout the book, he continually returns to the Dreams, the Dreams and their impact upon the dreamers.

I'm tempted to go further, to disclose more of the secrets that the small crew of the *Chronos* must uncover for themselves as they struggle with their Dreams... and with their life-threatening encounters with Black Holes, with nameless shadows and whisperings, with treachery and betrayal, with the enigmas contained within the derelict ship *Singularity*... and within their own imaginations.

I'm tempted... I will, however, restrain myself, and conclude with these few words.

*Read on. Enjoy. But be afraid to Dream.*

# ENDORSEMENTS

# ACKNOWLEDGEMENTS

When I published my first novel, there were so many people to thank that it seemed imprudent to attempt to thank them all by name. While that has not changed, I'm growing reckless in my old age. Or maybe there are just people who need to know exactly how much I appreciate them. So to my parents Mike and Sue who infected me at a young age with a love for books; to Erin who convinced me to start writing in the first place; to Marguerite and Anna who read this book and offered invaluable advice; to Annie whose endless enthusiasm and faith was infectious and kept me going when it seemed like I had hit a wall; to Christopher Payne for believing in me and this book, and to Dusty Parrish and all the soldiers and families who make the ultimate sacrifice so that we all have the freedom to put pen to paper—to you I give my thanks, my love, and my undying gratitude.

In the beginning God created the heaven and the earth.
And the earth was without form, and void;
and darkness was upon the face of the deep.
And the Spirit of God moved upon the face of the waters.
And God said, Let there be light: and there was light.
And God saw the light, that it was good:
and God divided the light from the darkness.

– Genesis 1:1-4


Und wenn du lange in einen Abgrund blickst,
blickt der Abgrund auch in dich hinein.

– Friedrich Neitzsche

# PROLOGUE

June 18, 2159

The dreams will stop. That's what they tell us will happen, if we succeed, at least. That was enough for me, for all of us. Sometimes, I think everything in my life comes down to those impossible dreams. They never were dreams, though. Not really. Not to me. I call them that only because that's what the lab guys, the scientists and the psychologists called them. Just "resonance in neural circuits." I guess that is why I am making this entry in my log. I hope they end, but I do not want to forget. I do not want to believe the lies. They have not seen. They do not know.

The last one was the same as the first. It was the same as them all. A valley opens up before me. But it is unlike anything I have ever seen. There are no majestic cliffs, no free-flowing waters or forests clinging to its sides. No. Hell has come to this place. The ground is scorched and barren. There is no life there, nor will there ever be. I can see dimly; the pallid yellow of the cloudless sky bears down on me like coming twilight. Even though there is no sun. Even though this place lies between the darkness and the light. In shadow. Though what casts that shadow, I cannot know, nor do I wish to. But the light is enough that as I walk down that valley toward its end, toward *the* end, as it narrows to a point where I do not know if I can go on, I can see *them*.

They stand along the valley's edge on both sides. High above me. Silent and unmoving. Figures, black. Hooded and cloaked, perhaps. But I think not. They are the shadow itself. Their eyes are ever upon me, though they do not move. For they do have eyes. Great pools of emptiness where their faces should be. And they speak to me. In whispered words and phrases. In wisps of cool breeze that seem to surround me, though the air is still and hot. What do they say? Can I know? Somehow I do. But whatever that truth may be, I cannot bear to repeat it here. I cannot tell what cannot be denied.

For ten years, I have walked down that valley. Every endless night I have seen them. And they have haunted me, even in waking. I have told no one, and neither will I. Wouldn't they think me mad? If I told them how the shadow figures watch me? How I see them sometimes, reposing under the streetlight beside my home? How they stand and do not move? Their cold, never-blinking eyes?

How I have found them in photographs, even those from my childhood? Lurking in the distance? Nameless sentries on the edge of existence and the frame? How I can feel them, standing behind me, even now? Their cold breath on my neck? And if I turn? How I catch them in the corner of my eye, even if they vanish by the time I look fully upon them? Yes, they would think me mad. And a mad man is most unwelcome in the void.

# CHAPTER
# 1

*Ten years later*

Aidan Connor woke to light. It was white and blinding and pure, but provided no heat. It held him, that light, and he wondered if he had died. He thought he had and that this place was Heaven. But his eyes cleared and the light sank into the steel ceiling above.

He tried to sit up, but felt pain burn through his body like molten lead. He winced and let his eyes veer down the white sheet that covered him to the robotic spider that crawled up and down his left leg. Then he noticed the hair on his face, the scratchy discomfort of a beard unkempt, one that he did not remember growing. For a second he thought it was a dream. No, not *a* dream, *the* dream, for no sleeping fantasy was ever so real as that. Then he remembered. The dream was always the same, and it was not this. No, this was no dream.

The world began to spin and he fell into blackness again.

He awoke to the sound of the door sliding open, and the first thing his gaze met was the image of a woman with chestnut-brown hair peering over him. She was dressed in white, as bright as the light above. She looked like his mother.

She had died when he was born, but Aidan had kept a photograph of her, taken when she was only nineteen. But something was off, something about this woman's eyes. They weren't right. Neither was her hair.

She smiled and tapped something on the paper-thin plastic sheet she held. It flickered and flashed a thousand different colors as she said, "Good, you're awake. My name is Dr. Jackson. I'm the medical officer on

~15~

board."

"Where am I?" he asked. He caught a glimpse of the spider as it marched across the sheet to his other leg.

"Sick bay," she said as she turned and pressed a button on the wall. A glass screen retracted and she removed a vial of liquid from inside, placing it in the back of a long tube. "You don't remember anything?" she said, taking his arm.

"Nothing."

"This is going to sting."

He heard the whoosh as the medicine was injected, but did not feel it. He looked up at her and arched an eyebrow.

"Hmmm," she said. "Well, it's not to worry. A little sensory collapse is not unusual. All in all, you're pretty lucky."

"And what about that thing?" Aidan said, pointing to the mechanical arachnid now making its way to his toes.

"Charlotte? Well, you had some burns on your legs. She's just fixing you up. Are you up to talking some more? I think Lieutenant Oxford wants to speak with you."

"Lieutenant?"

She smiled and put her hand on his shoulder. "This is probably going to come as a shock," she said. "But this is a military ship. The USS *Alabama*. The medical ship attached to the *Agamemnon* carrier group. We found you three days ago in a capsule, floating between Neptune and Pluto. You're lucky we came across your escape pod. I don't think you would've made it much longer out there." She smiled again and the compassion in her eyes scared him. "Anyway, I'll tell her you're tired, alright? That should give you a few hours."

"No," he said. When he grabbed her arm, he saw a flicker of fear race across her face, even though military training taught their personnel never to show it. "No," he repeated more quietly, letting her go. "I'd rather go ahead and see her. I've got some questions too."

She looked at him for a long moment and then the smile returned. "All right. I'll send her in."

Dr. Jackson walked to the far wall, the door appearing from nowhere and sliding away. He saw the world outside for a moment, as pure and white as the room in which he lay. She stepped into that world beyond and turned to him. She smiled and nodded and the door slid closed in a flash. Then it was just him and the whirring hiss of the spider as it seemed to devour his big toe.

Forty-five minutes—maybe an hour—passed before the door opened again. In stepped a woman. Well, a girl really, but something about the way her hair was pulled back tight, severely against her scalp, or maybe the way her blue Navy uniform hung loosely around her body, made her appear older. She saw Aidan look up at her, and when he did she smiled perfunctorily and without guile.

"Good evening, Mr. Connor. My name is Lieutenant Oxford. I'm happy to see you're awake." She walked over to the side table, removing a thin, flexible plastic sheet—a computer—from the pad of such sheets that sat upon it. In an instant, it interfaced with the ship's main system, loading all the information she needed to access. As she tapped the middle of her screen, Aidan did not think she looked happy. Then she simply stood, staring down at the image, apparently reading whatever it displayed.

"Ma'am?"

"Yes?" she said without looking up.

"Can you tell me what happened?"

"Well," she replied, sliding her index finger down to the bottom of the clear sheet in her hands, "we were hoping that you would help us with that. Do you mind if I record this?"

"No," he said, feeling worried for the first time. "Not at all."

She tapped the pad and a click resonated throughout the room as a camera turned on. "Now," she began, "tell me what you remember."

She looked at him and waited. He thought for a second but didn't remember much of anything.

"The last thing you remember."

It came to him suddenly and he didn't like it. He breathed in deep and started to lie, but as he glanced up at her, he got the feeling she had an ear for bullshit. So instead, he just sighed.

"Angela," he said finally.

"Angela?" He could tell by the expression on her face that the name was not in whatever folder she had been perusing. "Your wife?"

He chuckled for the first time since he had woken up. "No. No, my girlfriend. My ex-girlfriend. It was the last conversation we had before . . ."

He looked up at her with a start that had to tell her he had remembered.

". . .before I left on my last run."

"On the *Vespa*."

"Yes," he said, "the *Vespa*."

It was coming back to him in flashes, images and fragments of spoken conversations. He remembered that night on the beach, when Angela had asked him to give it up—to never fly another route or if he did to only do local runs. The nightmares had become too much for her. The nightmares that were but shadows, echoes of the dream. If only she could see what was in his head . . . Well, it might have driven her as mad as he sometimes thought he was.

But he couldn't leave. It was a good job. The best someone like him could ever hope to have. He tried to explain that, to convince her that staying on with the Merchant Marine was as good for her as it was for him. But she wouldn't hear his arguments and she left the beach behind, her crying and him confused and angry. Yes, he remembered that. He remembered everything before it. It was what followed that was hard, and he knew that was the most important thing of all.

"I'm sorry," he said, sensing her impatience. "I'm doing the best I can. I really am."

"Well," she said, "let's start from what we know. We found you in the trans-Neptunian void, at the edge of the warp zone. We had just dropped out of hyperspace and there you were. In fact, it appears that your escape pod had traveled some distance after the . . . incident." He didn't like the way she paused. "You had been in there six weeks from what we can tell."

"Six weeks!" She stared at him for a second before nodding. In truth, he had known it would be something like that, but it still shocked him to hear it.

"Six weeks. Your computer recognized you were injured, of course, and kept you in stasis. It's the only reason you are still alive."

"Thank God for modern miracles," he murmured.

"Yes . . . In any event, that means the accident happened beyond Pluto. And that's where we have a problem, Mr. Connor."

If it weren't for everything that had happened, this would all make sense. If he were in his right mind, he would know what she was implying, instead of lying there stupidly, Charlotte the spider the only being in the room not locked in some bizarre melodrama. Suddenly, through his fog-shrouded mind, he understood.

"We shouldn't have been there."

"No," she said simply, "you shouldn't have. Non-warp, trans-stellar travel is of course forbidden beyond the solar sheath, for obvious reasons. If a ship in warp were to—"

"Yes, yes," he said dully. It was one of the first things he had learned in flight school. "If a ship at warp speed were to intersect with one in normal space, the result would be catastrophic."

"Absolutely."

"So is that what happened to the *Vespa*?" he asked, knowing the answer as he spoke the words.

"No. If it were, you wouldn't be here, Mr. Connor. And besides, we have analyzed the debris field and there's only enough there for one ship."

Aidan sighed deeply; now there was no denying it. "So she's gone."

"Yes, she is. And then there is the matter of this."

She waved her hand and an image appeared in mid-air. Aidan found himself looking into his own eyes, and there was a bit of insanity and fear he found truly terrifying. The image flickered in and out, but he could hear words and fragments, even if there was seldom enough to make out a coherent story.

"This is a mayday from the private transport *Vespa*." He heard himself say. It was the last full sentence he could understand. "Warp core . . . we . . . facing catastrophic . . . cannot contain . . . maybe an hour . . . minutes . . . must abandon . . . please assist . . ." Then the screen flickered again and died.

"That transmission," the Lieutenant explained, "was picked up by our listening station orbiting Jupiter. Rescue ships were dispatched, but scans showed no signs of life and it was too dangerous to approach the debris field. It was most fortunate that anyone found you, Mr. Connor. It could have been years before that escape pod reached well-traveled space and by then, you would probably have been dead."

He stared back at her. All of this was becoming too much for his mind to process.

"So, can you tell us what that message is all about? Does it ring any bells? Jog any memories?"

In truth, no matter how hard he tried, it did not. He remembered none of it, and watching his own lips deliver a message he couldn't recall was perhaps the most disconcerting experience of his life. He looked up at her, the answer written in his eyes.

"Alright." She sighed. "That's understandable. Honestly, short-term amnesia is a symptom of both trauma and stasis, so it's not altogether unexpected. But we had hoped maybe you would be different. In any event, I wouldn't worry too much about all this. Our computers have analyzed the debris field and your message. They estimate a 98.3% probability that you lost warp containment upon entering hyperspace. That shattered your core grid and forced an abandon ship. The resulting explosion destroyed all the escape pods but your own. As I said, Mr. Connor, you are truly a lucky man."

She smiled at him, and although this one was sincere, Aidan Connor had somehow never felt more unlucky in all his life.

# CHAPTER
# 2

Aidan had never been a passenger on a starship. His work before had left him with precious few moments of down time, so lying in a bed in the ship's infirmary made the hours crawl by. Charlotte had become his constant companion, and the sight of the robotic arachnid scurrying about his body no longer brought a tingle of fear. Within a week, he could walk, and Dr. Jackson had given him permission to leave the sick bay.

It had not started well.

He had expected it. The sideways glances, the questioning stares. He had spent enough time in space to know the suspicion that follows a survivor, the weight that hangs round his neck. Yes, he had expected it, and it would be with him all his days. However, it was not company he sought, but distraction. And the ship provided plenty of that.

It was an older vessel, ten years or more, too big for artificial gravity even though the technology had been perfected since its construction. Thus it was long and cigar-shaped, a vast metal tube that housed enough medical equipment to treat the battle fleet of which it was a part.

The central portion spun, and in spinning, it gave the illusion of gravity to those inside. Since gravity was an illusion anyway, no one ever knew the difference. He studied every part of it from stem to stern and the captain was even kind enough to allow him a visit to the bridge. The only portal to the outside was there; windows were always dangerous and did nothing but weaken the structural integrity of a ship.

From the bridge he was able to see Jupiter as it passed them by. More impressive was the carrier group itself, the massive *Agamemnon* thundering above the medical frigate—by far the largest vessel he had ever been in—dwarfing the *Alabama*. Yet even the wonders of the ship were finite, and once he had seen everything, the boredom returned.

The days crept by and at times it seemed they would never reach Earth orbit.

"You might as well relax," Dr. Jackson would say. "It's another two weeks till we get home."

Aidan frowned. The cargo ships he was accustomed to moved at much greater speed, and he had never had to sit and wait around like this before. He didn't want to act like a spoiled child but he couldn't help it. Dr. Jackson saw. "The fleet moves at its own speed, Mr. Connor. You know that. It's not as if we aren't all ready to get home. I've only got two patients on this trip and that's two more than I normally have."

If Aidan hadn't been looking, he might not have seen. But he was, and he did.

"Two patients?"

Dr. Jackson paused, and in that pause, Aidan knew he had come upon something that she had not meant to reveal. "Well . . ." she began, "we had an incident."

"An incident?"

Aidan watched as the doctor blushed and part of him felt bad for pushing the matter.

"I really shouldn't say anything else. It's a long story anyway."

"Doc," he said, "I've got nothing but time."

Everything, every tenet of her profession, every piece of common sense, every rule of etiquette, dictated that she stop there. That she say nothing else. But for any number of reasons, she did the opposite.

"Well, our mission was to Eridani," she said. "And of course, we had to jump."

Aidan saw her pause and he worried that the story was slipping. "And?" he urged.

She exhaled deeply and let herself fall into a chair. "We've all felt it," she said. "All of us. If you say you haven't, you're a liar. I hate the sleep." She stared at the floor, as if Aidan wasn't even there. "I hate it. Everyone does. It's the dreams, you know?" She looked up. "But of course you do. You've seen it too."

They sat there together, silently. In their minds' eyes, they saw the same thing. But different. Unique. Special to them both, in the way that only something so horrible can be special.

"They have testing, of course. Special testing for the Navy. You don't make the fleet unless you are rated to the point that you never should crack. And most people never do. But this trip. . ."

"God."

"Yeah."

It happened sometimes, more often than the spacing guilds wanted to admit. The people who worked the deep space trade didn't often talk about it. It was taboo. As if talking about the creeping madness had the power to bring it about. But sometimes people snapped, whether you talked about it or not.

He had heard that space didn't always drive men mad. Back when all anyone did was float around the Earth, go to the moon. Then space was an adventure. But it wasn't like that anymore. People said that the problems began when men started going farther. To Mars. Venus. Beyond.

The general consensus was that Earth was the key. People were fine when they could see Earth. When it was just beyond them. Like they could reach out and touch it. But when it was no more than a great, big, blue star . . . when it was gone, truly, irrevocably gone . . . then they would break. And it's a dangerous thing, that. Nothing worse than a madman when you are oh-so-very far from home.

That was a lie, of course. A shroud to cover a darker truth, one that no one wanted to face. But he knew, just as they all did. It wasn't Earth. It wasn't the distance. Not just the distance, anyway. The distance probably had some effect, when the dreams came. And they always did. It was the dreams they all feared.

"I just feel so awful," Dr. Jackson said. "Lieutenant Felix was such a good kid."

"Was it his first trip?"

"How did you know?" she said.

He shrugged. "I've heard that's when it normally happens. If you make it through your first time, you can probably keep it together."

"Probably," she said. "But there have been those who have been in the deep for decades. And then one day . . ." She snapped her fingers, and Aidan shuddered.

"And that's what happened to Lieutenant Felix?"

"Yes," she said. "The fleet assembled a month ago at Armstrong. It was a routine mission, out to Eridani. We were on a six-month cruise. Basic maneuvers."

"But that's not how it worked out?"

"Not quite."

There was a chirping sound from Charlotte. The doctor pushed a button and Captain Gravely's face appeared in midair.

One command from the captain later, and Aidan was alone with the rumble of the ship's engines and the soft whir of the spider's computer. Jackson left him with more questions than answers, and he needed to know the rest. For the same reasons, no doubt, that Jackson wanted to tell him. And so he made a decision.

"Charlotte, what level is Lieutenant Felix being held on?"

A screen appeared above the spider's head and displayed the schematics for level two. It was probably a foolish decision, and he doubted anything would come of it, but his curiosity was too great. He left the infirmary behind.

He had become familiar to most of the crew, and though he would call none of them friends, they mostly left him alone. It was not difficult to find the brig. A lone MP sat at the console near its entrance, and if he was surprised to see Aidan, he didn't show it.

At first, he simply stood at the entrance. Of course, Aidan had known there would be a guard, but for some reason, he had not taken the time to think up an excuse. Thus he simply told the truth.

"I'd like to see Lieutenant Felix."

The MP looked at him for a while. He opened his mouth, like he wanted to say something but then his eyes went hazy and his face seemed to go limp.

"Felix, huh?" he finally said, looking back down at his console.

"So you want to see the murderer."

"Murderer?"

Aidan was shocked. Well, almost. But not really.

"They say he's crazy, you know?" the man said, standing up and walking over to Aidan, stopping only a few inches from his face. He was so close that Aidan could taste his breath. "That he didn't know what he was doing. That the dreams made him do it. Can you believe that? Not that he would be the first . . . or the last."

The man laughed but Aidan didn't laugh with him. They stared at each other for several awkward seconds that seemed to stretch to eternity, but then the man said, "I mean, we've all had them right? We've all seen it. We've all seen . . . *them.* But I never killed anybody. Have you?" Then he laughed again.

"I just want to see him," Aidan said. "If that's all right."

The man's smile faded.

"Be my guest," he said. "Maybe you can figure it out. They know where he got the ax, of course. Fire control. But when did he wake up? Why? And what did Ensign Kelly do to deserve that?"

"He killed him with an ax?"

The man cocked his head to the right and looked at Aidan like he was a fool. "Of course he did."

"Yes," Aidan said, "of course he did."

The MP shook his head and looked down at the computer in his hands. Aidan was about to say something else when a metal door opened that led to a long row of cells. Aidan stood there, half-expecting the guard to change his mind. But the man only stared at him.

Aidan stepped through the portal and shivered as the door slid shut behind him. The brig was no different than any other room on the ship. The same white walls, the same bright lights flooding down over him. Only one cell was occupied.

There was no door. No bars. Just an empty space where the door should be. Only the slight shimmer of the atmosphere, the electricity that tingled up and down his spine, let Aidan know that something other than thin air separated them.

Lieutenant Felix sat in the corner of his cell. His head was against the wall but his eyes were on Aidan. It was as if he was expecting him.

"Hello, Aidan Connor," he said. Then he smiled, and the look in those eyes told Aidan that he relished the shock in his own. Aidan knew the obvious question, but he refused to offer it.

"Hello, Lieutenant Felix."

"Well, now that the introductions are out of the way . . ." Felix trailed off into silence, and the two men regarded each other until Aidan asked the first thing that came to mind.

"Why are you here?"

The grin came slowly to Felix's face, but the laugh was hot on its heels. "Oh, Mr. Connor. I'm where I'm supposed to be. You, however, are not where you belong."

"And how would you know anything about me?"

Still grinning, Felix pulled himself to his feet. Aidan watched as he walked to the boundary between them, running his hand down the barrier, making the field crackle. "You ask as if you do not know," he said finally. "You ask as if I shouldn't know. But I know many things. I have witnessed many things. Many things indeed. Many things about *you*."

The smile faded and something about Felix's calm demeanor unnerved Aidan until he could no longer stand it. "You can play games with me, Lieutenant, but convincing me you're insane will do you no good." As he said it, Aidan hoped that this *was* an act. But somehow he knew it was not.

"Mr. Connor, I'm not insane. I've simply seen things that you have not. Seen things you cannot imagine. Seen you."

The air seemed to grow thick and heavy around Aidan, and the electric hum drilled into his brain. The image in front of him began to shake, to twist, to shimmer like it had when Felix had touched the force field between them.

Aidan wavered on the verge of collapse and he felt as though he might be sick. But the wave passed and there stood Felix, clear as day, glaring at him. For the first time, Aidan wondered why he had come here, why he had felt compelled to do so. Even as he wondered, he knew the answer to his own questions.

"I've never met you before in my life."

Felix grinned and looked at Aidan the way a parent might a child when faced with disappointment. "Come now, Mr. Connor, it's not of such ordinary things that I speak, as you are well aware. In life, we have never met. But in death? Perhaps."

"Why did you kill Ensign Kelly?"

"Why do you want to know?" Felix asked, allowing Aidan to change the subject. Silence greeted the question and Felix's eyes grew cold. "I killed him to save us all."

"To save us? To save who? From what?"

Felix's eyes now rested somewhere over Aidan's shoulder, in the middle distance between here and there. He spoke truth to deaf ears.

"All of us. This ship. The fleet. Maybe more. I knew they would not believe and so it fell to me. To do what I must. And in even your eyes I see the doubt; even in the eyes of one who should know."

"I don't understand."

Felix laughed. "There is a hole in your mind, Mr. Connor. A gap in your consciousness. But it is no matter. You will see them again. You will see the ones who took Ensign Kelly. Who would have taken us all. Who almost took me. In that moment, when they held me in their hands, my eyes opened. And I saw beyond this ship to worlds as yet unknown. To darkened seas and night-black suns. I saw you. I know what you did, Mr. Connor. Even if no one else does. I know. And I know this too—a time will come when you will be called upon. In your hands will rest the fate of many. Perhaps then you can redeem your lost soul."

Aidan did not speak as Felix backed away from him. He watched as the other man let his back hit the wall, sliding down to the floor below. The conversation was over, and Aidan had no more answers than when he came. He pressed a panel on the wall, and the door to the outside world slid open again. The MP spun around in his chair and looked up at him with a mixture of shock and fear.

"How the hell did you get in there?" he asked.

Aidan didn't bother to answer but walked back to the infirmary. Dr. Jackson was waiting as he stepped inside.

"Ah, Mr. Connor, I was just about to see if I could find you," she said, holding a vial of his daily medication in her hands. He smiled but said nothing as she injected it. It stung considerably now, a good sign.

"Did you make it down to see Lieutenant Felix?" she asked.

"I did."

"I knew you'd go. Too curious for your own good. I guess you managed to sweet talk your way past the guard?" Aidan nodded while she shook her head. "Well, I suppose that turned out to be an unproductive visit, huh?"

"What do you mean?"

Dr. Jackson looked up at him and smirked. "Well it must have been a rather one-sided conversation. Lieutenant Felix hasn't said a word since we found him."

\* \* \*

The evening was an illusion, the night a myth. In space there was no sun, no moon. Darkness, yes, but no night. Only the image of the thing, a creation of lighting and shade.

But the human mind is no more made for eternal sunlight than endless darkness and so every day at 7:03 p.m., the lights would begin to dim. By ten o'clock, the feeling of evening was complete. One might, if he were so inclined, mistake the gently curving corridors for the lanes of a Paris neighborhood, the sidewalks of Central Park.

Aidan sought solace there, when sleep would not come. He found himself wandering the halls of the ship at night, feeling the emptiness within. As long as he avoided the glare of the bridge or the engine room, he could almost believe that he was not millions of miles from Earth.

So it was that night, the last night that he left his room, before he decided it was better to stay locked behind his door, hoping that it would not open on its own. It was a night not that different from most nights.

The gentle hum of the engines, ever-present, no matter how far from them one might be. The ripple of the video walls, never really off, ready to deliver messages to whomever might require them. The soft kiss of the circulator breeze, refreshing the air and cooling the skin. Perhaps it was for that reason—how normal the night was—that he noticed the change just before he turned the corner of an otherwise insignificant hallway.

At the time he noticed only a tingle—a slight pulse of electricity as it rolled up his arm. When he thought on it later, he remembered more, things that he had not known then, though he should have. Remembered the smell, acrid and sharp, like the scent of burning leather. Remembered the tremor, as if the ship shifted from its place— moved to somewhere beyond where it should be. Remembered the sound, the tinkling timbre of chimes on the back porch at the house he lived in as a child when the wind would blow from the north. Remembered the cold chill, the one that seemed to come from within rather than from without, and remembered that even in the night, the world around him seemed to grow darker.

If he had known these things then, if he had felt them, sensed them, in any way other than his subconscious, maybe he would have turned and ran. Fled from whatever was before him, back across whatever threshold he had crossed when the world changed. But he did not. Instead, he paused for an instant, cocking his head to the side to hear a sound that he didn't even know was there, only to keep walking without another thought. He did not walk for long.

He saw it as soon as he turned the corner, but even as he stopped dead, he whispered to himself it was just an illusion. A trick of the mind. Or of his dreams maybe, a half-remembered nightmare lived and relived over those last twenty years.

It stood at the end of the hallway, reposed in the depths of that unnatural night.

He watched it for a long moment, one that seemed to stretch into infinity, and later he would wonder if more time passed in that hallway than he had thought. He stood and it stood, though it did not stand still. There was motion all about it, though what moved and what did not, he couldn't tell. Or maybe he simply shook so profoundly that the world moved with him.

It happened in an instant, and somehow he knew it was coming. He watched as the thing took a step forward. Lurched might be a better description, as he could not say whether its body had legs.

Looking upon his nightmare, Aidan couldn't run. Yet even in his fear, he knew that it had not come for him.

There was a crackling hiss and Aidan felt his legs go weak and his vision go black. He grabbed the wall and his sight cleared. The hallway was empty. The smell was gone, and the light was as dimly clear as always on those gray half-lit nights. Aidan was alone, the gentle rumble of the ship his only companion.

He did not linger long in that place, nor did he leave his room in the nights that followed. Whether the figure was figment or dream would remain unknown to him; his mind could not handle the notion that it was more than a shuttering weakness in his brain.

He probably would have dismissed it as such, had Lieutenant Felix not been found dead in his cell the next day. Dr. Jackson would call it natural causes, though even she was unable to say what in nature could make a young man's heart explode in his chest.

# CHAPTER
# 3

Before the warp channels opened, mankind was confined to the solar system. He strained against those bounds, fought against the limitations, but there was no use. Technology was his enemy, and no incremental change could save him. Thus he remained locked to the Earth and the feeble colonies of the moon and Mars, awaiting the day of his liberation. Nonetheless, when the *Armstrong* reached Alpha Centauri, the celebration was short-lived. There was no time to waste. Not when there were such worlds to conquer.

They went. Men and women who could find no succor on the planet that had given them birth. Earth had not failed them. It was not the air or the water or the land that chased them away. Although every generation had foretold her doom, she kept chugging along.

No, it was from their fellow men that they fled. From their rules and their laws, from the chains that kept their minds enslaved. There was nothing new under the sun, and when they went, it was for the same reasons that their forefathers had in the days that men set forth on rickety wooden ships across monster-infested seas. But the travelers could not enter warp unless they were sleeping. And with sleep came the dreams.

\* \* \*

Caroline Gravely watched the cross she had worn around her neck since her confirmation—the one her grandmother had given her on a rainy Easter day decades before—float in midair, a foot from the tip of her nose. She reached up a hand and spun it with one finger. The golden flecks sparkled in the sunlight that flooded into the shuttle through the small windows lining its sides.

Yes, Caroline had worn that cross since the day she was confirmed, but she had never really looked at it. She waited until the chain had wrapped itself into a single tight strand before she reached out and grabbed it, untangling it and tucking the cross back into her shirt.

She listened as the clamps holding the shuttle in place released and felt the pressure as the vertical thrusters fired, pushing the small vessel down and away from the landing bay. She looked out the portside window and watched, as the station seemed to drift into the distance.

She noticed, as she always did when she was this close, that the space dock was dirtier than she remembered from her childhood. From when her father called it Luna because it shone almost as bright as the moon in the summer night sky. She thought it was beautiful then. In her eyes, time had not dimmed it, and it didn't matter how many people told her differently.

Then the rear thrusters fired, and the shuttle took a hard turn to the right. Through the window, she could see the mighty American capital ships of the Fourth Fleet. Even across silent space, she could have sworn she heard the splendid rumble of the *Agamemnon* as its massive central structure spun in the void. The *Alabama* was out there somewhere, the ship she had once called her own, the vessel she had captained for the last decade. The fleet would leave soon, back into the deep, but this time with another at her helm.

The thought brought sorrow, even though she had sworn it would not. She had done her part for the Navy. She had lived up to her family's legacy, the one that stretched all the way back to the ancestor who was little more than a legend: Samuel Gravely, the man who had been the first of his race to command a ship of the line, back when such things mattered.

The shuttle banked to the left, and Caroline felt her stomach rise into her throat. She would never get used to that, no matter how long she spent in space. She wondered how the shuttle pilots did it, their boats too small for the artificial gravity of the capital ships and too cheap for a gravity generator. A life of weightlessness.

The intercom crackled to life and she heard the voice of the pilot call her name.

"Captain Gravely? There she is out the starboard window. The *Chronos*."

Caroline leaned her head against the glass and stared out across the shuttles that swarmed past. The *Chronos* was below in space dock and she had never seen anything so beautiful. It was her own. Truly her own. Not just her ship to command but one built with her blood and her sweat and her tears.

"Is she everything you thought she'd be?"

Caroline smiled. "No," she said, "she's more."

\* \* \*

The first time Cyrus walked into the crew compartment of the *Chronos*, he could hear someone vomiting in the room beyond. The door was cracked open, and he didn't hesitate to push it the rest of the way so he could get a better look. He grinned when he saw the man in the suit on his knees, head over the toilet. "Civilians," he thought to himself, "always the same."

"First time in an orbital shuttle, I take it?"

The man didn't look up. Instead, he held himself perfectly still, balancing with his hands on both sides of the bowl, hoping that his calm would transfer to his stomach. It did not. As he lost it again, Cyrus turned and walked back toward his bunk.

He opened his bag and removed the only three things he never left home without. The statue of Mary his grandmother had given him when he was thirteen years old was first. He crossed himself twice before kissing it lovingly on the forehead. Then the compass he always kept in his pocket. That was a gift from an old girlfriend. A perfectly useless thing really, much like everything else that had come out of that relationship. But he loved it, and it gave him direction. And finally a pennant from the New England Patriots' last Super Bowl championship. That had been a present to himself.

He was attaching the flag—he was old-fashioned; there wasn't a hologram on the thing—to the cold silver metal behind his bunk when the man in the suit finally emerged from the head. Cyrus watched him as he tried to dust the dirt off his knees. He thought back to his first time in zero g. It had been no different.

"Better?"

The man nodded his head and smiled weakly.

"It gets easier," Cyrus said. "Seriously, the next time, you won't even notice it."

"Hopefully," the man said, speaking for the first time, "there won't be many next times." He was British, and Cyrus made a mental note of his accent.

"Nah, there won't be. Only the orbital shuttles don't have a-grav these days. On the big Cap ships, you got your whole hab complex spinning. It's really pretty impressive. That way, you think you got gravity even when you don't. Ship like this, of course, uses antimatter."

"Is that right?" the man said. He might have been trying to blow Cyrus off but Cyrus had never been one to take a hint.

"That's right." Cyrus leaned himself against his bunk and explained. "You see, antimatter is basically the opposite of matter in just about every way. So the more matter you got, the more of a gravitational field it creates. Antimatter, the less you have, the more gravity you get. You take a single atom of antimatter, and in a nanosecond, it'll be a black hole. Thing is so small it evaporates just as fast so no danger or anything. But anyway, every one of these freighters has just a tiny amount of antimatter. Costs as much as the engine."

The man looked impressed. "And how do you know all this?"

"Cyrus McDonnell, ship's engineer," he said, offering his hand.

"Jack Crawford," the other man said, taking it. "I'm just along for the ride."

"Ah, well that makes sense. Sorry about the accommodations but this is a freighter, not a passenger ship. Only the captain and the navigator get their own cabins. Even the ship's doctor is stuck back here with the rest of us."

"Right," Jack said, sitting down on one of the lower bunks. His stomach was still reeling but he had just enough control over it now. "It's a lot cheaper."

"And what business do you have on Riley?"

Jack smiled. "Just business."

"Your own business," Cyrus said, coughing out a laugh. "And I guess that's none of mine. Well it's not a short trip out there."

"Same as every other one, right?"

Cyrus didn't like Jack; he knew that now. Didn't like him one bit. Cyrus didn't like most people but usually it took a couple days or more for him to realize it. Jack was right, of course. The trip out to the solar rim always took the same amount of time and you were asleep during the jumps. Cyrus shivered. He didn't like to think about that.

"You all right?"

He looked down at Jack and found the man genuinely concerned.

"Yeah, I'm fine," he said.

"So," Jack said, trying to change the subject, "have you worked on this ship long?"

"Nope, you're in luck. This is her maiden voyage. I was on the Gliese run for a while, working the trade between the system and Earth."

"Not exotic enough for you?"

Cyrus frowned and looked down at his feet. "Actually, we lost our captain on the last trip out. Made the jump back and found him dead. Died in his sleep. Just like that."

"I'm sorry to hear that," Jack said.

"Yeah, well, anyway. I needed a job and this one was available. So here I am. But now, I've got work to do. I'm sure we'll talk later."

Jack nodded politely and watched him leave. He didn't bother to follow. He'd see him again in due time and didn't really care what Cyrus did or where he went. Jack had his own business to attend to. He pulled out the data pad from his inside jacket pocket. A beam from the screen scanned his retina in under a second, and he was in.

There was nothing new to report, so he opened the last message he had received, the one that had led to this assignment. The image was unfocused and the object at its center otherwise unremarkable. But it was a ship, of that there could be no debate. One that should not be. One that, according to the official records, never was. He tapped the screen and the image was gone. The mission was to proceed as scheduled. Now he just had to wait to talk to Dr. Kensington.

* * *

At that moment, Rebecca Kensington was standing in the crew's mess, looking out the only observation window on the entire ship other than the one on the bridge. It was totally unnecessary, as any ship's architect would tell you, and in fact, could be dangerous.

A window was a weak point, and the vacuum unforgiving. But Captain Gravely had insisted. Not unlike most captains. She said it was for ship morale, and the architect accepted the lie. The truth was, what was the point of going to space if you never saw anything? So while Jack Crawford puked his guts out three decks above her, Rebecca watched the Earth turn below.

She had always wanted to go to space, ever since she was a child. She would have made it, too. She certainly had the brain for it. She excelled at math and science. Tests were always easy for her, and invariably her scores were off the charts. But there was one test she had never mastered, one test she couldn't study for.

The first time she failed the psych evaluation, she laughed. The second time, she cried. No one ever got a third chance. There was too much riding on it, too much chance of doing horrible, terrible things. To kill and to maim. Only the strongest minds could handle the dreams and even some of them cracked.

She could have joined the Merchant Marine. The transport ships that went back and forth across the system and beyond had standards that were lower, and the cargo ferries that never left solar orbit were even less demanding. But that wasn't for her. It was to be the Navy or nothing.

So when her dream died, she found others and into them she poured her spirit and her soul and everything she had. But always, the regret. Still, she was here now and even though it scared her a little, staring out through her own reflection over that great, blue sphere . . . it was a dream come true.

And yet, something was off about this dream.

She felt it creep over her, a feeling that she was not alone. That she was being watched. She had felt it before but now it was palpable. So when she turned and found a man standing behind her, she shouldn't have been surprised. It didn't stop her from issuing the smallest of startled yelps.

He had been watching her for several minutes. She was the one who concerned him the most.

"Oh, I'm sorry," he said, raising his arms to show he meant no harm. "I felt I was going to startle you but I couldn't think of any way to let you know I was here without doing it."

"That's alright," she said. It wasn't a lie, not like it normally would be. There was something soothing in the way he spoke.

"I'm Dr. Ridley," he said, taking her hand. "Ship's physician."

"That explained it," she thought.

"You mean shrink."

There was a moment of awkward silence but then she grinned and he laughed, albeit uncomfortably.

"Yes," he said, taking a seat at a nearby table, "I guess you could say that. Though people are rarely so direct. Sometimes I think they'd rather just accept the fiction and move on."

"I prefer to know what I'm getting myself into," Rebecca said.

"In that we can agree. What brings you to our ship?"

"Passenger," she said, as vaguely as possible. But the doctor was here to pry. Of that she was certain. Or perhaps he simply could not take a hint.

"Ah, to Riley? Not exactly a popular destination."

"No," she said, "but this is not a vacation."

"Seems like your business would've provided you better accommodations."

"Are you always this inquisitive, Dr. Ridley?"

"Actually," he said, standing, "yes. That's my job."

"Well, my business prefers to save money when it can and

there aren't exactly a lot of passenger ships that service Riley. It was this or a charter. A charter to Riley would have been . . ."

"Considerably more expensive," Ridley said, sauntering to the window. "Beautiful, isn't she?"

"Absolutely," Kensington said as she walked over and stood beside him. Ridley looked at their reflections in the glass and was disconcerted to learn that she was taller than him.

"So I've read your file."

He got the reaction he expected. Kensington jerked her head around and glared at him, open-mouthed. In an instant the look was gone and had he not been watching, it would have been easy to miss. Still, she cursed herself for the weakness, in spite of all her training, particularly as she knew he had noticed.

"I'm glad to know you are on top of things."

"Yes, well, it's one of the less pleasant aspects of my job." Dr. Ridley looked down at his feet and rocked back and forth on his heels. Repose was a trait he lacked and he was always fidgeting, one way or another. It was a habit his mother had tried—and failed—to break.

"Imagine that."

Kensington looked straight ahead. Dr. Ridley scared her, in the way that people of his ilk always had. She had drunk her fill of them, back when she was only a child. During the testing. When the decisions and judgments they had made murdered her dream. She hated them, really. Hated the way they looked at her. Hated the way they nodded their heads and murmured "um-hm" whenever she answered their questions.

Then they scribbled on their little pads or tapped their fingers across computer screens, always doubting. Every look was an accusation, every word more evidence of disbelief. In their eyes, she was a liar. Both to them and herself.

"Just a safety precaution, of course."

He stood there now, waiting for her to respond, she guessed. Waiting for her to give him something more he could judge her by. Instead, she glanced around the dining hall, admiring the stark metallic sheen that covered every surface. A throwback to a time when such minimalist decoration was in vogue.

Her intent was to hold out, to make him speak first, no matter what he might prefer. But her heart wasn't in it, and she was never one for silence. "Of course," she finally answered, far too long after such a response was expected. And then, "I suppose you are afraid I'm going to murder you in your sleep? Remove your heart with a carving knife?"

She was surprised that the doctor's chuckle seemed genuine. "It must seem like that, right? But no, actually. Not that at all. I suppose you've never seen your file, have you?"

"Of course not," she said. "Apparently, my own mind is classified."

"Yes, well, I've never thought that was quite fair, especially with someone like you."

She gave him the same disgusted look as before, and he held up a hand as if to defend some imminent physical attack. "I meant no offense," he said. "Far from it. Indeed—and I know it probably doesn't mean much coming from me—your record is extraordinary. You would have been a true credit to the fleet. If anything, you were overqualified."

"Yeah, well, too bad I'm crazy."

Dr. Ridley looked down at his feet, and she could almost feel his disappointment. "I'm sorry you grew up believing that, especially since it's not true. The truth is you're not crazy at all."

When Ridley looked at Rebecca this time, confusion met his eyes.

"There are many neuroses associated with warp travel," he continued. "The most widely known, of course, is Braddock's Syndrome, or what the space jockey's call, sleep insanity. Something about the dreams causes people to lose themselves, often with violent consequences. And it is true that the testing indicated that you may have a heightened susceptibility to its effects."

He paused, and she waited. When it became clear that she wasn't going to speak, he continued.

"In truth, you were only just across the cutoff line. If what they tell me is true, were you to take the tests today, you would probably have passed. In any event, you aren't crazy. And everything about your psychological makeup tells us that you never will be. Were it not for the fact that you are also susceptible to CNF, I wouldn't be concerned at all."

"CNF?" Rebecca repeated.

"Oh I'm sorry, Dr. Kensington," Ridley said, although he secretly relished having the upper hand in at least one area, "I thought you knew. Critical Neural Failure is another condition. Far rarer than Braddock's. We don't really understand it, not that we understand Braddock's either.

"The sufferers of CNF don't go insane. Something in their brain simply snaps. And then it shuts down. They go to sleep and never wake up. That's what they were afraid would happen to you, even more so than the other. In any event, I just thought you should know now where things stand, before we depart. While you can still change your mind."

Rebecca released a breath she had been holding for some time. "That's all right, Doctor," she said finally, "I have important business on Riley, and it's worth the risk."

"Well," Dr. Ridley said (he had expected no other reply), "if you ever want to talk . . ."

"If I ever need to talk," she replied as she started to walk toward the door, "I'll be sure to make an appointment." Then she turned and was gone.

# CHAPTER
# 4

Aidan had heard once—and he had no reason to disbelieve it—that sailors at sea in the age of wood and iron included in their pay a measure of rum, a measure that each man treasured almost above his own life. He had also been told that mutinies were more likely to result from a deficit in this remuneration than other, seemingly less trivial, complaints.

Whatever was or was not correct about that story, he could say for certain that it was no longer true. His ship, or the ship that was his, before it blew up in deep space with only one lonely survivor, had nothing of the sort, and alcohol was forbidden to the crew. So, when the fleet finally reached space dock in orbit around the Earth, the first thing he did was seek out a bar. He found one on the second sublevel, wedged in between a tattoo parlor and a pawnshop.

It was a Merchant Marine pub and it should have been a place he felt at home. But as hooded eyes turned suspiciously his way, he felt the urge in the depths of his stomach to back away. To run from those looks, to hide from them. It wasn't that he was a stranger. No, they were expecting him, even if they didn't know it was him they were expecting. As he walked to the bar, he felt the eyes upon him, fading only as he approached the bear of a man who apparently ran the place.

The tavern had a dirty feel. From the walls hung nets and anchors, oars and old ships' steering wheels. The Interstellar Guilds claimed an affinity, a direct lineage really, to the seafarers of old, and he had never been in a guild tavern that didn't look exactly like this.

He glanced up at the mural over the bar, a tacky bit of ostentation that nevertheless seemed completely appropriate for the place. It was of an ancient mariner, floppy yellow hat pulled down over his eyes almost to his beard, gray great coat hanging loosely around him. His arm was extended, grasping the hand of another man, this one tall and clean-shaven, the guild emblem emblazoned on the shoulder of his blue jacket. "Unto the Ends of the Earth and Beyond," was written in cursive above them in metallic gold leaf.

As Aidan sat down at the bar, the crashing cymbals and metal buzz of the end of some neo-cosmic rock song he didn't know assaulted his ears. When "Sweet Home Alabama" started, he longed for simpler days.

"Bourbon," he said. "A double on the rocks."

The bartender stared at Aidan for long enough that he was afraid the man recognized him. But then he turned and grabbed a bottle, pouring a long, thin line of whiskey until the glass was nearly overflowing. Aidan finished half of it in the first gulp. He looked down into the brown liquid and spoke to no one. But he couldn't help hearing.

"Fleet's in," said a man twice Aidan's age, who sat beside him. At first, Aidan worried he had spoken to him, but a sideways glance alleviated that fear, though the man's unguarded voice boomed loud enough that Aidan could hear every word he spoke to the portly woman, who perched herself on a stool to his right. She was drinking some orange liquid that Aidan did not recognize. "We should hear about the *Vespa* soon enough."

A chill ran down Aidan's back at the sound of his old ship's name. It was only a heretofore unknown reserve that kept him from shaking so violently that everyone in the room would notice. He leaned in close to the man, and in that moment, it seemed as though his ears became attuned to his voice, like he and the woman who sat beside him were the only people in all the world.

"Something's wrong there," she said, "but I don't think you'll learn anything more than we've already heard."

"And just what have you heard?" the old man asked. "I've heard nothing but rumors and I don't know that I believe any of them. Nobody's been out to the crash site but the fleet."

"That's just it, isn't it? Nobody's been out to the site because it's trans-Neptune. In the void. No ship should be out there. Not unless it's at warp."

"Well, maybe the ship blew up in warp."

"Impossible. Ship goes critical in warp and there's nothing left. Just bits and pieces spread across a billion miles of empty space. No, sir, if that had happened, then they'd just say the ship vanished, like so many others you hear of these days. Not destroyed. Besides, there was a survivor."

"Aye, so I've heard as well. But I didn't believe it."

"It's true, if Jackson out of communications isn't full of it. The fleet radioed it in. They gave a full report. Found him near Pluto, just beyond the warp zone."

"That's the end of your mystery then," the old man said, downing his drink. "He's the cause. There can be no doubt."

The woman clicked her tongue and shook her head. "You'd be wrong there or at least that's what the fleet says."

"No!"

"Apparently, they think it was an accident."

Aidan glanced at the man just as a look of disgust spread over his face. "Barkeep," he said, "I'm gonna need another drink."

"Maybe they're right," the woman said, lifting her drink so that it hovered just beneath her mouth. "I heard the captain of the ship that found him examined the evidence herself."

"So that's just it? She gets to decide all on her own? No inquest? No investigation? No trial? Nothing?"

"Did you expect anything else? The debris field's in deep space. Whatever happened out there, for good or ill, we'll never know. Besides, you and I both know how it is. No one in the fleet cares about the transports. Merchant mariners are disposable. If it weren't for the guild, who knows where we'd be."

"Amen to that. But I'll say this and it's the God's honest truth," the old man began, holding his drink in the air. "Whatever anybody says, I'll always believe the survivor was to blame. And it will be a long time till he finds work on any freighter around here, mark my word."

And there it was. Aidan knew what to expect when he got home. It would be an eternity till they'd forget. It was space, but the men who worked the trade were still sailors, and superstitions ran deep. Aidan threw back the rest of his drink and then ordered another. He took it with him to a small booth in a corner of the bar, a good place, he thought, to get roaring drunk and be left alone. He probably would have succeeded too, if she hadn't come in.

He didn't see her until she sat down across from him. When he looked up, he saw a face that was familiar even if couldn't quite place it.

"I'd hoped I wouldn't find you here. But I admit it was the first place I looked."

"I'm sorry, I didn't know . . ."

"No, you wouldn't have. I'm Captain Gravely."

Now Aidan remembered where he had seen her before. "Captain Gravely," he said, "from the *Alabama*?"

She nodded. "And while you couldn't have known it, the mission where we found you was my last in the Navy."

"Well," Aidan said, slurring his words and raising his glass, "congratulations on your retirement. Grab a drink and we'll celebrate together."

"That's just the thing, Mr. Connor. I've left the Navy but I'm not looking to grow tomatoes in the back yard."

"No?"

"No. I wanted a ship of my own and now I have one. But I need to assemble a crew. I've got most of one, but I'm looking for a helmsman and a navigator. The fact is, you're the best available."

Aidan coughed out a laugh and the captain frowned. "You're drunk."

"What can I say?" he said, still chuckling. "This is an unexpected surprise."

"Be that as it may, there's nothing in your file that indicates your latest misfortune was anything but that—simple bad luck. But you know as well as I do, no one here," she said, gesturing to the room behind her, "is going to believe that. They won't be giving you any second chances. They think you're cursed. Bad luck. Who knows how long it will be before you get a job on a ship again. You'll be loading freight just to pay your bills."

"Is there a point to all this?" Aidan asked. Suddenly, he felt very sober.

"The point is that I need you on my team. But I need you sharp, and I need you sober. The truth of the matter is that something really bad happened to you and not everybody's ready to go back out after that. It's not just superstition that'll keep these people from hiring you. It's a justifiable fear that the next time you go out there you'll freeze up at the wrong moment or crack under the pressure. And then it won't be an accident."

She was right, and Aidan knew it. It was what they all feared, especially on the smaller ships. One madman was all it took. He had never been good at accepting charity but he knew how grateful he should be for what the captain was doing for him. This was an opportunity he could not have expected or even hoped for.

"Yeah," he said. "Yeah. I'd be honored."

"Good," she said. "She's the *Chronos* out of Dock 23. We leave in three days."

Aidan stood as she rose to go. The captain nodded once, and when Aidan offered his hand, she took it.

\* \* \*

Captain Gravely believed everything she had said to Aidan. She just hoped it turned out to be true.

\* \* \*

It was a crisp, nearly autumn Saturday across most of the United States, and the first day of college football season was on the forefront of many people's minds. But on the *Chronos*, only Cyrus cared about such things, and he was too busy to notice. He ran his fingers along the computer control panel, preparing the ship for its most important test of all—today he would run up the engines for the first time. It was unlikely, but if something went wrong, they could be stuck in port for as much as a month for repairs.

They were already behind. The cargo of construction materials bound for Riley was finally loaded a full two days past schedule after an accident had occurred. A grav-loader malfunctioned and dropped a ton of freight on one of the dockworkers. That his death was quick made it no less gruesome.

Captain Gravely heard the whispers. A bad omen, the people at the dock had said, even worse that it was a new ship, one perhaps cursed from the beginning. Hiring Aidan Connor as helmsman had turned into a bit of a scandal and the accident only made it worse. In response, Gravely had driven her crew to the point of exhaustion. The sooner they sailed, the sooner they could put this incident behind them. So when Cyrus heard the roar of the engines firing after a successful run-up, it was nigh on a religious experience. Two hours later, the ship was prepped and ready to embark.

"*Chronos*, this is tower one. You are clear for go."

Aidan glanced at Captain Gravely who nodded once in response.

"Tower one, this is *Chronos*. We are go."

"Smooth sailing, *Chronos*."

Aidan disengaged the magnetic locks and the bridge shook as the ship floated free. He grasped the manual controls and felt the rumble of the engines in his hands. Gravely watched him maneuver away from the dock, with approval. The computers could have handled it, of course, but the best pilots never let them. The best trusted themselves more than they did the machines and it was that bit of self-confidence that could make all the difference in the deep.

"Alright, Mr. Connor," she said. "You know the way."

Somewhere below, Cyrus was smoking a cigarette while Dr. Malcolm Ridley sat in his office, drinking scotch and reading the files of his new shipmates. He ran his hands through his thinning salt-and-pepper hair and selected Rebecca Kensington's file. It was she who interested him the most. Kensington, who looked oh-so-much like his mother had when she'd been young. Long before Malcolm's parents had even dreamed of him.

In the passenger compartment, sitting across from Jack Crawford, Rebecca shuddered. But the feeling was gone as quickly as it had come, and she forgot it, passing it off as a physical reaction to the brief moment of weightlessness she had experienced as the ship flew free. Jack was going over the procedure again, explaining what he hoped would happen and the contingency plans if that fell through.

"Gravely is a Naval officer," he said, "and even if she is retired, she'll follow orders."

Kensington nodded along, but she was no longer listening. Her mind was somewhere else, somewhere she had never been before. And yet the picture in her mind was so clear that she could almost reach out and touch it. It was only when Crawford put his hand on her arm that the images of dead leaves and screaming, painted horses disappeared.

"Are you with me, Dr. Kensington?"

"Of course," she said. But then more honestly, "I'm sorry, Jack. I guess I got distracted."

He frowned, and she immediately felt guilty. "What's wrong?"

She hesitated, feeling stupid for even worrying about it. "It's just . . . well, what if the dreams are as bad as everyone says they are?"

He laughed. "I'm sure they aren't. You have to remember, the people who have the worst reactions aren't like us. Kids on their first trip out. Your rank and file sailors. I think we'll be fine." But it was the moment before the laugh, the one he hoped that Kensington didn't notice—when he swallowed hard and his skin blanched—that told the truth of his feelings.

"Good. That's good." She breathed deep and exhaled in one long sigh. "I'm sorry, Jack. I was just being foolish."

"No," he said. "No, you weren't being foolish." And that was the truth.

\* \* \*

On the second night out, Captain Gravely hosted a dinner for the crew and her passengers in the dining hall. The great metal doors that covered the window on the port side were open, and they were close enough to the moon to see the sparkling lights of Lunar One below. Gravely had always loved the city, the first of Earth's colonies.

The settlement was built on the moon's termination point, where the moon's dark side met the light. But even though the dark side of the moon was a misnomer, Lunar One never saw the day. It had been built deep in a crater, where the sun's beams did not penetrate and the frozen ice that remained in the shadows could provide the water the base needed to survive. Gravely had trained in the city many years ago and she would often walk the streets beneath the great glass dome that covered it, bathed in perpetual twilight.

The dinner was a special treat, something she had always wanted to do but never could in the Navy. But she had another purpose as well. The trip to Riley was long, the space they had to traverse deep, and Gravely didn't know her crew. She wanted to trust them as she had trusted those on the *Alabama*. But the old assurances, the training, the testing, the experience, it was all lacking here.

She knew a day would come when she would have to put her life in the hands of these men. She needed to be able to do so without hesitation. And that's why Dr. Ridley passed the evening mostly in silence, watching the interactions of the group. Listening to their words, learning their mannerisms and their particular habits. Finding out their demeanor when they were at their most relaxed, most calm, so that he might better tell when one of them was about to snap.

It was well after the final course, when the meal was finished and the dessert had passed, that the several bottles of Prosecco they had consumed started to take their effect, and the awkwardness that had marked dinner began to fall away.

"So, Dr. Ridley," Rebecca said, "how did you end up out here?"

"On this ship?" he asked.

"No," she said, laughing freely. Even if he weren't a doctor, her flushed cheeks would have told him that she was slightly drunk. "In space. Couldn't you have stayed planet-side?"

"Ah. Well I suppose you might ask that of anyone here. But as for me, this is the last great clinical laboratory," he said. "This type of experience is simply unavailable on Earth. It's a sacrifice I suppose, but well worth it."

"So we are your lab rats then, Doctor?" Aidan asked as he filled his glass. Dr. Ridley blushed and tried to laugh it off.

"That is one way to put it, but no. It's just that most of my fellows are professors. The fact is, the psych drugs are so good these days that few people planet-side really need a doctor. Not when they can take a pill and make it all go away. Drift off into some happy oblivion and wake up, as good as new. No analysis needed."

"If the drugs are so good, why not use them here?" Rebecca asked.

"Well . . ." Ridley paused and then coughed. That the answer was obvious didn't make it any easier to give.

"It's the dreams," Cyrus said. "You need a clear head for the dreams."

Aidan glanced from Cyrus to Rebecca to the doctor. A cold chill, a shadow, had fallen over the room at their mention, but Cyrus was right. So many of the things they did were inspired by the dreams, so many of their procedures revolved around them.

"You know, I hear so much about these dreams," Rebecca said tentatively, trying to blow off her fears as mere curiosity. "Are they really so bad? Are they nightmares? I mean, the way you people talk about them, I imagine you must see all sorts of horrible things. Demons, dragons, the creature from the black lagoon." Rebecca laughed for a second but no one else joined her.

"They are not nightmares, not in the traditional sense of the word," the doctor explained. "In fact, I would argue that they aren't even dreams."

"They are too real," Cyrus said before Rebecca could ask the doctor what he meant.

"And you don't forget them," Aidan added.

"No," the doctor continued, "no, your typical dream you might remember right after it happens but even then only briefly and only in parts. I think it is safe to say that we all remember the dreams."

One by one, starting with Cyrus, every person at the table nodded. Even the captain.

"Wait . . . you remember every one of the dreams you have ever had? How is that possible?"

"They are always the same," the doctor replied.

"More or less," the captain added in a whisper that only she heard.

"That's amazing. How is that possible?"

The doctor shrugged. "No one knows. We barely know anything about the dreams, really. Not yet. It is one of the last great mysteries of the mind. Now you can see why I'm here."

"But if the dreams are so bad, why not just stay awake?"

"Well, the regulations require it, of course."

"But why? Surely there is a reason."

"To understand that," Dr. Ridley explained, "you have to appreciate what a warp drive does."

"Right," Cyrus said. "Faster-than-light travel is impossible, of course. And even if it weren't, you've got that whole time dilation thing."

"A year for you is a decade for everybody else," Aidan interjected.

Cyrus took a drink of his wine and nodded. "Warping is not traveling faster than light. In fact, it's exactly what it sounds like. The warp drive warps space."

"How so?" Rebecca asked. Jack glanced at her but she ignored him. She knew all of this, of course. One might call it her specialty, what she did for a living. But she wanted to hear them explain it. Dr. Ridley was enjoying the discourse as well. He'd read her file. He knew the truth. Something about Rebecca intrigued him, however, and he had no interest in revealing her charade.

Cyrus explained, "Well, that's a little bit more complicated. But basically, it stretches and compresses space. Twists it all up and then unravels it. Traveling at warp isn't about moving through space at all. It's about moving the fabric of space itself. Ripping a little hole in it and slipping through."

"More like riding a wave," Aidan said.

"Yeah, whatever."

"So you can imagine what that would do to the mind," Dr. Ridley continued. "To see everything you know about the universe ripped apart and reordered? It would be the very definition of insanity, I think. But it also explains the dreams, at least partially. It's the mind's way of dealing with what is going on around it."

"But no one's ever seen it? No one's ever stayed awake? Just to see?"

Ridley hesitated. "No."

"What about the *Hypnos*?" Cyrus asked.

For the first time that evening, Jack Crawford looked interested.

"The *Hypnos* is a myth," Captain Gravely said. "I don't think it ever existed."

"I don't know, Captain," Cyrus said. "I've always believed it, and I think most people in the trade do."

"What is the *Hypnos*?" Rebecca asked.

"It's a ship," Captain Gravely said. "Or it was a ship. The story goes that the *Hypnos* was the first warp ship."

"But that's not right," Jack interrupted. "Everybody knows the *Armstrong* was the first ship to go warp."

"Right," Cyrus said, "that's the official story. But some people think that the *Armstrong* was just the first successful ship. Well, in that the crew survived, at least."

"Or didn't go insane," Aidan offered. "That's the way I always heard it. That they went crazy. Before they died."

"Wait," Rebecca said, "I'm confused. What exactly happened?"

"You have to understand," said Cyrus, "it's probably just a story."

"A conspiracy theory, more like it," Aidan added.

"Right. Anyway, my father used to talk about it. He said that there were rumors about a test. Decades ago. Years before the *Armstrong*, even. The ship went out beyond Pluto with a crew of four. A short warp test to Proxima Centauri. When the time came, they fired the engine and went to warp. The relay station at Jupiter was the first to hear from them. They had received a beacon from Proxima Centauri as soon as the ship dropped out of warp, and the celebration was already underway.

"Champagne, speeches, the whole deal. But then, the transmission came in. My father's best friend was a communications guy in the Navy. He had a buddy who was assigned to Jupiter Station at the time. He said the crew never radioed in. Jupiter tried to contact them but they couldn't raise them.

"At first, they didn't think it was a big deal. You know, warp does funny things to the equipment. But then something strange happened; the ship started heading toward Proxima Centauri. Slow at first, but then faster and faster. They sat there and watched them fly the ship right into the star. Nothing was left, and nobody ever knew why."

"That's pretty much the story I heard," Aidan said. "But I was told one other thing as well. After the *Armstrong*, they sent out a ship to see if they could find out what had happened. Turns out, when the ship started to break down and melt, the computer fired off an information packet. But it was too close to the star and too far from a listening post to broadcast. Anyway, the rescue ship found it."

"Where they able to figure out what went wrong?" Rebecca asked.

"Depends on who you ask. Some people say there was nothing but static, that all the circuitry was fried. Makes sense, given how close it was to the star. Others say that there were voices but you couldn't make them out. But some people, some people say that you could see and hear everything. The bridge was mostly destroyed. Two of the crew were dead. The other, who knows. But the captain was still alive. Still alive and in control. It was he who drove the ship into the star. He turned to the camera for only a moment. And he only had one thing to say."

"Well?"

"The last broadcast, the last thing they heard from the *Hypnos* . . . 'They are here.'"

"They?" Rebecca whispered, but to that question, no one had answers.

"Like I said," Captain Gravely offered, breaking the silence that had suddenly fallen over the room, "it's probably a myth. But in any event, you see now, Ms. Kensington, why it is worth the dreams. Cautionary tale or reality, it's dangerous out here, and we take every precaution, for your safety as well as ours."

* * *

"You really think it was a good idea, letting them talk about all that?"

Gravely poured two glasses of brandy and handed one to Dr. Ridley, who stood perusing a faded yellow newspaper clipping hanging from her wall. He recognized the man in the photo as an ancestor, the first to join the Navy. Gravely sat down behind her desk, leaning back in her chair till she was almost horizontal to the floor.

"People talk, Dr. Ridley," she said, taking a long drink from the glazed, crystal snifter engraved with the name U.S.S. *Alabama*. "Better to have them get it out in the open now. Especially Ms. Kensington. Or should I say Dr. Kensington. What do you think about that whole charade she played today?"

"You mean the talk about warp technology?"

"Given her background, we weren't telling her anything she didn't already know."

"Who can say," Ridley offered, his glass already near empty. "Perhaps she was just making conversation. Maybe she was humoring the boys, Aidan and Cyrus, letting them show off some of their own knowledge. I stopped trying to figure out why people do things like that a long time ago. Maybe she's afraid of the dreams and wanted to hear some reassurance."

"In any event, her fears are legitimate, don't you think?"

"The fact is," Dr. Ridley said, gesturing with his glass, "no one has ever proven that the dreams cause insanity. It is my theory that it is the anticipation as much as the dreams themselves. That people work themselves into a frenzy. It's a self-fulfilling prophecy."

Ridley looked at Gravely and saw her grin. Then she said, "Dr. Ridley, you've been on this trip before. You've experienced the dreams. Do you really believe that?"

Ridley smiled and finished his drink. Then he stood and walked to the door. He turned and hesitated for a moment as he glanced at the scale model of the *Alabama* Gravely kept behind her desk. Then he looked at her and said, "Touché."

# CHAPTER
# 5

Rebecca found him on the bridge, even though she didn't know she was looking. Just wandering aimlessly through the ship, passing the days until they reached the warp point—days that seemed to crawl by in the vessel's cramped and twisting quarters. Aidan was seated at his station, feet propped up on the panel in front of him, watching Jupiter as they passed by. He heard the doors open behind him and wasn't surprised when he heard Rebecca gasp at what she saw.

"It's beautiful."

"Yep," said Aidan, "it truly is."

"I've never seen it before," she said. "At least, not like this. I've only been as far out as Mars."

"I've seen it a hundred times. But I never get tired of looking."

"You mind if I sit?"

"Of course not, make yourself at home," Aidan said, sweeping his arm over the chair beside him.

"So what exactly do you do here?" she said with a smirk, only half-kidding.

"Well," he replied, looking at her for the first time, "I'm your navigator."

"Is that what you're doing now? Navigating?"

Aidan cocked his head to the side as he grinned at her. "As a matter of fact, yes. But you're observant. The computers can do most of the work these days. All of it, really."

"So why do we need you?"

"Regulations call for it, for one."

"Ah, Navigators Union particularly strong?"

"As a matter of fact, the Interstellar Guild is very powerful. But that's not it. At least, not all of it. The computers do break down on occasion and trust me; you don't want to get lost. Not out there." Aidan pointed to some point in the distance, some point beyond.

"I hope that doesn't happen often."

"No, not often. Usually only after the warp. Screws with the system sometimes. Maybe even most times. Nine times out of ten you come out of warp and something's wrong. Sometimes the whole computer is fried. Not permanently," he said, seeing the look on her face. "It only takes a couple minutes to bring it back up, usually. Every now and then you can't get it done. That's when it's good to have a navigator."

"Ah. So that's why you sit up here all day? Just in case something goes wrong?"

"Do I spend all my time in here?"

"Yeah, as a matter of fact you do."

Aidan looked back at the screens. For a second he was quiet and Rebecca was afraid she had said something that offended him. But that wasn't it. There were darker things on Aidan's mind.

There was no reason for him to be here. No ordinary reason. The computers could take care of themselves and if something did happen, he could be in the control room in plenty of time to handle it. No, he liked to spend his spare moments staring into space for other reasons.

Rebecca sat beside him still waiting for an answer.

Aidan supposed her curious nature lent itself well to her job as a scientist. And while inquisitive people often bothered him, there was something about Rebecca he liked.

"No," he finally answered. "That's not why I do it."

"Why then? You just like to look at the stars?"

He sighed and rapped his hand on the console three times in quick succession. "If I tell you," he said, "I'm afraid you'll think I'm crazy."

She smiled. "I won't think you're crazy."

"Don't be so sure." He picked up a glass of water and took a sip. She simply stared and he knew she wouldn't let it go.

"Ten years ago I was on a transport ship like this one. We were carrying mining equipment out to Anubis in the Omega quadrant, one of those industrial colonies past the Scutum-Crux."

"You've been to Anubis?" she almost whispered.

Aidan nodded once. They both knew the truth; Anubis wasn't just any colony.

The images flooded back to him, ones he rarely thought on if he could help it. Anubis was a place of dark legends, carried mostly on whispers that floated through the spacing guilds, growing more mysterious with every telling. It wasn't just that it was deep in space. That added to the mystique, of course. But it was everything else that sealed that planet as a place made of nightmares most God-fearing people preferred to forget.

Anubis sat in the middle of a part of the galaxy that many scientists called simply, "strange space." It was an appropriate moniker, but didn't quite capture it. The guild navigators had another name for it— the necropolis. Because all that once moved there was long dead.

Space was not a void. It was a thing unto itself, a great sheet of emptiness on which sat all that was. And like any sheet, it could be torn. For reasons no one had yet explained, the nebulae of the Omega quadrant had built stars so massive that they bent the very fabric of space. In that one magnificent place, all the golden glory of the universe was concentrated in those radiant spheres.

Aidan sometimes wondered what it must have been like. Or what it would have been like, if there had been anyone there to see it. A thousand great red and blue giants, burning in the night sky. There would be no night in that perpetual light. No darkness, no shade. It would have been what Heaven must be like, he thought. Worlds, if worlds there were, where the sun never set.

Who can speculate what civilizations might have grown there? Bathed in warmth that never ceased. Building monuments and temples to the great globes of fire in the sky. Never knowing darkness. Never cowering in fear of a Plutonian night. Never wondering if the sun would ever rise again. But alas, Nyx could not be denied forever. And when she came, she came in fire and death.

Some stars ended in crackling hypernovas that thundered across the void with such violence that the heavens rang with their sound. Others fell upon themselves, devouring fire and gas and matter until there was nothing left but a black abyss, impossibly emptier than space itself.

And as the void was twisted and torn, as it was ripped and stretched until the laws of physics no longer mattered, whatever cities and civilizations, monuments and memories, that might have been were simply washed away, like sand castles before the rising sea.

What was once a shining beacon in the night sky fell into darkness, and the Omega quadrant would likely have become little more than a curiosity, intriguing to few but a handful of astrophysicists. Except that one star remained.

It sat in the very center of the Stygian night that was the Omega quadrant. Officially, it was called Kruger 27-B, having been so branded in a time when scientists, rather than artists or philosophers, named the stars. It was tiny by even common standards and but a speck of dust compared to the mighty giants that once ruled Omega. But the star remembered, for it had been one of those giants in days gone by. Before the nova rippled across its surface and gravity collapsed its shell into a diamond-dense spinning pulsar.

A planet turned about that glowing gemstone, zipping so quickly around its center that it fell to the star's watchtower pulsating energy beam twice a day. Kruger 27-B Prime those same uninspired scientists called it. But it had another name. The men who provided supplies and carted away the rich ore that poured from the planet's mines called it Anubis.

Anubis, the Egyptian god of the Underworld, "he who sits upon his mountain," the mountain of death. The mountain of madness. If the ancient Egyptians had ever seen Kruger 27-B Prime, they would have agreed with the appellation.

Nothing lived on Anubis. It was a dead world, as every day the beam of radiation scoured its surface clean of life. Nothing moved on Anubis but the men who had come there to dig out the precious ore from its soil . . . if men they still were.

Aidan couldn't say. He had been to Anubis only one time and only then to Dejima, the quarantine port. It was forbidden by the men of Anubis for outsiders to go beyond Dejima's walls and the few who had tried had all met an end as mysterious as Anubis itself. The old mariners, the ones who had been but children in the early days of the colony, claimed that it had not always been so. That when the first settlers arrived on Anubis, clad in the full body suits that protected their lives but gave them an inhuman look that added to the planet's legend, it had been no different from any of the other mining colonies.

But it was said that the miners found something there, in the excavation. A relic from lost worlds, from one of the civilizations of light that had flourished before Omega was cast into darkness. Whatever cyclopean temples the men of Anubis had discovered changed them, for some things never die. Some things merely sleep.

Aidan recalled clearly when he first met them. The image of that moment was burned into his mind. They came to collect the supplies and supervise the loading of their cargo. They bought only meat; he remembered that too. Their leathery-plastic suits tugged tight at every inch of their skeletal frames and they did not walk upright, but rather bent and hunched over. That you couldn't see their eyes—hidden behind thick black glass as dark as the Anubian sky—only made it worse. No, the black men of Anubis never left Aidan. He saw them often in his night-haunted dreams.

It was always the same image: the last one he saw as the cargo ship lifted from the pad in Dejima. The airspace over the planet was tightly restricted but there were things one could not help but see as the ship cleared the walls. On that day, as Aidan looked out from the forward portal, it was them that he saw. Thousands of them, the colonists, all dressed in the same dark black suits that he had seen before.

The unnatural leather shimmered in the dim light, making each entity seem to quiver as if shaking from the cold. They were in every street, in every open space. Each man and woman, if you could still call them that, staring up into the sky at the purple star that barely gave any light. As Aidan watched, the rotation of the planet and its revolution around its sun fell into perfect alignment. A great wave of pale violet fire rolled across the surface of the planet, covering buildings, streets and people alike.

Aidan's eyes had fallen upon one of the beings below. He would never know precisely why this man had drawn his sight, but the reason did not matter. All that mattered was what he saw. As the beam of light rolled over him, as the purple fire that had left all others behind covered him, he was suddenly gone. Disappeared. Vanished. None of the others reacted. It was as if they had expected it. They simply shuffled away to wherever they went when they weren't there, until the streets were empty. Then the wave moved on. Rolling along the planet, to some other city or place. Perhaps to take yet another offering.

Still, that was not why Aidan found himself staring out into space on most days.

"So yeah," he continued, "we were on our way out to Anubis. At the time, Anubis was the most distant colony, until we settled Riley, which is a few light years beyond. We had finished the run, no problem, and were heading back out of the system. We had just hit the jump point.

"It's hard to describe what it's like at the edge of a system, you know? Especially a system like that. When you think of space, you think of the sun, the planets, and their moons. But out there, it's just empty. Just nothingness. All you have are tiny little points of light. These faint dots in the distance. You can see them pretty well since the only other illumination is coming from your own ship. And you can just feel it, the emptiness, if that makes sense."

Aidan shook his head. "It's crazy, you know? I was sitting on the bridge, one just like this one. I was looking up at the screens. Paying attention, but not really. . ."

Aidan paused. He had never told this story and he wasn't really sure why he was telling it now. He couldn't think of how to describe it. No, that wasn't true. The description itself was fairly easy. It was the believing of it that was hard.

"Go on," said Rebecca.

"So there was no one else on the bridge with me," Aidan continued. "And I'm looking up at the screen and I can see the stars. And then . . . it was like a shadow moved over us."

"A shadow?"

"Yeah, a shadow. I know that's a weird way to describe it. But I only knew it was there because, as it moved, I saw the stars wink out of existence one at a time and then reappear as it passed. It only took a second and it was gone. Then, everything was back to normal. Like nothing happened. The stars were there, the lights of the ship. I don't know. Part of me says it was nothing. But I know what I saw."

"What could it have been?" Rebecca asked.

"Beats me. All I know is that that there are still some things out there we don't quite understand. Still a lot of things we don't know about. And I believe—I'll always believe—that out there on the rim that day, on the very edge of explored space, I saw something that shouldn't be there. So I figure either I'm right, or I'm crazy. But maybe if I sit here long enough, I'll see it again. And then I'll know for sure."

Rebecca raised an eyebrow. "How will you know it's not just you being crazy again?"

"Well . . . huh . . . good point."

They both laughed.

"Tell you what," she said, "how bout I stay here and watch with you?"

Aidan looked at her and saw a spark in her pale blue eyes.

"I think that would be just fine."

She leaned her chair back and then they were both staring up at the screen. She said, "I was just kidding, you know."

"About what?"

"About you being crazy. I don't really think that."

"Well, I don't think you're crazy either."

He stared straight ahead, but he felt the change as her head fell to the side and she looked at him and he knew enough about secrets to know what she was thinking.

"I read your file," he said. "Maybe I shouldn't have, but Riley's a long way away. I like to know who our passengers are. Was surprised to learn you're a warp engineer though. Can't say I saw that coming."

"You read my file?" she repeated. Rebecca had always been a private person and while she liked Aidan, she felt violated.

"It's not a crime," he said. "If you are a passenger on a transport, your life is an open book. I'm the navigator on this ship. I just wanted to see whom I was dealing with is all. Didn't mean any offense."

Of course he didn't, she thought. She wasn't really mad at him anyway. She was mad at herself, at her one great weakness. The one that made her question who she really was.

"Look, I know you failed the test. Plenty of people have. I've worked with a lot of good guys who failed it too. I've never had a problem with any of them. Most people out here have never even taken it. You'll be fine. It's just a bunch of government bullshit."

"But what if it's not?" she said. "I mean, the way everybody talks about the dreams . . . what if it's not?"

"Well . . ."

Aidan didn't really know what to say about that. If it was true, if she really was weak, there was a good chance she was about to lose it out here, and she would never get it back. Nobody liked to talk about the Kirkbride Institute. Nobody in the trade, nobody in the void, nobody at all, really.

Most people had probably never even heard of its existence, though they must have known of the need for it. It was the place people who had lost their minds from the dreams went, assuming they didn't die on the trip. It was virtually a myth, its location hidden, its population a secret. But they were there.

Aidan knew only because he had seen a classified document once on a run he made ferrying some government guys between Earth and Mars. And it had mentioned Kirkbride, a place navigators in the guild only whispered about. There was no hope for the people there. Dr. Ridley and his psyche meds couldn't reach them. Their minds were gone forever.

Some of them claimed to be prophets. To know things that other men did not. To see truths that other men could only guess at. To see the future even, all the way to the end of time itself. And then there were the screamers. Aidan had been on a ship once with one of those. It had been the kid's first time. He had made the initial jump just fine. But when the ship warped back into solar space, Aidan awoke to the man's terrified shrieks.

The boy had never stopped screaming, the rest of the trip. Even though they had isolated him, they could still hear his desperate cries through the walls, and he was still screaming when they turned him over to medical. The screaming had not ceased long enough for him to tell them what he saw. The consensus seemed to be that he was living the dream over and over again. Seeing it, even in his waking life. Whatever images of horror that had driven him mad, they never left his sight.

"You'll be fine," Aidan said finally. "You'll be fine."

"And how are you gonna be?" Rebecca asked. She lowered her head toward him, conspiratorially. "You're not the only one that can read a file."

"I'll . . . I'll be fine," he said, after a moment's hesitation.

"You know it wasn't your fault, just because you made it back," she said. "There's no way it was your fault."

"Yeah, I know. I mean, I know that on some level," he said. "But I can't remember it. And as long as I can't remember it, I can't help but have doubts about what exactly happened that day."

"Well," she said cheerfully, "at least we've got each other. Two screwed-up peas in a pod."

"Yeah." Aidan laughed. "At least we do."

The ship rumbled beneath them, and the screen showed only the blankness of space and the stars beyond. But had they been watching it more closely instead of laughing with each other, they might have seen, if only for a second, a shadow pass over them. As abruptly as it had come, it faded away and was gone.

# CHAPTER 6

Caroline Gravely sat in her office, slumped low toward the floor, her back leaning uncomfortably against the wall. In her left hand was a glass half-filled with bourbon and a recently opened bottle of Maker's Mark remained on the floor beside her. In her other hand she held a piece of paper—folded, creased, and refolded many times over. It dangled precariously between her knees, and one who saw it would have thought that at any moment it might slip away and fall, as if she cared nothing for the letter or its contents. In fact she kept just enough pressure on its edges to prevent that.

She had received maybe five paper letters in her life. The first was from a boy in high school who, lacking the boldness or charm to approach her directly, hoped that the gesture would win him a date to the prom. Perhaps surprisingly, it had.

She had never felt more excited than when she opened the envelope, felt the crisp folded paper in her hand, smelled the ink and the processed wood. So much more permanent, so much more real than words on a screen. Yet she still had access to every email she had ever received, while four of the letters had passed to dust, forgotten somewhere in a life that spanned millions of miles of space and decades of time. But this letter—the last one that she had received to date—this letter remained and she kept it close at all times.

She had found it, quite unexpectedly, sitting on her desk on the *Alabama* some ten years prior. She immediately knew the hand, even before she read her name in jagged sharp angles on the front of the envelope. The only other name it contained was her father's. On two fragile sheets of paper were written the final thoughts he would ever convey to her.

He had passed the letter to her through a mutual friend on the ship, though she never discovered who had been the courier. Her father knew full well that his communiqués were scanned before they left his computer. Given what he had written, he must have also been completely aware that the words contained therein would surely be the end of him, were anyone but her to find them. Or maybe he just wanted his daughter to have something solid, something tangible to hold on to. It was clear he never expected to see her again.

Each time she read it, she knew that whatever had befallen him had been no accident. His disappearance, although officially a warp core breach, had a very different and terrifying explanation. He had broken, somewhere in the night and it had cost him, and those with whom he served, everything. So she read the letter again, as she had done before each jump for these last ten years. To remind her what was at stake.

There was a soft chime. Aidan, she thought. "Answer, audio only. This is Gravely."

"We've reached the trans-Plutonian void, Captain. Warp space reads clear. Based on the schedule, it looks like we have an eight hour window."

"Excellent, Mr. Connor. Prep the ship and the crew."

"You got it, Captain."

Another tone sounded, lower pitched, and he was gone.

"Computer," she said. "External video, aft."

A ripple seemed to roll across the far wall and then a flash of light. What had been a blank gray canvas changed into an image of the outside of the ship.

"Reverse angle, computer."

Another ripple. The ship was gone, replaced by the emptiness of space. She gazed back behind the ship, across time and distance, to a single point of light. The tiniest of spheres, with just enough dimension to not simply be another star. It was the sun, bright guardian of day and master of life. Here it gave no warmth.

* * *

Somewhere a deck below, Cyrus sat in the comm chair and pulled a helmet down over his head.

"Log in ready?" a gentle female voice asked.

"Ready," he replied.

There was a soft whirring buzz. He felt two pads press lightly against his temples. The sounds of the outside world disappeared as his ears were covered. A flash of light followed, and Cyrus felt like he was falling away from reality and into something else. Then another flash, and he was no longer on the ship.

He stood in the midst of the breakfast nook of a kitchen. His kitchen. The windows were open, the bright light of the sun streaming through, the breeze blowing the curtains up in great white billows.

"Daddy!" Emily cried. He turned and saw her running toward him.

"Hey, shrimp," he said, bending down and picking her up. As he did, impulses gathered by the synthetic's neural network were sent in an instant across millions of miles of space via warp tunnel relays. It was a means of communication that was expensive and drained a great deal of energy. Crew were permitted only one such call, and only immediately prior to jump.

"I'm not a shrimp!" She giggled on queue.

He, or the synthetic, rubbed his hands through Emily's curly auburn hair. He felt the resistance of each strand and its coarse, scratchy texture, as clear as if he were there himself.

"Emily?" he heard his wife call.

"Momma, it's Daddy!" she squealed, with the unbridled enthusiasm of the young and innocent.

Cyrus raised himself up and looked at his wife. She put her hands on her hips and smiled back, though he saw the same fear on her face as always. It was almost cruel to make these calls before the jump, the most dangerous time of all. How many had made their last call this way, one foot home, one in the unknown?

They chatted for a few minutes about nothing. It was awkward, as it always was. His wife had never gotten used to the synthetics, and even though a customized image of Cyrus was projected onto its skin (one he had designed himself, with slightly less heft and a little more muscular definition than the real thing), it still made her uneasy. But it didn't matter. He couldn't keep her long. And he didn't have much to say. Nothing but that he loved them and he hoped he would be home soon.

\* \* \*

Rebecca sat at a table, staring down at the latest communiqué Jack Crawford had received from the command. The same blurry image of a strange, arrow-shaped ship as before, no real information except a guess based on its configuration. And its location, just beyond the Anubis system. She took a deep breath and looked up at him as he walked over to her.

"I think we should tell them."

Crawford didn't look surprised. Setting down the cup of tea he had made for Rebecca and sitting across from her, he leaned forward, his hands flat on the table.

"And why do you say that?"

She hesitated. It had taken her all morning to work up the courage to say it, but she had expected a different response. Jack had a reputation for never straying from the mission, for sticking to the present parameters at all costs. It was one of the reasons his assistance was valued above many other agents. It was also a sign of the importance central command placed on this mission that he was here, with her. But now, even though she was suggesting they break protocol, Jack seemed entirely too calm. Almost disinterested. She could have handled yelling. She wasn't prepared for reasonable.

"Well," she said, "they seem like good people, the crew, and no one likes to be deceived. We both know they will find out eventually. You know how they are going to react. Why not tell them now? We will need them, Jack. I can't do this alone."

Jack leaned back in his chair and crossed his arms. "I guess telling you this is not up for debate won't suffice."

"No, Jack. No it won't. Because you know I'm right."

"No, Rebecca, I don't. You know our orders." She started to protest, but he held up a hand. "Look, we've been over this a hundred times. The computer will drop out of warp automatically when it reads a derelict ship in normal space. This is a commercial transport. There is a very good chance that they will want to salvage the vessel. Then the crew doesn't have to know anything. We wait till they deliver the ship to Riley. They receive their salvage award, and unknown to them—we get the ship. The plan is flawless."

"But, Jack . . ."

"Rebecca, please. We've been on this ship for less than a week, and you already think you owe these people something?"

Rebecca had worked with Jack at the agency for five years. He had not been the first person in her life to tell her she was too emotional, but his words had cut the deepest. Jack was an operator, a cold man, who accomplished his goals through brute force and cunning. He had abandoned friendships and more, when necessary, and he certainly didn't care about anyone on this ship.

But Rebecca was different. She fell easily and fast. She probably did care too much, and in the few days she had spent on the *Chronos*, she had made friends whom she wasn't ready to manipulate.

"Look," he said, his voice softening, "just tell yourself you are following orders. And remember that this opportunity fell into your lap. We do this and you're out. You were never cut out for it anyway."

She might have taken it as an insult, but it wasn't meant that way. She *wasn't* cut out for this, and she couldn't say that fact upset her too much. Especially now.

* * *

"Captain, this is the bridge."

"Go ahead, bridge."

"We are a go. Ready to set the countdown."

"We'll be waiting."

The comm channel went silent and Rebecca took a deep breath. It was happening. Right now. In ten minutes, according to the soft female voice (why were they always women?) that echoed through the chamber, the engines would fire and it would begin.

The door opened and Aidan walked in. He looked over at Rebecca and nodded. There was no time for sentimentality. Aidan's pod was directly across from hers. He sat inside and then lay down. There were eight minutes remaining.

A hundred different, random thoughts ran through her head. The pod was remarkably comfortable, though she wished she had a bigger pillow. She was afraid she wouldn't sleep, though she knew she'd be drugged. She wondered what she'd dream. What if she couldn't take it? What if these were the last sane thoughts she ever had?

Five minutes. Her breathing was fast and shallow. She was sweating. She was starting to panic. In a few more seconds, she would lose it. Then she was likely to leap from where she lay and just run down the corridors of the ship until the warp engines fired and she really did lose her mind.

Then a cooling calm wafted over her. Her heart rate slowed. She felt like she was floating. Her rational mind knew that the computer had read a spike in her vital signs and reacted, dosing her with just enough morphine to cause her not to care one whit about what was soon to happen. She didn't resist.

At three minutes, the glass domes that covered the pods lowered and locked themselves in place. At two, there was a sweet smell, a gentle, fruity breeze that kissed at her face. She smiled and felt her body rock back and forth, though in reality it didn't move. She thought to summers on the back porch of her house in Pensacola, evenings where she would climb in the hammock that her father had strung from one end of the veranda to the other.

On those cool nights as the wind would blow in off the bay, she would listen to the birds, the crickets, and the cicadas. Sometimes her father would sit in a small, wicker chair across from her and read. They didn't speak, for in those moments it was enough to be together. The silence and the peace was something to be treasured. It was a place she always felt warm and safe. A feeling she had never really felt since, until now.

These were the emotions that stirred within her on that day, as the computer counted down and the world faded. She fought against sleep, not because she feared it, but because she didn't want to leave this moment behind.

At ten seconds, her eyes fluttered closed. "Five seconds" was the last thing she heard. The computer continued dutifully.

Five,
four,
three,
two,
one.

The words echoed through the long hallways and darkened corridors of the otherwise silent ship, though there was no one there to hear them.

# CHAPTER
# 7

Rebecca was standing on a street, one she had never seen before. Her tawny hair hung loose and straight over her shoulders instead of twisted up in the back like she preferred. She was barefoot and a white cotton dress clung to her body. It was an Easter dress but it was not spring, not here.

Rebecca gazed down a cobblestone road that was more like a corridor. There were buildings on either side. Not tall ones, but more like the row houses and storefronts she had seen on fall visits with her father to his native New England. They were strange, built wall to wall, no alleyways or sidewalks between them. It was that way as far as she could see, until the road curved right, a quarter of a mile beyond.

She couldn't remember how she'd got here and she had no recollection of walking down this road. No memory, she realized, until she came to this very spot. She turned around, determined to retrace her steps but what she saw froze her in place. There was only darkness behind her. Just a flat, impossible wall of blackness.

It was as if an ink-black curtain had fallen between where she stood and whatever was behind. She followed that Stygian wall to where it seemed to terminate on her right side, slicing in half what had been a local pharmacy sometime in the distant past. The same had happened on the other side to a diner. "Bottomless Coffee" a sign read, though whatever price the place had charged was lost to the darkness.

Rebecca wanted to panic but her rational mind would not allow it. "There's always an explanation," she whispered to herself. When she didn't believe it she said it out loud.

Then a desire struck her, one that in another setting she might have called mad. She raised her hand toward the ebony wall, extending her index finger. Closer and closer, until she was but an inch away.

A voice thundered in her mind. "No!" She jerked her hand away and turned her back to the darkness, determined not to look at it again. From somewhere behind her, the wind blew, lifting her hair, and with it, the pale white fabric that covered her. It seemed to her that the air was colder than it should have been and she shivered. Dead leaves swirled in crackling vortexes as the wind thundered down the road and away. Rebecca started to walk.

She looked at the storefronts and row houses on either side of her. She had seen images like this before, but only once, earlier in her career. It was the job of a warp engineer to twist the fabric of space. Maybe even to break it, depending on whom you asked. That was both an awesome power and an awesome responsibility, so everyone in her field was required to visit the Exclusionary Zone, a fifty-square mile parcel of forbidden and forgotten land in north-central Pennsylvania before they could receive their degree.

The town of Fiddler's Green had once been there. In fact, it was there still, dominated by the great cooling towers in the distance of the NuCo Nuclear Power Plant. But it wasn't the plant that had brought Rebecca and her fellows there.

What was left of Diego Quantum was located a mile from the reactor, the only power plant in the country that produced enough energy to power the quantum accelerator buried beneath five square miles of once-fertile Pennsylvania soil. It was there that they journeyed, like penitents on a pilgrimage, to stand upon the platform that jutted out over the blackest abyss she had ever seen.

The black hole would have swallowed the Earth, devouring land, sea, cities and towns were it not for the massive electromagnetic field generators that held it suspended between earth and sky, fed by the nuclear power plant, its sole purpose to provide the immense amount of energy that, if interrupted, would release the beast that slept in their midst.

The people of the town had been evacuated so quickly that everything was left behind, from merchandise in store windows to food on dinner tables. The people had been told they could return, of course. That was a lie. The only people that visited Fiddler's Green now were scientists like her, either studying the destruction or being reminded that technology giveth as well as taketh away.

That's what these buildings recalled to her mind. They were devoid of life or purpose, frozen in time from a century before. But they were out of sorts somehow, as if randomly thrown together by a city planner who had never quite mastered his profession. Pharmacies next to apartments next to feed stores. Three diners in a row, all identical, all broken down. Shattered window fronts and collapsed-in doors.

Rebecca had been walking for what seemed like hours and yet the orange glow of the setting sun never faded. Maybe it was always so, but the dim sun did nothing to illuminate the darkness within the buildings she passed. It remained thick and impenetrable, just like the shroud that had seemed to cover her exit before. Whatever existed beyond the broken windows and doors of the structures on either side of her remained a mystery she had no intention of exploring.

She was scared. The fear had crept into her bones the minute she opened her eyes. The silence—broken only by the leaves being crushed between her bare feet and the cobblestones or crackling in the constant breeze—chilled her more than an icy wind ever could. She wanted nothing more than to see another living person, but the sensation of being watched was so powerful it made her tremble. Yet it wasn't the shrouded gazes of hidden observers that made her hair stand on end—it was the whispers.

At first, she blamed the breeze. A trick of swirling wind through broken glass. In her heart, though, she knew.

Some of the voices were subtle, others harsh and coarse. They came from the stores and the shops. From those who watched just beyond the light. There were too many to make out and whatever they said became jumbled together and distorted. But she heard some words. One in particular.

"Rebecca!"

Her name, over and over and over. Called and cried and cursed. Screamed at times, if one can scream in a whisper. Running into each other. Doubling over. Rising in a crescendo and dying into a denouement. The whispers grew in both number and intensity. Elevated to such an unintelligible roar that she raised her hands to cover her ears, but it didn't help. The whispers weren't coming from without. They were in her own head.

*Ding, ding!*

The sound of the bell on a child's bicycle would have stopped her heart from shock, had the voices not disappeared in the same instant. She didn't have time to turn before a girl rode by on a pink bicycle, white streamers caught up in the breeze as her bike bumped along the cobblestone street. Rebecca's mouth hung agape as she watched her ride by in a blue jumper and white sneakers, brown hair in pigtails.

"H—hey!" Rebecca stuttered, shocked at how loud her own voice sounded, bounding off streets and buildings. The girl stopped her bike and turned around. For a split second, Rebecca wondered what she would see, if the girl was really some hideous beast, a basilisk that could kill with a glance. But when she turned, it was only a little girl, bright eyes as happy as her smile.

"Hurry up, silly! You're gonna miss the festival!"

"The festival? Honey," she said, squatting down to the girl's level and holding out her arms, "come to me baby. It's not safe."

The little girl giggled and when she did, it sounded like a dozen children were laughing. The sound doubled and redoubled, building and breaking on itself. Then the girl rode away.

Rebecca didn't think; she just ran after the girl. Maybe, if there had been more time, she would have wondered what a child was doing here. But there was no time. Instead she ran, stumbling over cobblestones but never falling. Chasing the girl whose laughter still echoed down the cavernous tunnel of abandoned stores and homes. She didn't even notice the whispers had returned. They called to her from the darkness. Her eyes were on the turn of the street, the one that approached her now, more slowly than it should have given the distance. When she reached it she stopped dead, as if she'd run into a wall.

She had never passed out before. Never fainted. But now she

felt the blood flow from her head and the blackness close in. She would have let it take her, but knew that to do so was to invite horrors unimagined. She steadied herself as best she could. There was no way to stop the shaking.

She put her hand over her mouth. To stifle a scream, or perhaps just because that was what people did when they see something they couldn't believe. It wasn't that what she saw was any more frightening than what she had seen before. The street behind was merely familiar, a place she had been, even if it was only in her dreams.

The street opened into a grand plaza, so big that she couldn't see where it ended to the left or the right. In the plaza was a fairground, or it had been, many years before. Now it was a lost place, as dead and decayed as the frail brown leaves that swirled about the grounds, whipping past old carnival rides and empty booths. In the far distance, somewhere beyond the plaza, smoke was rising, and the acrid smell of burning wood invaded Rebecca's nostrils. The girl was sitting on her bike in front of the gate, grinning at her.

"Come on!" she said. "It's just on the other side of here."

"Wait!" Rebecca cried, but it was too late. The girl had already darted through the entranceway, her bike racing through the eternal dusk, the scattering of leaves and the *click-click-click* of her bike the only sounds.

Rebecca didn't want to follow, but she couldn't go back. There was nowhere to go back to. She took a few steps toward the fairgrounds, passing through the broken turnstile. She would have sworn she heard it click even though no bar remained to count patrons.

Or maybe it was just the haunted sound of rusty metal swinging in the wind, a creaking that grew louder with every step. It was the gate of the old bandstand that stood before her, chipping paint and a broken-in roof leaving no memory of the past. Back and forth the gate swung in the wind, slowly wearing down what was left of the hinge that had held it for untold decades.

Suddenly though, the creaking was drowned out, replaced by the distant sound of music. The notes of a jazz band, so soft that she wasn't sure she really heard it. In front of her, then to her right, and finally behind, the direction changing as she circled the bandstand and then passed it.

She walked on, past broken bumper cars and a shattered house of mirrors but saw none of it. There was only the thing that lay at the center of the plaza, the entity that had haunted her dreams since long-gone childhood. Images of dead leaves and screaming, painted horses assaulted her eyes. The carousel sat before her, spinning slowly on its axis, as if the wind were strong enough to turn it. As it turned, she could almost see the children on the animals' backs, laughing despite the beasts' crazed eyes. Their haunted, horrified gazes.

It wasn't possible, she thought to herself. It couldn't be. She considered for the first time that maybe this was a dream. But it was all too real, too solid. She had never felt more awake at any moment in her life. Then she remembered. It was a dream, just one unlike any she had ever experienced.

Flames came into view just beyond the carousel. Rebecca knew that the little girl was there too and soon she would see what else awaited her. Then she heard the scream.

\* \* \*

Dr. Ridley was walking. His dream always started the same way, walking down a long drive. A tree-lined approach, their arms forming a canopy of foliage above him. Probably a tunnel of green in the spring, but it was never spring. Always cold, dead winter. Not that the trees would look any better in the spring. They had been left to go wild by whoever had once tended them, and now they looked like ancient, dead giants, frozen fast in the ground with great, long fingernails that continued to grow despite their end many years prior. Their eyes still watched Ridley as he walked down the ruined street and he felt their gazes ever upon him.

He remembered the first time he had come to this place, how he tried to discover a way not to visit the accursed structure at the road's end. How he had studied the shadow wall that lay behind him. He had considered touching it. Diving into it even. Perhaps he could reach the other side, he thought. If there was another side.

Something told him no. A voice in his head seemed to scream it. He decided that if he didn't listen, there was a good chance he would end up like many of the madmen he had treated earlier in his career. Maybe that was the solution. Maybe it wasn't the dreams that got you. It was curiosity, an unstoppable desire to know what lay beyond the wall of sleep.

He didn't stop to think on it anymore. Now he just started walking as soon as it began, even though each step was as if they were footsteps of doom. Even though every fiber in his being told him to stop. He didn't know if it was true but he had a theory that the less he fought it, the quicker the dreams would end. He had no proof of that, but who had proof of anything in a place like this?

The wind blew through the trees. They began to sway and in the crackling of their ancient limbs, Dr. Ridley heard words. He told himself he didn't but that was a lie. For words there were. Whispers. Of what did they speak? Secrets, maybe, of the mind. Things only the trees knew. There was only one word he really understood—his own name. He hoped he never had to answer it.

On he walked and the house—the prison—at the other end grew larger. He had seen places like this before, if for the most part, only in his studies. Those books of history that chronicled the long trek out of darkness that his profession had endured. Books that told of a time when men and women with broken minds were locked away from the rest of the world and forgotten till they died and were buried, often with nothing but a number to mark their final resting place. For him it was more than just history. He had experienced it first-hand.

And that was what sat brooding in the distance ahead of him. A jailhouse with the face of a plantation. All antebellum columns and white, shining walls. Or that was what it had once been, back when the trees weren't wild and the road wasn't deformed. The paint had long since faded and chipped, the windows shattered. The building's façade now mirrored the horrors of what had gone on inside.

Ridley stepped from the boney cover of the trees into the pale sunlight of a darkened red sky. The brick drive that he had followed now formed a circle, in the center of which stood a fountain. He looked up at the statue that rose from its midst. He shivered, but not from the cold.

There was a great stone figure, hooded and cloaked, though within the shroud one could still see the face of a woman. Her eyes were cold and bitter, locked on the trembling boy who stood before her. Her face was angry, but the boy's was terrified. The reason why was in the woman's outstretched hand.

It was a small piece of metal, incongruous with the marble hand that held it. What looked to be a small stone, shining like burnished bronze in the dying light. He could almost see the smoke rising off its surface, as it hovered, an inch in space and a second in time, from touching the lips of the quivering boy. Ridley reached up and touched his mouth. He could still feel the scar, even if it had faded with time.

"Then flew one of the seraphim unto me, having a live coal in his hand, which he had taken with the tongs from off the altar: And he laid it upon my mouth, and said, Lo, this hath touched thy lips; and thine iniquity is taken away, and thy sin purged." It was the only verse of the Bible he knew by heart.

His mother had not always been insane. There had been a time when she had been a good and gentle woman. It had begun, they suspected, the day he was born. She had lost more blood than she should have, and something in her brain had gone wrong. His father had tried not to blame him for it, but every now and then, Ridley saw the creeping resentment in his eyes.

Whatever the cause, there was nothing that could be done to stop her slow spiral into madness. His father had tried to ignore it at first, passing off her increasing periods of delirium as the product of an overly emotional mind. Then came the day when he could ignore it no more.

Before her mind slipped, his mother had been a devoted Christian woman. After his birth, her religion became her obsession. She was drawn, as the mad often are, to the more esoteric and apocalyptic writings of the Bible. Her favorite was Isaiah.

What had he done that day? What crime had he committed that needed to be expunged? He could not say. For years he had obsessed over it, thought it through again and again. Perhaps he had spilled something. Broken something. Made noise when he should have been quiet. Been quiet when he should have made noise. It didn't matter.

All that mattered was when she dragged him into the front room where the fire burned wild and hot in the hearth. She reached in, removing a red-hot coal from its midst. In her religious fervor, she didn't even feel the pain. But he could smell the burning of human flesh, and the stench of it made him scream all the louder when she placed the coal to his lips.

The next day, his mother was committed to an insane asylum on the other side of the country. He never saw her again, not until her body lay in a casket.

He looked up at the face behind the shroud, the perfect image of his mother. He wept for her and he wept for himself. He wished that it could all be forgiven, because that was what the statue represented.

The cleansing of sin. His sin. Yes, it was built for him. *They* had built it. Not so he would never forget. He needed no memorial to spark his memory. The evidence was still on his skin. No, it stood here so that he would know that they knew. That they knew everything.

It had been years since water had come forth from that stone. Indeed, years since rain had touched the barren soil that surrounded the antebellum structure, stretching forth to the thick, dead forest that bordered it on three sides and probably lay beyond the shadow wall as well. He spat into the bone-dry depths of the fountain. Some people ran from the dreams in fear. He faced them in anger.

He walked around the statue and looked up at the broken windows of the abandoned edifice. He could feel their eyes upon him. He had never seen them but his patients had. And he knew they had eyes. Great pools of emptiness where their faces should be. The whispers began again, calling him.

"Show yourselves!" he shouted to the nothingness. The laughter of a woman answered him. He looked through the open door, all the way across the main hallway to a large courtyard through yet another open portal. She stepped from the shadows and into the light only for a moment, passing through the shard of the dying sun that poured through the open door.

Even from that singular moment, he saw she was beautiful, just as she had been before he had known her. He was able to draw that conclusion from so little because he had lived this moment a hundred times, every time he had the dream.

He walked through the broken door of the asylum. The wind blew the leaves in behind him and he jumped as a crystal from the chandelier above fell to the ground and shattered. He cursed himself under his breath. No matter how many times it happened, he was always surprised.

He stepped gingerly across the broken tile and listened to the *bang* . . .

    *bang* . . .

       *bang* of a door somewhere in the distance.

There were two long hallways, one on either side. The woman had walked from his right to left, not that he really had to think about it. He turned down the hallway on his left. He could see all the way to the end. Rows of rooms, cells really, lined the corridor on either side. He waited. She appeared again, walking from one empty room into another. Ridley snorted out a laugh.

"It's always the same game, isn't it? Well, Mother, let's finish this."

He took a step into the corridor but that's when he heard the scream.

# CHAPTER
# 8

Caroline Gravely stood in the center of a plain of golden grain. Fields that went on forever in all directions, as far as her eyes could see. Down into valleys and up hillsides. All the way to the horizon. An undulating sea of amber that made the wind look like a thing itself dancing among the stalks.

There was no black wall of shadow, as she had heard so many others describe it. There was no need. She knew, through some preternatural sense, that nothing lay beyond the planted field of waist-high wheat. If she walked forever, she would never reach its end.

There was more than just a carpet of gold, though, and the bright blue sky above it. More than the thick, white, puffy clouds that cast moving shadows upon the field. There was a cabin several hundred feet in front of her. A rickety, worn-down shack of hewed logs and unplaned wood. She wondered sometimes, stupidly, she thought, where the wood had come from. As if anything here had to make sense.

Gravely stood and imbibed as the scene moved around her. It did not move as it should. The world was slowed, as if time itself had been split in half. All was slow motion and when she raised her hands or took a step, it felt like the air was molasses. Only her thoughts ran at full speed.

The breeze that rustled the wheat caressed her hair and made the only sound she heard—that of heads of grain beating against each other. The cabin door was open, but inside showed no light. The doorway had the appearance of a dark maw that might swallow her up, made all the worse by the bright, shining sun above.

As if to mock her feelings of something sinister within that darkness, a man emerged. Neither his skin nor hair was as dark as they had once been, for age had coated them an ashy white. But even from where she stood, she could tell that his eyes were still bright and strong. She had seen those eyes before. Every day when she looked in the mirror.

But she had never seen her grandfather like this, dusty blue overalls and dirty white shirt underneath, great hands calloused and torn from labor. No, he had been a naval officer. This was another ancestor, from far longer ago, a man who had once been a slave. He looked at her, standing in the midst of the field. She watched him as he slowly turned and she saw, rather than heard, him say something to the darkness beyond.

Then, longer than it should have been, another figure emerged. A woman, once beautiful, but whose youth had been stolen by too many years of bright sunlight and the dirt of the field. Now they stood next to each other, two people from her past and her present and, no doubt, her future.

Her grandfather raised his hand, slowly, inexorably, like it had a weight attached to its end. He was waving at her. The woman joined in, beckoning in slow motion for her to come to them, to join them inside. She could almost hear their voices, telling her that there was lemonade and homemade sweet potato pie. A warm bed with clean sheets where she could sleep away the crushing weariness. She wanted so much to believe that. And maybe she would have, were it not for the whispers.

They roared from the cabin on a sudden gust of wind that blew at half-speed across the field. She comprehended nothing, but recognized the rhythm and cadence of speech. Then a word she knew, "Caroline," whispered almost lovingly.

It chilled her, that voice, even in the midst of a sun-drenched field. Her ancestors continued to beckon, urging her to join them. To convince her that it would be all right. There was peace here. And love. She wanted to believe. She had fought against that call for so many years. Every time she came here. Every time she saw the one thing that she never had in life.

But the swirling darkness that waited inside the cabin spoke black truth to that lie. She could feel eyes upon her. Empty eyes.

She started to shake. She wrapped her arms around her shoulders and her chest but no warmth came. The two figures on the porch turned and walked back into the house.

"No!" she wanted to cry, but the word would not come. Those two people were not her family. They were a myth, a trick of light and shade. Bait to lure her to her demise.

Caroline fell to her knees. The golden grain swayed around her at eye level, more whispers from their ears to hers. She collapsed down on her side and started to sob. The clouds crawled across the sky. The grain danced in the breeze. And she prayed that whatever waited in the darkness could not abide the light. She was still praying when the scream ripped through the whispers and echoed across the plain.

* * *

Jack Crawford was standing in the foyer of what he would come to learn was a grand ballroom. He looked down at himself and rubbed his hands along the stiff fabric of the tuxedo he was wearing, one he had never seen before. All of this was new to him. Jack had done most of his work on-world and the few times he had left Earth, he had stayed within the solar system.

"Well this is different," Jack said as he fingered what appeared to be a solid gold cufflink on his left sleeve.

Music wafted through the double doors that stood closed before him. He turned and tried one of the exits. Somewhat to his surprise, it opened, but Jack did not leave. His eyes met what appeared to be black smoke. But too thick for smoke. Too solid and consistent. More like a wall of flowing oil. Something about it repulsed him. He let the door slam and he did not think of leaving again. Not till much later, at least.

He turned back to the sound of music. The deeply carved doors were illuminated by an ornate chandelier that hung above, its thousand different crystals both gathering and fracturing the light, throwing it in grotesque patterns upon the wall.

Jack Crawford took a few steps forward and grasped the handles of the double doors. He heard laughter from inside and wondered what he was about to find. He pulled them open and the music and the light washed over him. The ballroom was an appropriate location, for this was a ball. The men were dressed like him in sharp, black tuxes and white ties. The women in ruffled fabric. Gloves with sleeves that stretched all the way to their elbows. Their hair, piled high in delicately placed mounds, always an instant from collapsing like an avalanche down their shoulders.

Jack's stomach twisted in knots and he felt the bile rise in his throat, that uncomfortable wave of nausea that spread over one about to be sick. He looked out over that crowd, trying to understand what it was that made him so uneasy. Trying to remember. For he thought the key was locked somewhere inside, deep within his mind. If he could find it, all of this would make sense.

A gloved arm slid around his neck, but Jack was still too confused to be startled. He looked over to see a woman brushing gold ringlets from her blue eyes, smiling at him.

"Jack," she purred, "so glad you could finally make it. We've all been waiting for the guest of honor."

She was familiar and frightening at the same time. What scared Jack all the more was his inability to remember why she was either. She beamed up at him but there was something sinister about those straight rows of perfect, pearly white teeth. There was no joy there.

She released her grasp on Jack's neck, letting her arm slide down his back and around his waist, and then over to his hand, which she took.

"Shall we?" she asked. Jack merely nodded.

"You don't remember me, do you?" she said as they walked down the steps to the ballroom floor.

"I . . ." Jack began.

"It's alright," she interrupted. "I'm no fool, Jack. I know I wasn't your first, or more importantly"—she laughed—"your last." She finally ended his suffering when it became clear that Jack was no closer to remembering. "Elizabeth. Elizabeth Akers."

Now Jack had a name, the familiarity of which matched the face, but did no more to dispel the mystery of who this woman was, where he had seen her before, or what role she had played in his life. She pulled him close to her when they reached the floor and whispered in his ear, "I need to go to the ladies' room. Get me a drink. You know what I like."

He started to protest, to say that, in fact, he had no idea, but she had already slid away from him, disappearing into the crowd of people beyond. All of whom, he noticed, were eyeing him with some interest and, if he read them right, familiarity.

Jack hesitated, until the voice of a man calling his name pulled him from his thoughts.

"Mr. Crawford," said the man. Jack turned and saw that he was standing in front of a bar, even though he had no memory of moving to the side of the room in which it sat. "Hello, Mr. Crawford. Such a pleasure to see you again, sir."

"Again?" Jack said.

"Well of course. I never forget a face. Certainly not yours."

"No," said Jack, "I guess in your business that's a good trait to have."

"Yes, and I suppose in yours it is better simply to forget."

The man grinned, his salt and pepper black hair slicked back over a burgeoning bald spot, while Jack stared stupidly back at him. Before Jack could say anything else, the man continued. "But this is actually not my trade. I'm simply filling in for the event. Every party needs a bartender, after all."

"Party?"

"Ah yes. A reunion of sorts, you might say. All in your honor, of course."

"Of course," Jack murmured.

"So. What'll it be, sir? As you can see, we have a fully stocked bar. Mixers of every variety and every sort of alcohol you could imagine. I assume you'll be drinking top shelf."

"I'll take a Manhattan," Jack said.

"A Manhattan, and easy on the vermouth, I assume?"

Jack frowned. "How did you . . ."

"Just my job, sir. I can tell you are a man who likes his alcohol with a little bite. And for the lady?"

"The lady?"

"Yes, I believe you are with Ms. Akers."

"Yeah. . . yeah she'll have a . . ." Then it came to him like a clap of thunder. "Vodka gimlet. With a twist."

"Ah yes, that is her favorite. Classic drink, yes, Mr. Crawford?"

Jack had no idea if that was her favorite or not, nor did he know why that drink tumbled forth into his mind like the bourbon the bartender was now pouring into a glass.

"Here you are, sir, a Manhattan for you and a classy drink for a classy lady. And, Mr. Crawford," he said, as Jack began to turn, "I do hope that you enjoy the reunion. After all, none of us would be here without you."

For a space of two seconds that seemed like an eternity, the men stared across the bar at each other. The bartender's eyes told Jack all he needed to know. Most of what he said was a formality, like he had been playing a game. A part, a role that had been given him. But that last bit was true, a bitter truth riding on the bartender's cold glare to fill the space between them.

Jack turned around and scanned his surroundings. Trying to find something, anything to help him understand what was going on. He knew the dreams sometimes took the form of old memories. Although he searched for a landmark in that great hall, he found none. If this were a memory, it was not one he recalled. If this was a place he'd frequented before, he had forgotten it.

Of course, there were those that speculated that the dreams were visions, pictures of the future. Images of things to come. Jack had never believed any of that nonsense. Jack put his faith in the cold, hard truths of the world. In the facts that could be seen and the things that could be known. A man in his profession didn't think too much about the future. Didn't think much about fate or God's will or the afterlife.

Jack had long been a tool that shaped worlds but he did not like to think of himself as such. He liked to believe that he was what he had chosen to be and that in so choosing, he had been more instrumental in deciding the future than most men would be if they lived ten lifetimes. Jack didn't like to believe in destiny because it detracted from what he was, undermined the power that rested in his hands.

No, fate didn't decide how men's lives would end. Jack did that. And a man like Jack Crawford never liked to feel out of control. In his profession, such a feeling could be fatal. But it was one he could not avoid here, where every person in the room seemed to know his face, yet he recognized no one. But it was just a dream. Just a dream. He would ride it out, and then when he woke, none of it would matter anyway.

He turned and saw Elizabeth gliding toward him. She held out her hand and took the drink from his. She took a sip and the alcohol lit a fire in her eyes. She smiled decadently, saying, "Robert always did make a fantastic vodka gimlet." She looked past Jack, raised her glass and nodded. Jack turned in time to see the bartender bow slightly in response.

"So you know this Robert?" Jack said, cautiously probing the edges of the mystery, trying to find the common thread that bound all these people together, other than himself.

"Oh, I've known Robert for a while. He was here when I arrived. He helped me, just like he helped so many of us. With the transition. It's not an easy one, you know? Well you wouldn't. But you'll know one day. Hopefully one day soon." Elizabeth laughed, and the sound of it gave Jack chills.

"Yes," Jack said nervously. "So . . . what do you do here?"

"Here? Here we wait. We've been waiting for you, of course. To join us. It has been," she whispered, tilting her head back and closing her eyes, almost as if in unimaginable pleasure, "so long. Longer for some than others."

The music picked up. He did not know from whence it came; it simply was. As much a part of the chamber as the floor or the ceiling or the air. Or these people.

"Shall we dance?"

"Of course," Jack answered. Jack's training with the agency had begun when he was very young. His father had been an operative before him. It was a job he was born to do. His education had been wide and varied. Everything from firearms and explosives classes to the social graces. Jack was as well versed in the Argentine tango as the KV-27 rifle.

His training had also prepared him for situations such as this. If you don't know what's going on, play along. The situation will eventually explain itself. It had always worked before, Jack thought. No reason it wouldn't now.

As the others danced around them, Jack looked down at the woman who clung tightly to his neck, black dress hanging low and loose from her shoulders. She was gazing up at him. In her eyes was a mixture of so many emotions that he couldn't make a single one out.

Then that changed. The smile faded. Her mouth began to quiver. Her skin went pale. Fear came into her eyes. She grabbed his shoulder and squeezed so hard it hurt.

"Elizabeth?"

She uttered a pitiful cry and slid down on her knees. She looked up at Jack who stood dumbfounded above her. She opened her mouth, but nothing came out. Then she released him and fell on her side. Around them, the others danced. The music did not stop. As she lay dying, no one seemed to notice.

Jack looked down at Elizabeth's motionless body. He considered just leaving her there. No one seemed to care about what was going on, about the dead woman in their midst, and the feeling that he should flee was becoming overwhelming. There was no understanding this situation. Only getting away from it.

"You just gonna stand there?"

Jack shuddered. It was a voice from his past, a voice he had never expected to hear again. His father, Austin Crawford, stood beside him. He was wearing an Armani tuxedo, a beige pocket square, and a crimson bow tie. Even as he stared at this phantom, Jack could think only that his father had always known the best things in life when he saw them, and he was never shy about spending the money it took to acquire them.

"This is a dream," Jack mumbled.

His father knelt down beside Elizabeth's body. "It's a not a dream. Well, it is, I guess," he said, looking up at his son. "But only for now. It will be real all too soon."

His father gave the same toothy grin Jack had often seen in life. He looked down at Elizabeth and nudged her in the side. "Hmm. Let's see what we have here." He grasped the body with both hands, pulling her toward him. As he rolled her over on her back, her still-open eyes locked on Jack. Most men probably would have looked away. Jack stared back.

"Poison," Austin said as thick foam poured from Elizabeth's mouth. He picked up a shard of the shattered glass that lay on the ground beside her and took a deep breath. "No doubt about it." He looked up at Jack. "Definitely cyanide." He stood, brushing off his hands on his pants. "Your specialty if I remember correctly."

"Never cyanide," Jack said. "I wouldn't be so stupid." For a moment, for several actually, Jack had stood, staring stupidly at the resurrected phantasm of his father, dead these past ten years. But the old resentment had returned. He was not afraid and somehow, he wasn't shocked anymore either.

"No," said Austin, "no, I guess you wouldn't."

The two men stood face-to-face, so close to each other that their noses almost touched. They could have been mirror images of one another, were one man not twenty years older.

Finally, Austin looked away. "I need a drink." He stepped over Elizabeth's body and walked to the bar. "Gin and tonic, Robert. Double."

Jack glanced down at the woman he did not know one last time and then joined his father.

"Another Manhattan, Mr. Crawford?" Robert looked up at Jack expectantly, bottle of bourbon in his hand. Jack ignored him.

"What the hell is wrong with you people?" Jack rarely lost his composure but it was all but gone now. "That woman"—he pointed behind him—"was your friend. You knew her. She . . ." Jack looked back toward where she still lay. Her head had fallen to the side and once again her open, dead eyes met his. "She's dead," Jack said. "Somebody killed her and none of you even care."

His father slung back half of his drink and looked up at Jack. Then he laughed. It started as a murmur, then grew to a low chuckle. A rumble that began deep in his stomach and burst full born into a roar that echoed around the great hall. Bounding up and down, multiplying and reverberating so loud that Jack put his hands over his ears to stop the sound. But it was still there, inside his mind as much as beyond it.

It died down slowly, matching the sound of the music and then succumbing to it. Jack noted clinically that the music had switched to a waltz. The couples danced almost mechanically, circling around the room and Elizabeth's body.

"So," Austin began. He had produced a cigarette from seeming thin air and Robert was leaning in to light it. "All of a sudden you've developed a conscience. How charming. I didn't think you were capable of caring. Only when it suits you, I suppose."

"Ha! Whatever I'm capable of, it's what you made me."

Austin slammed his glass against the counter so hard that ice cubes went flying along the bar, though Robert was ready with a towel.

"I know exactly what you are capable of," he said, stepping forward. Austin grabbed the collar of his own shirt. He pulled it down sharply, popping buttons that went skittering along the floor. Thick red lines ran parallel around his neck, meeting and overlapping in the middle.

Jack didn't look. There was no need. He had seen them before. "You made your own choice, Father. You should have known what would happen."

"Don't patronize me!" Austin snarled. "I never turned. They knew that. And worst of all, you knew it too. It was a test. To see just how far you would go. Well you passed, didn't you? And now you're theirs for life. Their good little dog. Just waiting for them to tell you what trick to do next, isn't that right?"

"Oh this is rich. Is this why you came here? You self-righteous bastard. How many people did you kill? You always knew how it would end. You died for a reason. If it wasn't me, it would have been somebody else. I decided I would rather take care of it myself. You deserved that much."

"Is that right? Well tell me this, why did you kill her?"

Jack followed his father's finger to Elizabeth's corpse. It was only then he realized that the music had stopped. The people at the party had stopped dancing too, and now they surrounded Elizabeth in a half circle. But they still did not seem to notice her. All their eyes were on Jack.

"I told you. I didn't kill her," Jack said, suddenly uneasy. "He's the one who fixed her drink. Why don't you ask him?"

Robert coughed out a laugh, and Austin gave him a knowing grin.

"It wasn't Robert, Jack. Take a look at her again. Take a good, long look."

"I don't know her!" But even in his own voice, Jack heard doubt. He looked back at her, at the gracefully curving lines of her body. The well-defined cheek bones, the high and haughty brow, her eyes and her lips. Within him a memory stirred.

"Not so sure, anymore, are you? Her name is Elizabeth Akers. Elizabeth Akers Adair."

Adair.

"Oh God." Jack fell back against the bar, his hand covering his mouth. "It can't be."

"Anything can be, Jack. Anything can be here, in this place."

Elizabeth Adair. Yes, he knew her now. It had been years. Fifteen, if he remembered correctly. Her husband was David Adair, the head of a banking conglomerate that had found involvement with terrorist organizations to be a lucrative business opportunity. His target had been Elizabeth. The Company didn't want David dead. Killing him would only open the door to some other cutthroat SOB who would follow the money to the exact same policies David had pursued. No, David needed to be sent a message.

He had met her at a bar on the North Side of Chicago, just down from Wrigley Field. He had followed her there several times, whenever David said he was playing poker with his buddies but instead was ensconced in one of the city's finer gentleman's clubs. One where touching was both allowed and encouraged, for the right price.

Elizabeth found peace in that little baseball-themed bar, three blocks from where she had grown up. It reminded her of simpler times, before she gave up her dreams for a life in a penthouse apartment in midtown. Most people thought she had done well for herself and she didn't have the heart to tell them otherwise.

He found her seated at the bar, talking to a no name drink jockey who was paying attention only because her neckline seemed to plunge all the way to her stomach. Jack bought her a vodka gimlet. He had found that women were always on the lookout for a sign, something to assure them that whatever they were doing was the right and proper thing. That God or fate had ordained it. For most, ordering their favorite drink without prompting was like a bolt of lightning from the heavens.

"How did you know?" they'd ask, just as Elizabeth asked that night. And Jack would smile and say he could just tell by looking. "I've been watching you for three weeks" was far less romantic.

He'd had no trouble taking her to a room in the Four Seasons. She was desperate for something, anything to drag her out of her pain. He was there and willing. He'd slept with her, even though that was not part of the assignment. He wasn't sure why he did it. He had felt sorry for her, somewhat.

When he thought back on it, he guessed that the least he could do was give her one more night of pleasure. One last good memory to float off on. David had killed her spirit all those years ago, when he plucked her from a nice middle-class life with nice middle-class dreams to be a trophy for presentation. Now David had killed her body too, even if he didn't know it.

Austin had been right; it was cyanide. Jack resorted to poison only when he wanted a death to appear natural or accidental and so normally he would never use the drug. Too obviously murder. But here he wanted to be obvious. Elizabeth had died to send a message.

Not that David heard it. His response was to hire new security. Jack wanted to be the one to finish him off, to make him pay. But another agent got the assignment, and at least when David's car exploded in his driveway, the bank's next CEO realized that criminal associations, while good business, were bad for one's health. Still, Elizabeth had died for nothing.

"Yes, Jack, you know her, don't you?"

He did, but it wasn't Elizabeth that made his mouth go dry, that made his blood run cold in his veins. He did know Elizabeth, but he knew others too. They stood in the crowd, every one of them staring daggers at Jack. There was Bryan Truant, a man he had shot with a high-powered rifle for his involvement in a Martian separatist movement.

Philip Hayman, poisoned in his home for reasons Jack never cared to know. Grace Craft, stabbed in a back alley behind a bar. Robbery gone bad, the papers had said. There were so many. Some he knew. Others he didn't, either because he didn't remember or because they were collateral damage. A necessary price to pay for progress.

And then there was Robert. Yes, Robert Graves. An accountant in Boston who wrote a holo on the side, one as popular as it was judged dangerous. Robert Graves, the first man he had ever killed.

"We're all here for you, Jack," his father said, as he and everyone else in the room took a step forward, closing in a half-circle around him. "All for you. We've been waiting for you to join us."

"But this is just a dream," Jack said, pushing himself against the bar so hard that one might wonder if he thought he could dissolve into it.

"Perhaps, Jack. Or maybe this is something more." His father's face was inches from his. The others were crowded around, bathing Jack in their hot breath. "Maybe this is a glimpse of the future. It will be here soon enough, and when it comes, we'll be waiting."

His father started to laugh, and perhaps Jack would have screamed. But at that instant, another scream rent the air, and the room dissolved into darkness.

# CHAPTER 9

Something wasn't right. Aidan hated the dreams as much as anyone, but there was comfort in their familiarity. The way they were always the same, no matter how many times he dreamt. This time, it was different.

He always awoke in the bowels of a ship, a massive one that was altogether unfamiliar to him. He would wander through the deserted, darkened corridors, alone, save for the whispers that echoed up and down its halls, and the shadows that walked with him. For they were there, just beyond his sight. Smoldering night personified.

Yes, the dreams were the same. Almost. He could change them, if he took a different turn or chose a different path. Not that he was free to do whatever he wanted. Often he would open a door and peer into a darkness so thick that he thought it a solid thing. The shadow wall, others who had found it in their own dreams called it.

Sometimes he thought about challenging that darkness, plunging into it with body and soul and seeing what it hid. But he never did. Instead, he always locked it behind doors that slid closed with a thud, temporarily drowning out the roar of those interminable whispers. Then he would push on, searching through winding corridors for something, though he could never say precisely what. Not until the last time when he found it.

He had gone farther than ever before, his path guided by those dark walls that prevented him from turning aside. Whatever lay behind that darkness, whoever called his name in a language he could not comprehend, was leading him. It wanted him to find it, what was hidden. When the final door opened and the whispers ceased, he knew he had reached his destination.

He emerged into a large open room, one that he recognized immediately as the bridge. It was different, though, than any he had ever seen. The command center was the same, but when he looked up, he saw that the entire ceiling was made of glass or something like it, clear and transparent, leaving the darkness of space to shine down on him.

As he stared up at that openness, he knew that there was something wrong. For it was as pitch black as the shadow walls behind him. He had never seen anything like that. Even in the deepest parts of space, there was always something, even if it was only the tiniest pinpoints of light from the most distant stars. Not here. Here it was just darkness, one that the glass dome above made seem utterly infinite.

He walked over to the computer and ran his hands across it. To his surprise—but somehow not—it sprung to life.

"Command, Aidan Connor?" it asked. He never even questioned the fact that it knew his name.

"Location?"

The answer should have come instantaneously. Instead, the computer sat silently, the whirling sounds and flashing lights from within telling him it was still working on the solution to a simple problem.

"Cannot ascertain location," it finally answered. Aidan frowned.

"Run diagnostic," he said, knowing how foolish such a request must be in the midst of a dream.

Almost instantly the computer replied, "Diagnostic complete. All systems functional."

"Computer, display the nearest star."

Another unusually long period later, "No stellar activity detected."

A shiver ran down Aidan's spine, and despite his best efforts to control it, the panic started to set in. The stars were his guideposts, shining beacons in a dark sea of infinity. And if the computer could not find one, then he was truly lost.

He looked up at the black dome above him and an impossible

thought crept into his mind. A dawning realization of a horrible possibility, made all the worse by the fact it was the only one that made any sense.

"Computer," he said, "locate the nearest gravity well."

It appeared in an instant, the physical representation of insanity made manifest. A swirling darkness on the computer screen. The black hole was only a moderate distance away, but far enough that Aidan did not fear the event horizon.

"Computer," he said, "zoom out ten light years."

The screen changed, the image stretching and expanding, the small whirling darkness shrinking to a mere black dot. Then it multiplied and a hundred more black holes filled the screen.

"Computer," Aidan whispered, "zoom out, maximum."

For several minutes Aidan waited, the only sound that of the computer collecting data from as far as the ship's sensors could reach. Collating and arranging it into a graphical representation of space that he could understand. Then the computer displayed what Aidan expected, and he felt his sanity slip.

Thousands of gravity wells appeared, spread across what had been the galaxy. Splotches of blackness on an already inky sky. He looked up again at the great dome of glass above him. One intended, he supposed, to allow men to gaze out at the glories of the universe. Glories long dead. And finally, Aidan understood.

He had awoken then, just as the *Vespa* had dropped out of warp somewhere beyond Pluto. It was the last warp jump he had ever taken, the *Vespa* having not made another one successfully. But now, he had been prepared to see it all again, the heat death of the universe. A vision of that which must one day be.

Billions of years in the future, a time when every star had died, and every civilization with it. Burnt out to charcoal cinders, exploded to nothingness, or collapsed into black holes. He had steeled himself for that ultimate darkness, that infinite shade. How surprising then when his dream began somewhere completely different.

Well, not completely. It was a ship, but not an unfamiliar one. Nor were the corridors darkened and empty. No, it was just as he remembered it. Alive and full of light. For when Aidan awoke to the dream, he found himself on the *Vespa*, standing on a hallway that led from the engine room to the bridge. It was her final voyage. He knew that instinctively.

Mark Anderson, the ship's engineer, came through the door to the bridge on the far side of the corridor. He walked toward Aidan with eyes directly upon him. Aidan started to say something, but then a cold realization dawned on him—Mark could not see him. He then had the most disconcerting moment of his life as Mark seemed to pass straight through his body, walking toward the engine room beyond. The door opened, and the shadow wall appeared. But Mark did not seem to notice it.

"No!" Aidan cried out. Mark didn't hear him, either. He simply passed through, with nary a ripple. As horrific as the old dream had been, somehow this was worse.

Aidan took a few steps toward the bridge, and tried to get everything straight. He wasn't on the *Vespa*, not really. So the sensors on the door would not recognize his presence. But when he reached them the doors opened, just as they should. He didn't bother to pause and think on it, instead stepping through them, feeling the whoosh of air as they closed behind. It was then he found himself standing face-to-face with his doppelgänger.

There he was as he had been only a few months before, standing at attention, wearing the same blue flight suit he always did. Aidan shivered as he recognized just how much these last few months had aged him, but the scene he was witnessing was a recent one. The only things he couldn't explain were why his twin seemed to be sweating so profusely, and why he had no memory of this moment.

"Aidan," he heard a voice say. He spun on his heel to see Captain Marcus standing behind him. His mouth fell open and he started to answer. But the man's eyes were fixed beyond his left shoulder. He wasn't addressing him. At least, not his present self. "Aidan, I'm sorry, but I don't understand what you mean."

"Sir, I don't know that I can explain it. But my gut says there's something wrong here. I think we should wait."

"Wait? Wait on what? Mr. Connor," the captain began, and Aidan heard a twinge of sympathy in his voice. The older man moved forward and Aidan stepped to the side to avoid the awkward feeling of having the captain stand in his spectral presence. "I know you had a tough go of it last time. We've all been there. But you've got to move on. Listen, when this mission is done, why don't you take a break? A vacation. A couple months would do you good."

A feeling of lightheadedness rushed over Aidan and he had to grab the chair next to him for support. He half expected his hand to slide straight through it as he fell to the floor, but it held his weight.

He had long tried to avoid thinking about those days, the ones following that last horrible sequence of dreams. After he had stared into the final fate of all things. He had experienced what might be called a nervous breakdown, and had even spent a couple weeks under the care of a psychiatric doctor in the infirmary. It was nothing serious.

Not the sleep-madness at least, and everyone accepted the doctor's diagnosis that Aidan had simply been working too hard for too long and needed a break. But now he knew what Captain Marcus had always understood: it was more than that.

He watched the man put a hand on his twin's shoulder, and it struck him once again that he had no memory of this event, just as he had no memory of most of that final, fateful trip on the *Vespa*. Had any of this actually happened? Was any of this real? Or was this all *their* creation? But for what purpose? To confuse him? To scare him? That, he could not say.

He glanced around the bridge, searching every dark spot, every shadowed corner for their empty, watching eyes. But he did not see them, and more importantly, he did not feel or hear them either.

"I promise you," Captain Marcus said as Aidan looked back at the man he had called friend, "nothing is going to happen on this trip. You and I, we've done this for years. Done this dozens, hell, hundreds of times. This one is no different."

The other Aidan nodded once, and Captain Marcus accepted it, even if no one in the room was convinced. Then a computer voice broke in, the same female voice as always. "Warp point reached," it said.

Marcus looked at Aidan's twin. "Alright," he said. "I'll be with the others. We'll see you shortly, right?"

He didn't wait for an answer. Instead, he turned and walked to the door, stopping there to cast one last glance back at Aidan. Then he was gone, off to his destiny.

Aidan and his double were alone. Aidan looked over at the man who had been him and he didn't like what he saw. He was shaking, whatever self-control he had mustered for the captain was now gone. The other Aidan looked down at the controls. The computer had opened the warp console. He need only input a few numbers, mark a few coordinates, and his work would be finished. But he did not move. He just stared, the trembling in his hands spreading to the rest of his body.

"Go on," Aidan said, even though his twin didn't hear. The man's trembling stilled and in his face Aidan saw a conclusion reached, a decision made. He reached down and with a swipe of his hand, closed the warp console. "What are you doing?" Aidan shrieked as much as asked. In a few seconds, he would have known the answer, but then a scream echoed through the bridge like the sound of thunder.

# CHAPTER
# 10

Cyrus was smoking a cigar. The paper band wrapped around the cut end said it was Cuban, though he had no recollection of buying it or lighting it for that matter. He took a deep draw and the glowing embers of lit tobacco glowed so fiercely that for a moment they almost lit the dim rear compartment of the Rolls Royce. Cyrus blew thick smoke into the air and grinned. He'd smoked the same cigar dozens of times over the years and it always tasted just as sweet as the first.

As if on cue, the driver turned to him. "We're here, Mr. McDonnell."

"Of course we are," he thought. The script was so familiar to him he could almost count the beats to the next event, the next phrase. Especially the beginning. The beginning was always the same. The same sweet cigar; a touch of orange peel and the taste of leather. The ancient Rolls Royce, curving lines of steel that trumpeted wealth to the world. And the driver. In a way, Cyrus was frightened by him. It was his black, soulless eyes, and Cyrus was glad their interactions were brief.

"Thank you, Charles," Cyrus said. Whether the man's name was Charles or not, he couldn't say. But the appellation seemed appropriate and the man had never objected, so Charles it was. "I'll take it from here."

Cyrus stepped out into a rain-slicked Chicago evening. He stood and buttoned the middle buttons of his suit jacket, pausing a second to fix the cuffs of his shirt. "Just part of the ritual", he thought. "Just part of the night."

Before him sat a tall granite building, cyclopean in its construction. It rose up like a modern pyramid in the center of the city, disappearing somewhere above the rain-full clouds, their bloated forms threatening to break at any moment.

On either side of the building was a shadow wall. Each pulsated like a living thing, rippling and roiling as the seas might on a stormy night. He watched as cars emerged from and then disappeared into those implacable barriers. People on the sidewalks did the same, not seeming to notice them, or not caring if they did. "A barrier only to you," Cyrus thought.

He had wondered, when he first dreamed, what lay beyond them. He was an explorer at heart. He had joined the guild for adventure. To see beyond what others saw. Space had called to him like the sea must have called his ancestors centuries before.

But the walls were not necessary to stop him anymore. Cyrus had no desire to go beyond them. No, what he wanted was in the building in front of him. Or more precisely, below it. He rubbed his hands together and smiled. Cyrus didn't hate the dreams like the others. He loved them.

Oh, he kept up the lie. He told people that he feared the dreams as they did. He would recount the terror he experienced vaguely, never in too much detail. Which was fine. No one ever talked about the dreams, not really. The dreams were a gift in a funny way. A treasure of the sleeper. Unique and yet the same all at once. Like falling snowflakes.

Cyrus walked down the long, dark alley next to the building. He loved how clichéd and wonderful it was. Like something out of a movie. It was barely lit and bathed in shadows, every one of which threatened to hide some unnamable evil or danger. Steam rose from open pipes that protruded from the alley walls. Cyrus stopped and listened carefully until he heard the sound of an empty bottle skittering across the ground, as if an angry man who intended evil against man and bottle alike kicked it. Cyrus almost laughed. The regularity was humorous in a way.

He kept walking until he reached a door in the massive building's wall, a dim bulb hanging naked above it. He remembered still the first time he had the dream. It had not been much of a search to find this door. He had walked straight to it, as if guided by some preternatural sense. He had found it, even if he had not known he sought it.

He knocked loudly. Three times, pausing a half beat between each. He had known to do that the first time, too. A wooden slat slid away in the center of the door. Two unfriendly eyes peered out at Cyrus. Then the look changed to recognition.

"Mr. McDonnell!" the voice that came with the eyes exclaimed. "So good to see you again, sir." The slat slid back in place and the sound of the unbolting of many locks reverberated down the door and into the alleyway.

The door swung open and a man who Cyrus felt like he had known his entire life appeared. He was a giant. From his shaved head to his muscle-bound arms to his massive fists, one of which he opened and offered to Cyrus, everything about him made one think he'd been built instead of born. Created for the sole purpose of winning a fight. The man's hand enveloped his own and Cyrus winced from the power of that grip.

Cyrus had learned over the years that the man had been a professional boxer before he was a bouncer. His career had gone so far as to land him in a championship fight in a division that was not heavyweight and thus that Cyrus did not recall—assuming, of course, that this man existed in the real world. In any event, he had lost that match, and his career with it. Cyrus often mused that anyone who could defeat this man in single combat was not a person he had any desire to meet.

"Who's on stage tonight, Tom?" Cyrus asked. He knew the answer. It was a question he had asked a dozen times. But he had come to feel that he had a role to act out in this play. It was incumbent upon him not to stray too far from his part.

Tom grinned. "Sidney, of course. But you know that."

Cyrus did know it. It was strange, though. He never recalled Tom knowing that he knew it before. Perhaps this abnormality should have given him pause, and maybe it did deep within that reptilian part of the brain where the instincts live. But he brushed the inconsistency away. He had no time for such silly things.

Tom led him down a darkened hallway to a spiraling staircase that curved down to a floor below. Gesturing toward it with a sweep of his huge hand, Tom said, "You know the rest of the way, Mr. McDonnell. Do enjoy yourself, now. I hope you have a . . . pleasant evening." Tom smiled, and for the first time Cyrus noticed he had the same coal-black eyes as the driver.

Cyrus began his descent, curling down the stairs, his feet making a

*clank*

    *clank*

        *clank* sound with every step.

It ended in the opening to a hallway. Another large man in a suit stood at the entrance. He nodded to Cyrus, just as he always did. Cyrus had never spoken to the man and he occasionally pondered what would happen if he did. He suspected the man would merely nod, regardless. A robot, programmed to do a single task.

The hallway beyond was darkened by clouds of smoke billowing from chambers to each side. Cyrus stepped into that smoke, smelling the sweet, sappy fragrance, the decadent tang. The gift of the poppy. The side chambers were no more than open pits where men lay, most of them emaciated and slack-jawed. Their eyes were still open, even if they no longer saw. Their lives given to the opium that still burned within pipes they clutched in their hands.

Cyrus shivered. He tried to keep his gaze straight. To not look upon the men. But his eyes always wandered. Why was this part of his vision, he thought. What did this have to do with him? It was with great relief that he reached the end of the passage and left the Stygian abyss behind.

The corridor opened into an antechamber where another mountain of a man stood. His purpose, Cyrus suspected, was to keep the haggard ghosts of the cells behind from mixing with the club's more respectable clientele. Cyrus surmised that, for most guests, a bit of a confrontation could be expected here, while the man who guarded the gate to yon paradise determined whether you were one to be protected or one to be protected from.

Not so for Cyrus. The man knew him. As all did here. As all had here, since the beginning. And even if he had not recognized Cyrus, his suit and the attendant trappings of wealth would have sufficed to gain entrance. Men like Cyrus had their vices and their drugs. But they remained respectable.

"Mr. McDonnell," the man thundered, if only because his voice filled his frame. "Good to see you again, sir."

He rapped twice on the door. The sound was muffled by a thick layer of crimson velvet that clung tight to its surface. Apparently, it was loud enough, though, as in an instant, it opened and Cyrus was inside.

It was a club, a speakeasy. Classic and decadent all at once. At one end was a bandstand where men in white tuxedos lightly tuned their instruments. The sound created a sort of quiet cacophony: a rich, ebullient mix of music and chaos. Along the chamber walls were plush leather booths, filled with men like him.

They wore suits, while the women that accompanied them donned dresses that hung close to curves and rises and dips, tasseled ropes of fabric and frills clinging to the edges like some sort of fashionable window dressing. Their hair was cut short in the style of the times, thin wisps that gave them a boyish quality, a hint of innocence that their eyes betrayed.

Cyrus had read of this era and loved it. He supposed that was why this was his gift, why this dream was his adventure. He had stepped back in time to an age of license and frivolity, of forbidden pleasures and underground palaces that would provide them. He breathed deep the sweet air, perfumed by cigars and cigarettes pressed tight against gently smiling lips.

"I'm back," he mumbled to himself. Oh to never leave!

Along the entire rear wall was a bar, its most prominent feature a mirror that stretched the length of it. Cyrus stopped for a moment to admire his own image in that mirror before speaking to the skeleton-faced man in front of it.

Cyrus had never been wealthy in life. Not that he had been poor, but always scraping, barely making do. He acted happy. That was his part to play. But here, he was what he had always dreamed of being.

"Mr. McDonnell," said the man behind the bar, pushing forward a martini that he had already mixed. "Your favorite, as always."

Cyrus took the glass and raised it in salute. He then turned, making his way to an empty booth that sat only a few feet from the stage. He had never paid for this martini or any other drink he'd had here. Apparently, his money was no good in this establishment. Yet another aspect of the dream that pleased him.

Cyrus sat down and waited. He pulled another cigar from his inside jacket pocket. There was a gold-plated cutter there as well, a tiny pair of scissors that could serve only one purpose. He snipped off the end of the cigar and picked up a book of matches that sat on the table in front of him. Written in bold letters across the front were the words,

*The Abyss.*

Cyrus removed a match and struck it hard. The end exploded in a flash and the smell of sulfur stung his nostrils as flame erupted to consume the flimsy piece of wood. Cyrus brought the flame to the end of the cigar, the fire flaring with every breath. It took two more matches to light the damned thing. Not that he cared. Cyrus was in a state of bliss. In that moment, there was nowhere he would rather have been.

The band had fallen silent, the tuning and re-tuning of instruments having finally stopped. Now they, and the other patrons, waited. Cyrus felt the tingle of anticipation kiss his skin, the electricity in the air that seemed to visibly spark. No matter how many times he had seen her he always felt the same. Excited, exhilarated, full of light. She brought that light. She carried it with her everywhere she went. In her eyes and in her voice.

In an instant, the house lights dropped. Cyrus and all the rest were plunged into darkness, save for the burning ends of lit tobacco and the flash of an occasional match. It only lasted a moment. There was the loud crash of a large switch being thrown, and a single spotlight burned down from the ceiling. It landed upon her.

When Cyrus was a boy, he had known a girl named Sidney Driskal. She grew up four houses down from him in Chesterfield, one of those quaint New England towns in Western Massachusetts that time and progress—and all the good and the bad that come with it—never quite reached. She'd been a tomboy and that is what drew him to her when he was young, before he appreciated girls for their ability to do things other than climb a tree.

She wore overalls in those days. The same pair every day, it seemed. Faded blue with fraying cuffs and holes in the knees. Her dark hair was cut short and he might have mistaken her for a boy, were it not for her general softness. She was too pretty, even then, for one to make such a mistake. Not that either one of them knew it at the time.

In the summer they would climb trees and explore the forbidden forests that lay behind their houses. During the winter, on days when the bitter cold wind did not blow so fiercely, they would build snowmen and snow forts, hurling packed balls of ice that stung when they hit and left bruises as proof of contact.

It was the fall they longed for the most, even if its coming did bring the start of school on its heels. Those fall days, when the sun was waning in the west but had not yet died and the leaves on the trees gave the illusion that they were aflame, were the days they loved.

For most children, Christmas was the occasion to be wished for, the night to anticipate. Not for Cyrus and Sidney. They awaited days of carved pumpkins, spiced cider, and harvest festivals. Tales of ghosts and witches and things that went bump in the night. The ancients called their celebration Samhain, held the final day of October, their new year. And so it was with Cyrus and Sidney, for when October passed, the year died with it.

But with every death comes new life. The wheel turned for them together. Always cycling to something new. Until the day came when they themselves were that new thing. Until Sidney's hair grew long, and her straight, rough edges began to curve. Cyrus began to see her not as a friend, but as a woman.

It might have divided them, that change. Sent them apart like so many childhood friends when childhood ends. Instead, in each other they explored mysteries that bewitched them both. Shared secrets never to be told. Experiences, whole lives it seemed sometimes, that they said they would never regret. Cyrus never did, and he believed, had she lived, that Sidney never would have either.

It was the blood Cyrus remembered most clearly. The blood and her eyes. Crystal blue eyes that in that final moment seemed to shatter. He didn't remember much else. Only that they were driving on the Forest Dale Road, between her house and their school. A trip so short it barely merited a thought.

He didn't even remember how it happened. He only recalled, when he woke, his shirt was wet with his own blood, his eyesight gone as if a shroud lay over his face. But when that mist cleared, he was staring into her face, Sidney's. Paler than it should have been, life having poured out from a hole in her throat that a shard of glass had made.

He had been the last thing she had seen. The last thing she had chosen to look upon. He knew that, for it was her eyes that met his when the veil was lifted. Her eyes that he peered into until he passed out again. Not to awake until he was lying in a hospital bed twenty miles away.

When the spotlight came on, everything else turned off. In the silence, Cyrus could hear his own heart beating and the gentle crinkle of slowly consumed tobacco as the fire burned the cigar he held in his hand. He barely noticed, even if those things were a roar compared to the perfect stillness of the room. His eyes, like all eyes, were on her.

She stood as still as death, her pale skin heightening that illusion. But there was burning inside her, fire that bespoke life and passion. Cyrus knew, in his rational mind, that it was the light that burned down from above that gave her illumination. But it did not seem so. No, she seemed to shine herself. As if whatever was inside of her burned so hot that it longed to escape.

Her ensemble completed the illusion. A dress that hung tight to her body, the fabric of which caught the light, reflecting it back as if she was covered in precious stones. The design evoked the Far East, for it was vaguely Asian in appearance. A light blue primarily, with a high collar that swept up her neck. Covering it to her chin. If the tightness on her throat bothered her in any way, her singing never showed it.

The men in the room sat in stasis, not daring to move, not wanting to be the one who broke the moment. In truth, the women felt the same. They all wanted her. Such was the power of the goddess in their midst. The whole world was frozen. Then she blinked once, and the edges of her mouth curved upward—almost imperceptibly—into the tiniest of smiles. They all breathed again; up to that point they hadn't realized they'd been holding their collective breath. Her eyes closed, her mouth opened, and she began to sing.

What did she sing? What were the words that she uttered? Were they words at all? Cyrus had thought on it but concluded long ago that it did not matter. Would one ask a nightingale the name of her song? Or the robin on a summer's day to explain its meaning?

No, hers was simply a voice as beautiful as any instrument, as heartrending as any violin, as uplifting as any trumpet, as dark as the lowest bass. She didn't need words. Yet somehow, deep within him, he knew this song was written for him.

How long did she sing? How long did she carry him from the heights of ecstasy to the depths of despair and all places in between? How long did she serenade him with such beauty that he thought his mind might break because of it? He lived a lifetime there, in that song, though it was only an instant. In that instant, he saw visions of what might have been. Images of a future long lost. Of a road not taken, but only because he had no choice in the matter. Yes, Cyrus loved the dreams. Because for him, that is what they truly were. Dreams. Dreams of more than one life lost.

It always went the same. He would come here and he would listen to her sing. When she finished, he would stand in the rain in front of the club and smoke cigarettes till the ship reached its destination, wherever that was. Every time went like that and he had every reason to think that it would always be so. But now, something changed. She looked right at him.

She had never done so before. She had sung her song and if she knew that he was there, she never showed it. Now their eyes were locked.

In any other circumstance, he probably would have wilted under that gaze, even though it came from a beautiful woman. *Especially* because it did. But he never wanted to look away now. He had waited for so long to look in those eyes again. Those crystal blue eyes.

She sang the rest of her song staring through the darkness at him. With the light upon her and he in the shadows, she couldn't have seen him. But that was wrong and he knew it. She saw, just as clearly as he. In her eyes, a million words danced, a thousand messages. He didn't always know what she said but his answer was yes. It didn't matter what she asked.

When the song ended, the lights came up and applause exploded throughout the room. They thundered for her. They called for her. They screamed her name and begged her to give them the merest glance, the slightest nod, the simplest acknowledgement of their presence. As always, she gave them none. But she did not simply turn and go as she had in earlier dreams. Instead, she walked straight over to Cyrus.

She floated across the room, her long dress giving the illusion that her feet did not touch the ground. She came to him, bending down low so that her mouth was at his ear and whispered, "In an hour, meet me behind the stage. Second door to the right." She cocked her head slightly in its direction. "I'll be waiting." She backed away, turning and smiling to the crowd, allowing them the slightest bow in response to the roar they gave.

Cyrus waited. He waited through interminable minutes that passed so slowly he wondered if the clock ran backward. He waited under the hate-filled gazes of those around him, their jealous eyes cursing the connection they all saw between Cyrus and the dark-haired beauty that haunted them. Cyrus wondered how he would escape them and meet her without the others knowing. What if they followed? But then he had his answer.

The lights dropped again, and a woman appeared on stage that he did not recognize. This was his chance. He inched himself quietly out of the booth, making sure to draw as little attention to himself as possible. He made his exit through the darkness, guiding himself by a mental map of the room burned into his mind by a hundred different visits. He felt his way along the wall, searching for the doorknob.

The woman's song wafted down to him from the stage. Her voice was not as beautiful, nor as intoxicating, but it snuck up on him. Seemed to bury itself in the back of his mind. In those words that were not words, he recognized a warning to turn back. That the silent siren call he followed would lead to his own destruction. His hand found the knob, and all was forgotten.

He stepped from one darkness into another, and silence came with it. He stood in the night, peering into the blackness, wondering what he should do. No candle or flame illuminated the shadow. No light guided his path. He stepped forward, sliding his foot along the ground, ensuring that always there was solid ground beneath it and that the floor did not drop away into some abyss that would swallow him, body and soul.

Then came the sound of wind blowing through the trees of a night-haunted forest. He felt no breeze but he heard it. And in that *crinkle-crick-creek* he could almost make out words. A chorus of them, whispering to him. Urging him onward.

He flattened himself against the wall, feeling along the moss-covered bricks of what he assumed was a hallway. Gradually, his eyes cleared, and as they adjusted to the darkness, he saw the thinnest ray of light in the distance. He edged toward it and he soon realized he was staring at the rough outline of a doorway. He grasped the doorknob. It turned easily in his hand. The door opened and Cyrus was awash in light so bright that he had to cover his eyes. When his pupils shrank and his sight adjusted, he stepped into that light and felt as though he had walked into the waters of the sea, even if the whispers, which had grown into an ocean-like roar, died instantly away.

The walls were white, if you could call them walls. But he wasn't sure there was anything solid there. They were more like boundaries, as if the great white sheets of light served no other purpose than to mark the dimensions of this room. Cyrus only thought they were walls because there was a door in the midst of the one across from him whose simple wooden frame seemed particularly incongruous to its surroundings. There was nothing in the room, save for a glass table on which sat two crystal goblets of red wine and a gleaming white couch. She rested upon it, her arms spread wide along its back, her eyes staring up at him above an almost mischievous smile.

She was nude. Or she would have been, were it not for a mesh of crisscrossing white linen strands that formed perfect square windows through which to view her body but did nothing to cover her nakedness. Her porcelain skin shone through those openings, unblemished were it not for the jagged scar that ran across her neck, a white-on-white reminder of the past.

"I've been waiting for you," she said, and though she barely whispered, the total silence of the room grabbed hold of her words, doubling and redoubling them until they echoed round the chamber. "I've been waiting for you for so long." Her voice was even and still but could not hide the storm that raged beneath it.

"I've come before. I've come so many times. But you've never noticed me."

"I noticed. But seeing and speaking are two different things. I was never allowed to speak. They never let me. Not until now."

"They?" She nodded, as if nodding answered all questions. "But I don't understand? Who are they? Where is this? Why are you here, now?"

"I'm here because you brought me here," she said. "Because seeing me was the thing your heart most desired."

"Is that what the dreams are? A fantasy? You get whatever you want most?"

"No. Not for all. But for some. And not fantasies. What you see here," she said, standing, circling the coffee table to where he stood, "is real. The air you breathe. The food you eat. Me. It's all real."

She grabbed the lapel of his coat and pulled him down to her. His lips found hers, and his hands ran up her arms to her shoulders, his thumbs rubbing her skin through the myriad holes of the thing that mocked the word clothes. This was what he wanted, he decided. His life had not been an unhappy one since that day in the August rain when her life was lost and his forever changed. He loved his wife and he adored his daughter, but this existence had not been his choice. A part of him—a large part of him—wondered what might have been.

Her lips were so cold.

She pulled away, looking up at him. "Do you want to stay?" she asked.

"I can't stay. The ship will drop out of warp. I'll wake up and all this will end."

"It doesn't have to be that way, you know? You don't have to go. You can stay with me, forever. If you wish. Will you stay? Please say yes. I don't know that I could bear to lose you again."

He turned over the options in his mind. He wondered what he would do if this choice was actually his to make. But these were only dreams, no matter how real they seemed. And all dreams must come to an end. It didn't much matter what he said, so why not say the one thing she wanted to hear?

"Yes. Yes, I'll stay with you. I'll stay."

When she smiled in response, it was so bright and full that he thought her face might rip from the joy. But there was something else there. He saw it, though in that moment he wasn't sure if his brain was playing tricks on him or if she was truly trying to hide something. For a split second, competing emotions raced across her face. There was joy there, yes. Perhaps even triumph, though over what, he didn't know. But there was darkness as well, and sadness, if one could see sadness in a smile.

"We must go then," she said.

"Go?" he laughed. "I thought you wanted me to stay?"

"Sometimes, in order to stay, one must go. In our case, we must go there."

She pointed behind her, at the curious door he had noticed before, the one set in the gleaming wall of light across from him. She stepped backward toward it, not taking her eyes off him. But he did not follow. Instead, he let his hands slip away from her. There was something about that door. She walked over to it, standing beside its frame.

"Come on," she said. "We must go, but only you can open it."

Cyrus was frozen in place. A thousand dreams had come and gone and he had never been afraid. It had been how he said he would survive them. By treating the visions differently from all the others who experienced them during the long sleep of the deep. By ignoring the notion that they contained danger. By believing that, in the end, a dream was just a dream, and that no matter what he saw, no matter what lay behind that door, in reality, it couldn't be that bad.

Even if he opened it to find the worst beast imaginable, it could not harm him. Then why did he fear? Perhaps, he thought, it is not knowing what lies beyond the door. If he were to open it and see, then no matter what he saw, it wouldn't be that bad after all. And yet still he stood, staring, wondering, thinking. But he had never been able to resist that smile, those eyes, that face. He had to play along, if only for a little bit longer.

He moved toward the door. It was nine, ten steps at the most. And they passed like one might expect nine or ten steps to pass. Quickly, without fanfare. They did not seem as though he was walking to his doom. They were just footsteps. He stood in front of her, his hand resting on the handle. She looked up at him and smiled. Now he was sure. There *was* sadness there, no matter how much she tried to cover it. He could still leave, he thought. He could turn and just walk away. That he had come this far said nothing about where he had to go. But standing there, with his hand on the doorknob, he felt as though he had no choice. He had to turn it, so he did.

Cyrus opened the door. There was nothing beyond it. There was no great beast waiting, no cosmic horror. No giant alien to devour him. Just more darkness.

Initial assessments, however, could be deceiving. As he peered into that darkness, its surface began to shimmer. To ripple, to flow. This was not just some darkened room beyond him. This was the same black shadow wall he had seen every time he had dreamed. The same one that stood guard on either side of the street above him.

The room wasn't quiet anymore. He could hear the whispered voices and for the first time, he could almost make out words. Some urged him to turn, to flee. Others beckoned him. Whispered lovingly to him. As the whispers washed over him, with as many begging him to go as pleading with him to stay, he looked over at the wraith beside him. The ghost, the image of Sidney. With perfect, crystal blue eyes. Her flawless skin, although it had not always been so pale, was just as inviting as ever.

"What now?" he asked.

"You must pass beyond the wall. You must go willingly and you must see this world as it truly is." She bent down and kissed him again. She smiled, and then she stepped through the wall herself. She turned before she passed beyond the black curtain and nodded once.

Then she was gone. It was not as he had seen it before. The other denizens of his dreams had passed through the shadow wall with no effect. She seemed much more real than they. He watched as the blackness rippled around her, covering her skin like oil before swallowing her whole.

"Sidney?" he whispered. From somewhere beyond, she answered.

"I'm here, Cyrus. I'm right here. All you have to do is come through. Then you'll see, and we can finally be together."

Cyrus reached up and did something he had always wanted to do; he touched the darkness. A ripple ran around his fingers. It was warm, almost wet, but not damp. There were none of the things he had always feared. No pain. Nothing grabbed him. His finger didn't dissolve away. He looked at it, from the top of the door to the floor, and made his decision. Cyrus took a deep breath, and then he stepped into shadow.

When Cyrus opened his eyes, he looked upon the beyond. He saw into the abyss. He knew what gave the darkness shape and what filled the spaces between space. As he began to scream, he felt his sane mind falling, falling, falling, as if into a deep well. Finally, screaming, he blinked out of existence.

# CHAPTER
# 11

The transition from the dream world to reality had not been a smooth one for Rebecca. One moment she was standing in the ruined city, staring up at a great fire that burned just beyond her vision. It had seemed so real.

But when the scream came from somewhere beyond that world, the whole of that reality cracked. She was suddenly pulled away, as if a great hand reached down from the sky and plucked her bodily up, up, up. As the world dissolved below her and the scream grew louder, she thought that this was what being born must be like.

She opened her eyes with a flutter, unable to shake off the shroud of sleep. That screaming, what had been an otherworldly shriek, now seemed so close. The world spun and she could find nothing to grab on to, no handhold of reality. She heard the sound of fighting. Other voices shouting. But always the scream, punctuated only by sharp intakes of breath.

Rebecca grasped the two sides of the bed on which she lay, pushing herself to a sitting position. Her eyesight was still confused. There were flashes of color, a mad dash of reds and blues and whites to go along with the cacophony of sound. When her eyes cleared, what she saw made her pass out straight away.

* * *

Aidan was the first to awake, having snapped back to reality far more quickly than Rebecca. After years of sleep stasis, the waking symptoms—confusion, disorientation, sensory malfunction—had largely ceased for him. So when he woke, it was a quick affair; an instant to leave the dream world behind in exchange for a waking nightmare.

There was no mystery as to where the ungodly screams came from. Cyrus was sitting in his bed, his roaring raised to a vocal cord-shattering level Aidan wouldn't have thought the human body capable of producing. But the scream wasn't the worst part. Cyrus's face was awash in blood from two, ragged crimson holes dripping a mixture of tears and viscera. His hands were mired in the gore of what had once been his eyes.

Aidan didn't think. He just leapt to his feet and ran to where Cyrus sat, determined to stop him before he hurt anyone else. Cyrus was not a small man, but he was no bigger than Aidan. Yet before he could begin to subdue him, Cyrus grabbed hold of Aidan and threw him across the room.

Aidan had never felt anything like it before and he sailed through the air for what seemed like an eternity. But down he did come, crashing at the feet of Dr. Ridley, who held a sedative in his hand.

"Get up!" Ridley yelled. Aidan raised himself, adrenalin masking the pain. This time, Aidan avoided Cyrus's grasp, wrapping his arms around Cyrus's throat, determined to hold him fast whether Ridley's drugs worked or not. But Cyrus had the strength of a madman. He reached back and grabbed Aidan, flipping him head over heels to the ground.

Aidan landed hard on his back with a sickening crack, smashing into Ridley's legs and causing the doctor to lose his balance, the sedative skittering away across the room. Aidan wasn't sure he could get up this time. A shadow fell over him and he saw Jack Crawford advancing from the side.

Cyrus lunged at Crawford, somehow sensing where he stood. With a speed that shocked Aidan, Jack slid to the side. For a mere second, Cyrus was off balance, but that was all it took. In that instant, Jack swung his clenched fist and connected with Cyrus's jaw. Like some bizarre recording, the scream was instantly silenced. Aidan watched Cyrus crumple into a pile, his body gone limp.

* * *

Aidan, Rebecca, and Captain Gravely sat in silence on the bridge. Crawford stood leaning against the back wall, his arms crossed over his chest. They had been like that for an eternity, it seemed to Aidan, though he knew it had only been a handful of minutes.

Aidan said a quiet prayer of thanks for modern medicine. He had apparently cracked some ribs, but the shot that Ridley had given him was enough that he felt no pain. He did wish someone would speak, even if none of them knew what to say. There were many questions to be answered, but only Ridley would have those answers, if anyone did. So they waited.

Finally, the door to the bridge slid open with a soft whoosh. Ridley stepped inside, wiping his hands on his pants as if he had just performed an operation. They all looked up at him expectantly.

"He's sedated for now. It took three doses of sedatives to accomplish what Mr. Crawford here did with one punch and I can't say how long he will be out."

"Three doses?" asked Rebecca.

"Yes. According to the scans, his mental activity is off the charts, even now. The computer is to alert me if he even begins to regain consciousness. I put him in the holding cell. I would say there is nothing there he can use to harm himself, but given what he did with his own hands . . ." Ridley stopped speaking when he saw Rebecca shudder. She would see that image in her dreams until the day she died.

"I don't understand," Aidan said. "Cyrus has been at this for years. Why now?"

The doctor threw up his hands. "It happens," he said. "I know that is not a very scientific diagnosis, but really I have nothing else to offer. It's true, as you all know, that the insanity usually strikes, if it ever will, on the first trip, but there are cases every year, few though they might be, where men who've been at this much longer than Cyrus break. I don't know what he saw there, but whatever it was tripped something that we simply don't understand."

"But why his eyes?" Rebecca whispered.

Ridley rubbed his own eyes with his hand. "That's not all that uncommon. It makes sense, in a way. Whatever they see, apparently it makes them never want to see again."

"I think I'm going to be sick." Rebecca stood up and walked to the back of the room. She glanced down at Aidan as she passed, and he had an almost uncontrollable urge to stand up and hug her as tightly as he could. Instead, he simply sat there and the moment passed.

"What do you expect when he wakes up?" asked Gravely.

"There's no way to tell. He may be in a catatonic state. He may never speak another word. Or, he may become manic. The screaming could return, incoherent babbling, rambling speech that makes no sense. Any of those things are possible. I really can't predict it."

"I don't understand how he got out of the stasis chamber," Aidan said. "In fact, I don't know how any of us did. I was always under the impression that they are supposed to stay closed."

"Well that's the thing," Captain Gravely said. She stood up and walked over to the computer console. "It's true that Cyrus's screams are what woke us all, but we were about to be awoken anyway. The ship had already dropped from warp."

"So we're at Riley?"

"No. We are four light years from Riley."

"Four light years?" Dr. Ridley said.

"You mean the Omega quadrant?" Aidan asked.

Gravely nodded. "About two light years beyond Anubis, it seems."

"Good God," Aidan said. "We're lucky to be alive."

"Very."

"What's this about?" Ridley demanded. "What do you mean?"

"They call it 'strange space.'"

"The necropolis," Aidan added.

"Right. The whole quadrant is riddled with black holes. We could have dropped out of warp right into one."

"Don't the computers correct for that kind of thing?"

"They do," Aidan answered, "but warp has a way of messing with them just like it does us. I don't understand though," he said, turning back to the captain, "why it would randomly drop us here."

"Not random," she said. "Computer. Display the object off of our port side." In an instant, the great blank screens above them flashed on, dissolving into the image of something that should not have been there. Rebecca glanced over at Jack. His expression was the perfectly choreographed bemused surprise of a man who did not know what he was looking at. Of course, Rebecca knew the truth.

Aidan gazed up at the image on the screen, not fully processing what he was seeing. It looked like a ship, but not of any design or classification he had ever seen.

It was long and sleek, made of some sort of shimmering metal that caught whatever faint light was left in this godforsaken backwater and reflected it back stronger than when it had arrived. The hull was thick on the back but tapering off to a point toward the front. It reminded him of the point of a spear.

"Is that a ship?" he said finally.

"I don't know what else it could be," said Gravely.

"Chinese?" Ridley asked.

"I **don't** think so. The colors aren't bright enough," Aidan said. The Chinese, everyone knew, preferred to paint their ships a vibrant red. "Besides, the Chinese have no interests in this sector."

"Maybe it's a prototype, a new type of ship they are trying to keep secret?"

"It's not Chinese," Captain Gravely said.

Aidan took a deep breath and let it out, turning the question over in his mind that they were all thinking before finally asking, "It's not alien, is it?"

"Not unless they write in English." The captain ran her finger up the console in front of her and the image in the screens changed. It zoomed in to a section on the front of the ship. A word was stenciled across the hull in large, evenly spaced letters.

"*Singularity?*"

"Strange name for a ship," said Gravely.

"Maybe it's a science vessel? Studying black holes? This would be the perfect place to do that."

"I thought that too. But I checked the books before we departed and there were no crafts scheduled to be out here. I ran it through the computer too, and it confirmed my suspicions. There shouldn't be any ships in this quadrant. Not here, not now."

"Maybe they forgot to check in," Ridley offered.

Gravely shook her head. "Unlikely. Particularly for a science vessel. But it gets better. I had the computer cross reference *Singularity* against the Domes Book of Registered Spacecraft. There is no such ship, not listed there."

Aidan felt the hairs rise on the back of his neck. If it was an American ship, it should be in Domes. All ships were listed there. All legitimate ones at least. "You don't think it could be pirates, do you?"

Gravely glanced over at Rebecca and Jack and wondered how they were taking all this. "I doubt it. But we can't be sure. That's one of the reasons why we haven't gone in any closer."

Ridley slumped down in a chair next to Rebecca. "One of them?" he asked.

"The truth is, I'm afraid to move the ship much at all. We know that we are safe here, but the computer is registering multiple gravitational anomalies, and I don't know if the sensors are going haywire or if we are sitting in the middle of a swarm of black holes. I need more information before we can go any farther."

"Did you try and contact them?"

"The computer's been hailing the ship since we arrived. No response. If there's anyone over there, they aren't interested in talking. Or they are unable to. They haven't moved either."

"Is she dead in the water, Captain?" Aidan asked. He didn't like anything about this, least of all the not knowing.

"I wish I could tell you that, Mr. Connor, but this isn't a military ship. Our sensors might be able to provide us with some answers if we were closer. But at this distance, all we have is the visual."

"I hope I'm not speaking out of turn . . ."

Everyone turned and looked at Jack Crawford. He had been silent up to that point, but now he stepped forward, walking over to where Aidan and Gravely stood. Rebecca watched him curiously as he passed.

"But is there any protocol for something like this? Is there a plan we are to follow?"

Captain Gravely looked at Aidan and frowned. She had not anticipated anything like this on her first civilian run and although she had tried to prepare herself, to learn the rules and regulations, a situation like this was so different from what she had experienced before that she did not know how to proceed.

"Well," Aidan said, glancing back at Gravely and seeing the gratitude in her eyes, "if she's derelict, then we have some decisions to make.

"We're required to wait twenty-four hours, unless there's some legitimate reason not to. Then we are free to call it in and get out of here if we want. Spacing regs say that she is ours if we salvage her, and looking at her, she'd fetch a high price on the market.

"We aren't required to do anything, though, unless there's some threat to the crew or passengers of the derelict, and only then if we can act without putting ourselves or the ship in danger." Aidan turned to Gravely. "But being in this area of space, Captain, I don't think we can do much of anything without some danger."

"I agree, Mr. Connor. We'll give it twenty-four hours, as required. In the meantime, I want you to work with Dr. Kensington here, if she doesn't mind, to figure out exactly what we're up against as far as gravitational anomalies. If there's a black hole out there, I want to know exactly where it is. Would that be agreeable, Dr. Kensington? I know you're just a passenger on this ship, but we are down a man and I could use your help."

Rebecca glanced surreptitiously at Jack Crawford who gave an almost imperceptible nod. "Of course, Captain," she said, "I'd be happy to help."

"Excellent. Dr. Ridley, keep me informed of any changes with Cyrus. If things go badly with him, I want to know immediately. I'm not risking his life, no matter what is going on with that ship. And, Aidan, put out a call to Riley and let them know that we're out here. I know there are no other ships scheduled to come through this quadrant, but I don't want to take any chances. But let's keep this off the bands when it comes to the ship. If she is derelict and we can claim her, I'd rather not have any competition."

"Understood, Captain."

"And let's hope nothing else goes wrong."

# CHAPTER
# 12

Dr. Ridley sat in his office, staring down at the image of Cyrus's brain on the screen. He glanced up into the cell. Cyrus was mercifully asleep and if Ridley had anything to say about it, he would stay that way until at least Riley and possibly Earth. His brain, however, was as active as ever. Lightning flashed across the screen, the visible representation of the storm of thoughts raging in the man's broken mind. There was simply nothing about Cyrus's mental activity that made sense, nothing that resembled any other brain scan Ridley had seen. Well, he thought to himself, that wasn't quite true.

In his career, he had lost three crew members and one passenger to the dreams. One of those, a ship's engineer from a nothing town in South Dakota whose name had long since fled his memory, had died in his sleep. The other three had lived and their minds wandered in the same incomprehensible manner as Cyrus's. Neurons firing at impossible intervals, waves of thought rolling through the brain in directions and speeds alien to anything he knew, visible evidence of their insanity.

The passenger had been the worst. Not that losing the crew wasn't tragic, but they accepted the dangers, knew what could happen every time they went out. Anna Lane—a name he would never forget—had not. When they came out of warp, she was foaming at the mouth and convulsing, her brain having turned to a sputtering mess.

How do you tell a family waiting at the spaceport that? What do you say to a child who wants to see his mom? How do you tell him that his mother is a drooling zombie, a brainless lunatic likely to rip his face off if she gets within range?

The afflicted were lost and they never came back. They never fixed themselves, and there was nothing in medicine that could reverse the damage, no matter how far the science of the brain had come. Society warehoused them in the last remaining asylums. Most were catatonic. Ridley preferred those.

He had friends who worked at the hospitals, the prisons, where the lost wasted away. They whispered about the other ones, the ones that could speak. Their ramblings had a way of getting in a sane man's head and making him feel perhaps he was losing his mind. The month Ridley spent amongst them as an intern was enough for a lifetime, and the last three cases he had treated as a ship's doctor had remained sedated for the duration of the trip. He would follow the same course here. He just hoped there weren't any more.

He had spoken to Rebecca after the captain left the bridge. He had called her over before he went to check on Cyrus. There was no one he could trust, not really, but better her than Jack Crawford. Something about that man bothered him, triggered some sense in the back of his mind that told him all was not right.

"You alright?" he had asked her. They were all shaken, but she was the worst.

"Not really," she said, trying to smile. "No, not really at all."

"That's natural," he offered. "Come by later and I'll give you something to help you sleep."

"No, no drugs. I never liked taking drugs, especially to sleep. I don't like feeling like I can't wake up. I think that's particularly true now."

**"That's understandable."** Ridley wished he had something more, but the fact that he was a psychiatrist didn't mean he was particularly good at comforting people. It was closer to the opposite; he'd become a psychiatrist because he *didn't* understand people. In any event, he thought that perhaps he should leave it at that and say no more. He pushed that thought aside.

"So, Rebecca, I know you've been through a lot, but have you been feeling all right? Any dizziness? Confusion? Hallucinations?" In the end, these questions were too important to leave unasked.

"What? No, nothing like that. Why do you ask?" The puzzled look on her face told Ridley that she was telling the truth.

"I know you've already been through so much, but there's something I need to tell you. The sleep-madness, it sometimes comes in swarms."

"Swarms?"

"We don't know why, but occasionally when one person goes, others will follow. They seem fine at first, but then . . ." Ridley snapped his fingers and then immediately regretted it as he watched her flinch. "It's very rare," he said, trying to save the moment, "but obviously very dangerous as well. Just keep an eye out. It seems that some people on this ship are more comfortable with you than me. If they are going to let their guard down, you will be the first one to see it."

As he left her behind, he was sure that she would be vigilant. It was her nature; that much he could tell. But he couldn't trust her. When he saw movement in the shadows out of the corner of his eye, he realized he couldn't trust himself, either.

* * *

Captain Gravely sat in the chair behind her desk, looking up at the image of the arrowhead-shaped vessel sitting a thousand miles off the starboard side of her ship. It was just one more complication.

"Computer." The female voice chirped back its readiness. "Music. Beach Boys. Sloop John B." The familiar chords started and Gravely smiled at her own joke. A metallic jingle interrupted, Gravely reluctantly admitted the visitor. It was Aidan.

"Have you already found something?" she asked.

"No, no. We haven't even started. Rebecca . . . Dr. Kensington was speaking with Dr. Ridley, so I thought I would take a moment."

Gravely gestured to the seat across from her and Aidan sat down.

"The Beach Boys?"

She nodded.

"I always preferred the Beatles. Two hundred years and we still haven't come up with anything better."

"You'll get no argument here. So what can I do for you Mr. Connor?"

Aidan didn't really know what he wanted to say. He felt for Captain Gravely. She had given him a shot when he didn't expect one, when he had resigned himself to some difficult, hard times with no food and less money. But things had gone badly for her. It had crossed his mind that some people would blame him. That they would question her judgment for bringing him on. After all, he was bad luck.

Superstitions never ended. It didn't matter how advanced the society, how plugged into technology. It didn't matter how secular or religious. Superstitions gave men power. When they were being flung through the deepest reaches of space, sedated and at the mercy of the warp drive and the machines, trapped in the midst of the dreams, they still had control.

They had worn the right shirt or played the right song. They had checked off the boxes of habit that had kept them safe all these years. As long as they didn't mess that up, as long as the candles stayed lit, the medals stayed around their necks, it would be okay. If something did go wrong, there must have been a reason. Someone must have made a mistake. How much worse to imagine it was all random chance? How much more terrible to believe that things happened for no reason at all? Just the result of the dial of dumb luck tilting against you. No, *that* was unbearable.

"I just wanted to say that this is not your fault. Cyrus, I mean. You couldn't have done anything about it."

Captain Gravely looked down at the palms of her hands, tracing the pale lines that cut across her ebony skin. "I appreciate that, Aidan," she said without looking up, "but the fact is, it doesn't matter. When you are in command, people put their faith in you. Their lives are in your hands, and whether it's your fault or not, when something happens to one of them, you feel responsible. You get over it. You don't dwell on it. But nobody ever forgets the ones they've lost."

It was what Aidan expected. He had said his piece and he guessed she had said hers. There was nothing else. He wasn't even sure he should have said that much.

"Well, I'll get to work then, Captain," he said, rising from his seat. "I've got a few ideas that I think might help us close in on that ship a bit."

"That's excellent, Mr. Connor," she said, looking up at him. "That is why I brought you on board. I do not regret it. Not in the least."

He nodded and turned for the door. As it opened, Gravely spoke again. "And, Mr. Connor, I appreciate what you said. But it's not your fault either."

He paused at the portal for only a moment before letting the door slide shut behind him.

\* \* \*

It was only when Dr. Ridley left the bridge that Rebecca realized Aidan had stepped out. It was the moment she needed. She found Jack sitting at a desk in their quarters, staring down at his computer.

"We need to talk," she said.

"Then talk."

"I think we should abort the mission."

He placed the thin piece of plastic to the side of the table and gestured at the chair in front of him. Kensington sat, though she couldn't help but feel like she was a child in the principal's office. Crawford's crossed arms and blank stare didn't help.

"This is the second time in so many days that you have come to me and suggested we deviate from our orders. I thought I made myself clear last time that we are seeing this through to the end."

"Well, Jack, I don't know if you noticed, but things have changed since then. You saw what happened to Cyrus. He needs a doctor."

"He has a doctor."

"He needs a real doctor."

"Last time, I checked, Ms. Kensington . . ." Her face hardened, and he knew he had hit his mark. She hated it when he dropped "doctor" in favor of "miss." "Dr. Ridley *is* a real doctor. And while you may not be familiar with Cyrus's . . . condition . . . I am. No one comes back from that. There is no 'help' for him. Besides, he's expendable."

Rebecca's face fell despite her efforts to mask her feelings. "How can you say that? Besides, Jack, we can always return here later. That ship isn't going anywhere."

The pounding headache Jack had suffered since the sudden end to the dream now thundered against his temples like the beating of a bass drum. He wondered if his skull might just crack open, spilling his brain out onto the table. His hand slipped down to the pistol he kept on his hip. Maybe he could pull it and shoot Rebecca in her right eye. The one that was just a little bit more closed than the other.

He had noticed it from the first time he met her. She was pretty he guessed, by the measure that most men count beauty. But the eye. That damned eye. All it would take was one bullet. Unfortunately, he needed her. And her eye.

"So what would you have me do? You want me to leave that ship behind with three witnesses knowing it's here? And you don't think anyone else would find out? You don't think we would have salvage crews scouring this area? Tearing it apart? Fighting to claim the prize? What am I supposed to tell Command? That you felt sorry for a dead man? Because he *is* dead, Rebecca. No matter how long his heart keeps beating. Now, what I need you to do is get in there with Aidan and figure out a safe path to that ship. The faster you do that, the sooner we can go.

Am I clear?"

Rebecca stood up, and the screeching of the chair as she pushed it away was like a nail driven into Jack's brain.

"Crystal."

\* \* \*

Aidan was in a deep discussion with the computer when Rebecca entered the bridge.

"I'm not interrupting anything, am I?" she said with a smile.

"Hey! Where'd you go? Sorry I started without you."

"Oh . . . that's alright. I had to get something from my room. Actually, you disappeared first."

"Yeah, I wanted to talk to the captain."

"How's she holding up?"

"She's a trooper. It shook her up, of course, but I don't think we have to worry about her. Anyway, I want to run this by you." Rebecca watched as he called up a protocol he had just written. "So the sensors on this ship are basically useless. We don't investigate or explore; we carry cargo. We also don't go wandering out into space where there might be random black holes, so in a way, we are completely blind. But we do have these."

A piece of U-shaped equipment materialized in mid-air, spinning on its y-axis. It was one Rebecca recognized immediately, though she didn't understand why Aidan thought it was significant.

"A Chandrasekhar Scanner?"

"Exactly. Every ship has one, because every ship in warp gives off Chandrasekhar radiation. The scanner is the only thing that warns the computer if two ships in warp are about to intersect. It's the one piece of equipment we have that's worth a damn. No telling how many lives it saves."

Aidan looked up at Rebecca like she should understand. She did not. "How does that help us?"

"Hawking radiation." He watched as the implications washed over Rebecca's face.

"We can modify the scanner to find it," she said. "They aren't exactly the same, but they are close enough."

"Do you think you can do it? I know the equipment, but the details are more your area of expertise."

"I can do it if you help," she said. She glanced at him with bright eyes over an open-mouthed smile. Her face was alive and happy for the first time since the dreams. He considered asking her how she was doing. But better to not open old wounds, he thought. "So," she said, tinkering with the computer, "what's next?"

"Well, we have a laser-based system on the ship for measuring distance. Basically, we fire a laser from the ship and whenever it hits an object the computer can tell you the distance down to the micron. The radiation will give us the general location of the black hole. The laser will tell us where the event horizon is located. We fire the laser at it and when the beam disappears, that's the point of no return. We can map the whole thing in a matter of seconds."

"Impressive."

Aidan wouldn't have traded a medal for that one word. "Okay, I think we've got it. Let's see how this goes." He tapped the screen once, waited a second, and frowned. "Damn it."

"What's wrong?"

"It's not working. Something's off," he said, gesturing to the display. "I must have done something wrong."

Rebecca looked at the screen. There were red pulses in no fewer than a dozen places, covering the entire screen, save for the narrow strip of space connecting their ship to the other.

"Aidan . . . I think you should try the lasers."

"There's no point. These readings are garbage."

"Aidan, just do it."

"Computer," Aidan said after a deep sigh, "run mapping protocol Aidan One."

When he was a child, Aidan's father had spoken of soul-stealing moments. He was, in many ways, a primitive man, particularly by that day's reckoning. Even though his father had been an expert technician specializing in the latest holo-simulators, he remained an old soul, somehow tied into the wisdom of days gone by.

*Soul-stealing moments*, he said, *were when you saw something so frightening, so amazing, or so horrible that it literally scared a little piece of soul from your body. 'That*, he told Aidan, *is why your hair stands on end, why you feel that cold chill ripple from head to toe.* Aidan didn't know if that was true, but he pretty much assumed it wasn't. He did know he had never experienced one of those moments. Until now.

The computer had started at the closest ping, but its calculations were limited only by how fast the laser could fire and that was several thousand times a second. They watched as the screen ceased to be blank space and the black holes quickly materialized, painted in by the laser as it fired into that eternal vacuum, cut off at the point where nothing ever returned.

They were all around the ship. Great, silent, whirling chasms of destruction. The ship was surrounded, as much as one could ever be surrounded in space. It was an impossible configuration, spread out in a procession all the way to the derelict vessel. But the worst was just beyond it.

The computer displayed a representation of what a black hole "looked like," though if such a phrase even has any meaning in relation to something that cannot be seen is unknown and unknowable. But as the computer sketched out that great darkness, a hundred times bigger than any of the others, Aidan felt true fear, as if he started into the very pit of Hell itself.

# CHAPTER
# 13

When everyone reconvened on the bridge, the screens above revealed the horror to them all. They said that seeing was believing, but Aidan knew that what they saw was impossible to comprehend and thus impossible to believe.

"This is our best representation of what we are dealing with. Even with the lasers, we can't know the exact location of the event horizon and we need to be very careful moving forward. The computer has charted a path to the derelict and I have every reason to believe it is a safe one, but we should all know the dangers."

"What's our present situation?" Gravely asked.

"Secure for now. As long as we stay here, we'll be safe."

"And the other ship?"

"Well, Captain, I have some bad news. With the help of Dr. Kensington, I was able to recalibrate our sensors. Get a little bit more out of them. It's not much, but I learned a few things."

Aidan tapped a control panel and the screen zoomed in on the derelict vessel. An ever-decreasing number appeared in the upper right-hand corner, though what it counted down to, only Aidan knew.

"Our initial readings told us that the ship was stationary. We now know that was incorrect. In fact, while at no great speed and apparently under no control, the ship is moving. Drifting, to be precise. And it is headed there." Aidan gestured to a massive black hole at the top of the screen. "The number at the top of the screen represents our best guess at the distance from the ship to the event horizon. It is my estimation—and once again it is impossible to know for sure—that the derelict will cross the point of no return in approximately thirty-six hours. At that moment she, and everyone aboard her, will be lost."

Captain Gravely stared up at the screen, watching the computer's graphical representations of two dozen black holes spinning in mid-space, black on black. Perhaps it was best, she thought, if the other ship was unsafe. It made the decision to stay or go all the easier. "Mr. Connor, what do you suggest, given what we know?"

"Well, Captain, although I can't say that our current location is the one I prefer, our ship is at least safe. That ship, however, is not. Our options are few, but if we are going to try to save the ship or its crew, we will have to send a boarding party. And while I can give estimates and say with some degree of certainty that we have time on our side for now, much of what I am giving you is little better than a blind guess. I believe we have a day and a half until that ship slips into the void. Could be less, could be more. But once it happens, that's it. If anyone is on board when it goes, there will be no getting them back."

"Any signs of life? Communication? Energy spikes?"

"No communication, Captain. The computer's been hailing them continuously since we arrived. Nothing. As for of signs of life, we don't have that kind of equipment. I can tell you that we aren't reading any activity within the ship. I think she's dead in the water. That would mean that life support systems are also off-line. If that's the case, a ship that size, depending on the crew, malfunctioning life support system, no air circulation? They could last a few days, maybe?"

"Hull breach?"

"None that we can find. If I had to make a call, I'd say the hull's intact."

"Then what we have is a derelict ship floating uncontrolled toward a black hole. No signs of activity and a dead system. They could have been here for days or weeks."

"No, Captain, not weeks. I checked the navigation log. A week and a half ago, there was a supply ship that left Riley bound for Earth. Its warp path would have taken it through this same quadrant. If the derelict had been here, we would have heard about it. So I've got to think it couldn't have been here for longer than a week."

"So what you're telling me, Mr. Connor, is that if there are people on that ship they have no way to contact us or anyone else, and depending on when their life support systems failed, they could be alive. But in less than thirty-six hours, they will slip into the black hole?"

"That's what I'm telling you."

For a long moment Gravely took in the two images on the screen. One of the map and its swirling chaos and the other of that mysterious triangular ship. "I'd like to hear from everybody on this. Any actions we choose are going to affect us all."

Ridley didn't wait for anyone else to take Gravely's offer. "I say we go, Captain. I've got a man two decks down in sick bay and I need to get him to a hospital as soon as possible. We've already lost enough on this trip. It seems to me there's probably not anyone alive on that ship. And even if we go over there, what are we going to do? I know I've never seen a ship like that before and from what all of you said earlier, you haven't either. What makes you think we can fix it? Especially without Cyrus?"

"Captain," Aidan said, "I certainly respect Dr. Ridley's position. But the truth is, I think we have some time. And according to our regulations, we are supposed to give it twenty-four hours in any event."

"Actually," interrupted Ridley, "I think with Cyrus in the condition he is in, leaving would be justified. The longer we stay, the longer a crew member is endangered. Not to mention the fact, if you send someone to that ship and they don't make it off, we don't know what fate you are condemning them to."

"Be that as it may, if there is anyone alive, I think they deserve at least a shot of getting off. If we leave them, then their blood is on our hands. If it were me, I'd hope someone would at least take the opportunity to see. I say we send a party to the ship, see its condition and the situation of the crew. Maybe we can fix her fairly easily. We'll take her with us and all make a lot of money. Either way, at least we will know."

"Alright, Mr. Connor. While I share Dr. Ridley's concerns, I know that if it were me on that ship, I'd want someone to try and get me out. I think it is safe to at least bring the *Chronos* alongside her. When we are in range, we can reevaluate the situation. Perhaps the sensors will be more useful at that point. What time frame are we looking at?"

"Eight hours. Any faster puts the ship at risk."

"Then eight hours it is. I recommend you all get some sleep. The next twenty-four hours may be long ones."

\* \* \*

An hour later, Rebecca was lying in Aidan's bed, her head on his shoulder and his arms wrapped around her naked body. Later she would lie to herself and say that she wasn't really sure how it happened, that it had just been something that came over them both and that they had given in to the moment.

In reality, she should have gone straight to her cabin. She was exhausted, both by the dream-filled sleep that gave no rest and the events of the past few hours. There was no reason that the path to the derelict—checked and rechecked by Aidan and designed by the computer—needed checking again. Still she found herself in his room, charts in hand, one thought in her mind, even if it was buried deep.

Aidan had seen it as soon as she walked in the door. The eyes were the most obvious—windows to the soul and all—but it was other places too. Her hair, the way she held her hips, the fact that she was biting her lower lip, even though he was pretty sure she didn't know it. He had made sure his hand brushed hers as he took the console. For a moment, they stood still, staring across space at one another. What followed was not unexpected. Neither regretted it.

"We should get some sleep," he said. She just laughed, and then he was laughing too.

"We should," she said. "But now I'm not tired."

"I could take a look at those calculations."

She slapped him playfully on the chest. "I don't think that will be necessary."

"Are you nervous?" he asked after a few more minutes of lying in silence.

"About what?"

"The ship. We're going to need you, you know. If the captain decides to try a salvage. I know my way around an engine, but you're the expert. Well, Cyrus was the expert, but obviously . . ." He didn't finish. There was no need.

"I hadn't really thought about it. Yeah, I guess I am nervous. What about you?"

He was, and he wanted to tell her that. Instead, he lay there in silence, thinking about the one time he had come in contact with a black hole.

It had been fifteen long years prior. Aidan had been a private fighter pilot tasked with escorting science vessels beyond the Parseus Transit. It was deep space, far beyond the charted regions and spacing routes. It was a routine job, left over from a time when pirates were an actual threat instead of mere legend.

That day, he'd been assigned to the *Hyperion*. It was a ship they only whispered of now, one of those legendary disasters that men sing folksongs about. They had dropped into a stellar cloud, their mission investigating the nebulae of the region. Aidan kept his fighter at a safe distance, listening to music and slowly circling the science vessel as it crawled along through the charged gases and swirling particles that would one day form stars and planets. Important work, he was sure, but nothing he understood or cared about. So he floated, spinning lazily around the ship, wishing somewhere in the back of his mind that something would happen to justify him firing his weapons.

They had completed two out of three surveys when it happened. The third nebula was the most distant. It was across a great blank void of space, a distance that would take four hours to traverse. The captain of the science vessel offered to let Aidan cross that distance on board the ship. He had seriously considered it. But his job was to remain outside, to guard against any threat, real or imagined. It was a decision that would save his life.

The investigators who descended on the area said that it was a preventable disaster. The scientists on board should have seen the signs. They should have recognized what they were dealing with. Maybe if one of the nebulae had been closer, the steady stream of energized particles leading to a vacant space of pure, coal-dark blackness would have warned them. Maybe they did know. Maybe they recognized their situation. Maybe there were frantic calls to the bridge, calls filled with confusion and misunderstanding, the dawning truth coming too late to prevent the tragedy.

All Aidan knew was that he had rolled his fighter to the port side of the ship a few minutes before it happened, and if he had been on the other side, he wouldn't have lived to see it. It started as just a feeling of discomfort. He felt sick, as he had in flight training when spun in a machine designed to demonstrate changes in gravity. Even his thoughts seemed sluggish and his mind didn't work like it should. When it happened, he thought it was an illusion, a hallucination.

The ship had just scraped the event horizon. As it did, the entire right side seemed to blink out of existence. It dissolved in an instant, and then the whole ship shuddered to a stop. The rest of it still existed, somewhere beyond that shroud. Aidan just couldn't see it, as the light it should have reflected was sucked down into oblivion. Then the visible part of the ship began to follow, sliding away from him, disappearing from the world that is into one beyond.

There was nothing Aidan could do. Nothing but fire his thrusters in reverse and pull as far away from the ship as he could. From there he sat and watched as the rest vanished, listened to the men and women who remained inside. Their terrified cries. Their pleas for help. Then there was silence upon the surface of the deep. Nothing remaining to tell what lives passed before. Beyond the curtain, the ship and the people within were ripped to shreds by forces that man mercifully is incapable of contemplating.

If Aidan had anything to do with it, he wouldn't watch that happen again.

"I'd be lying if I said I wasn't afraid. I think it would be foolish to not be. But that's why I know we have to do it. If there are people on that ship, we have to give them a chance. That's what I think."

Rebecca found herself pulling Aidan close to her, hugging him tight. It was exactly what she expected from him. He was exactly who she thought he was. She just hoped that when he found out the truth about her, it wouldn't be the end of this, whatever this was.

\* \* \*

Captain Gravely found Ridley on the observation deck, staring out into the swirling darkness. The black holes themselves were invisible, but now that he knew they were there, he could see the strange distortions as the light from distant stars was bent by the gravity wells. In some places there was pure darkness where light should be; there, he knew, lay the singularities they must avoid at all costs.

"You can't see them, you know.

Ridley coughed out a laugh. "Oh yes you can. If you know where to look."

"Perhaps," she said, joining him in front of the great windows. "I know you are uncomfortable with my decision. I wanted to give you the opportunity to discuss it, if you are so inclined."

Ridley looked down at his feet and chuckled dryly to himself. "It's not my job to decide such things," he said. "I just offer my opinion. I understand why you and Mr. Connor feel the way you do. I suppose it is what one would call 'the right thing to do,' no?"

"Yes," she said. "Yes, I believe it is."

A thin strand of blue electricity snaked across the glass of the observation window. It seemed to dance along it, to curve and slither around on itself, leaping and splitting and merging back together.

"Plasma," Gravely said. "Dr. Kensington mentioned that we

would see some of it. The competing gravitational fields of the black holes create a sea of highly charged particles."

"And we are in the midst of it all."

"Yes, we are."

Ridley took a deep breath and exhaled. "Captain, my job is not to make the tough decisions, but it is to know something about the way people work, in all their glories and all their flaws. This is our first trip together, but I can tell already that you are exactly what I would have expected." Ridley saw a quiver pass over Gravely's face and held up a hand. "I don't mean that like it sounds, not negatively. You were a captain in the Navy; it is no surprise that you would choose the noble course. But have you considered that you may not be getting the best advice?"

"I don't think I understand what you're . . ."

"Well let's start with Aidan Connor," Ridley interrupted. "A man who has managed to find himself at the scene of two great tragedies. First, the *Hyperion*. Then, the *Vespa*."

"Neither his fault," Gravely felt compelled to mention.

"Of course not," Ridley offered, though Gravely wondered how much he believed it. "While that is true, it is also irrelevant for our purposes. The fact is, Mr. Connor may feel, rightly or wrongly, that he has much to make up for. Perhaps he feels guilty, the guilt a survivor naturally carries with them. Even an innocent one. And here is his chance to save lives. What might he say? What dangers might he obscure, even subconsciously? No, it is not my job to make these decisions and it is not my job to be heroic. But sometimes, the heroic choice is the easier one. Sometimes it is easier to put lives in danger than it is to choose the safer path."

They stood there, staring out into the darkness, watching the occasional blue or purple flame kiss the ship. They did not look at each other, speaking to and past each other all at once.

"Dr. Ridley, I have every intention of keeping this ship safe. You have my word on that. Aidan may have his problems, but I trust him."

"There's one other thing you should know Captain." Now Ridley did turn and face her. "The mind is a mystery, but it is not entirely mysterious. It is a spiritual manifestation of a physical thing, if you forgive me the phrase. And like all physical things, it can be affected, just like those particles out there."

Gravely reached up and rubbed her temples. Suddenly she had a headache. "Doctor, if you are about to tell me that on top of everything else, the black holes can drive you crazy, too, I just may go mad right here, right now." Ridley didn't laugh.

"It's rare, Captain. But I'd say if there is anywhere it is a danger, it's here, especially after what happened with Cyrus. Black holes are powerful things, and the gravitational upheaval often causes physical illness. That, everyone knows. Some in my profession point to subtler effects.

"Gravity does more than bend light and distort space—it may slow your very thoughts, cause you to see and hear things that are not there. I'm not trying to cause a panic and I don't want to alarm the other passengers. I just thought you should know. We will be at the very doorstep of one of these monstrosities and better to be prepared than not."

"Of course," Captain Gravely said with a sigh. "Of course. Keep an eye out for any problems, Doctor. That's the last thing we need."

"Always." Ridley bowed slightly.

"And, Dr. Ridley," Gravely said as she turned and walked to the door, "let's keep this between us. People are liable to see ghosts even if we don't give them a reason."

Ridley hesitated, but before he could say anything, Gravely turned and was gone. As the door closed behind her, he could almost hear the sound of his mother's laughter.

# CHAPTER
# 14

The *Singularity* floated alone in space, drifting inexorably toward its end, swathed in total darkness. It had every reason to think—if it had a mind to think on it—that this was its destiny. That its descent into the abyss would pass unseen and unnoticed.

Then the floodlights of the *Chronos* exploded in a flash that split the darkness, sweeping the surface of the *Singularity* and bathing it in the warmth of their glow. Two silent explosions erupted from ports in the side of the *Chronos* and a pair of metal spheres raced through the void toward the derelict ship. At the last second, eight metal legs sprang from each, grabbing hold of the *Singularity* and then racing across its surface to the side that those within the *Chronos* could not see.

"The Charlotte's scanners coming on-line now, Captain."

The *Chronos* was now virtually on top of the *Singularity*. The laser array had been firing constantly and Aidan was sure they had at least twenty-four hours before they were in any danger. But the captain wasn't taking any chances. The first order of business, however, was to ascertain if the *Singularity* had suffered any hull damage during whatever befell her.

Without circling the ship, their scanners could only analyze the side facing them. The two Charlottes would have to do the rest. It only took them a few seconds. As the data poured in, the hazy image cleared, and they had a clear picture of the entire ship.

"She looks to be intact, Captain. Whatever happened, it didn't breach the hull."

"That's one thing then. What else?"

"No electrical activity detected. She's definitely dead in the water. Impossible to tell what the life-support situation is without going over there."

"Then I guess that is what we will have to do."

"Wait," Dr. Ridley interrupted. Gravely had given to allowing them all access to the bridge. This was not a military ship and they had not signed up for this. They would make their decisions together or not at all. "Are you planning on going over there?"

"I don't see why not, Doctor. We should be able to figure this out pretty quickly once we get a look inside."

"You should let me go, Captain," Aidan said. "No reason to risk your life over there."

"While I appreciate the sentiment, you are the only one that can get these folks home if anything goes wrong. No, Mr. Connor, you are staying here."

"You mean to go alone then?"

"No, not alone."

Gravely turned and looked at Dr. Ridley. It took him a moment to realize what she meant. Aidan wondered if he would protest, but he did not. Instead, he frowned and said, "And then we leave?"

"Then we leave."

"Okay. Let's do it."

Aidan maneuvered the ship to its side, flipping on the airlock cameras as he did. What he saw surprised him.

"Come look at this, Captain."

Gravely leaned over Aidan and peered at the screen, but nothing she saw looked out of place.

"It's the airlock," Aidan said. "It's not a universal. Every ship built in the last decade has a universal lock."

"Maybe she's older?"

"A ship like that? I just can't believe it could be that old. Surely we would have seen something about it? Anyway, it's not a problem; I can still engage her. It's just strange is all."

"Actually, Mr. Connor, don't engage."

Aidan looked up at the captain, not sure what she meant. Then the obvious answer came to him.

"You mean to grapple her, then?"

"I do. Smarter, don't you think?"

It was. All ships, even the oldest ones, had titanium metal bars jutting from the hull above the airlock. They had been most useful in the days before the universals, but now were used only when a ship was damaged or in need of a tow.

"This way," she continued, "we keep a little distance between us and that ship. And while I trust your calculations, should they be wrong, I'd like to have the option of making a quick getaway. If she starts to go, I'd rather not be air-locked to her. We can release the hooks in an instant. Airlock might be more difficult."

"Agreed."

"Captain," Jack said, "Couldn't we use the grappling hooks to tow the ship away from the black hole? Seems like that would make things a lot easier."

"Not a bad idea, Mr. Crawford. But the fact is, a ship that size drifting like she is—there's a lot of momentum there. We'd strip the engines and probably end up following her over the edge. Even if we didn't, our grappling lines aren't strong enough to handle the stress. No, Mr. Crawford, if we can't get her engines going, there's no saving her."

Crawford frowned and glanced at Rebecca. She simply nodded. That was her job and she could handle it. She didn't appreciate the doubt in his eyes.

Twenty minutes later, Gravely was pulling on the full body suit that she would need for the short trip from the *Chronos* to the *Singularity*. It clung tight to her skin, so thin and elastic that she almost felt naked. The suits were designed to give maximum protection while providing maximum mobility. They were not flattering. There was no hiding in them. Ridley joined her in the air lock, holding the glass dome that would fit over his head under his arm.

"Just for the record, I want to say I am still opposed to this."

"Noted."

"Also, Captain," Ridley said as he fitted the helmet over his head. When he spoke again, it had the electric tinge of the comm system. "You should know that as we approach the event horizon the danger of gravitational effects will increase. If you start to see things, or if the crew starts to act strangely, then we have to leave as soon as possible."

"Understood." Gravely slipped the helmet over her head and looked out the narrow slat on the airlock door to the ship beyond. She touched the wall and an image of Aidan appeared.

"Captain, I'm ready at fire control whenever you are."

"Alright, Mr. Connor. You may proceed."

Aidan let the computer do the work. It adjusted and aimed the grappling hooks and when the target was acquired, awaited a final command. Aidan gave it and the grappling guns fired. The hooks flew through space, wrapping themselves around their targets. A perfect shot.

"Got it, Captain," Aidan said.

Gravely turned to Ridley. He nodded once. She tapped a computer screen and the room sealed itself. In a few seconds, ventilation shafts removed the air from the room, leaving it as complete a vacuum as the emptiness of space without. Gravely spun the wheel on the airlock door and pushed it open. The steel line of the grappling hook hung above her, floating in the weightlessness of space.

Gravely removed a clip attached to a cord that ran to her midsection and attached it to the line above. Then it was just a matter of taking a leap of faith. For a moment, long enough to take one breath, she hesitated. Then she jumped. Her momentum carried her, and she felt an almost childlike exhilaration as she slid down to the open airlock below.

When her feet met solid metal, she removed the clip from the line and attached it to the wall of the ship. Ridley arrived few seconds later. From the bridge, Aidan, Rebecca and Jack watched the video feed from Gravely and Ridley's cameras on the two great screens above them. The cameras were mounted on the top of their helmets, allowing those who remained on the bridge to see everything they saw.

Gravely stuck a field generator to the wall of the ship and a solid — if invisible — wall appeared behind them, sealing the room from space. She tapped a computer console that sat next to the airlock doorway. To no one's surprise, nothing happened.

"Power's dead. Attaching battery."

Gravely slipped the battery cable into the ship's auxiliary unit. The battery console lit up, but the ship's computer terminal remained as black as space behind them.

"Dammit. Nothing."

"If we can't get the doors open," Ridley murmured, "this'll be a short trip."

"You seeing this, Aidan?" Gravely said, ignoring Ridley.

"We are, Captain. Check below the auxiliary node. Do you see a panel with a handle depressed into its center?"

Gravely looked down, and as she did Aidan saw what they were looking for.

"Yes, Aidan. I see it."

"Good. That's the manual release. Grab it and turn it clockwise. A quarter turn and it should lock in place."

Gravely grasped the handle and pulled. It didn't budge. She grabbed it with her other hand and tried again. Still nothing. On the third time, however, it turned ever so slightly. Then something gave and the handle spun freely until it locked in place just as Aidan said it would.

"Now what?"

"Now push it in. It should sink into the side. When it does, the magnetic locks on the door will release. Or they should, at least."

Gravely looked up at Ridley. "Ready?" He didn't answer, though she took the look on his face to be a yes. "Here we go."

Gravely pushed the handle and felt it slide into the wall. There was the sound of grinding metal. Somewhere inside the door, a lock released. It opened in one swift movement. A rush of wind followed as the vacuum in which they stood filled with air from the ship with a force strong enough to almost push Gravely over. Then there was nothing but silence and the deep, impenetrable blackness of the inside of the *Singularity*.

"Alright. So far, so good. Here we go."

\* \* \*

Minutes earlier, as Gravely and Ridley were pulling on their flight suits and preparing to leave the *Chronos*, Cyrus McDonnell, or his body at least, lay on a metal bed in the infirmary, separated from those outside by an invisible force field. One would never know it was there were it not for the occasional crackle of electricity that coursed down from its top to its bottom, rippling its surface.

Not that anyone needed to be protected from Cyrus. The drugs that Dr. Ridley had pumped into his veins were sufficient that he may never wake up. Not until they reached Riley, when the doctor planned on passing him off to the nearest hospital.

Someone else's patient and someone else's problem.

But then Aidan pushed a button on his computer screen, and the grappling hooks were fired from the *Chronos*. As the hooks latched on to the other ship, as the *Singularity* and the *Chronos* went from two separate entities into one being, the lids that covered two pitted eye sockets opened and . . .

. . . Cyrus McDonnell awakened.

# CHAPTER
# 15

Gravely and Ridley stood on the precipice of the airlock, the cold waste of space behind them and perhaps something even darker ahead. The computer in Gravely's suit sampled the air, reporting the readings on her heads-up display.

"Are you getting this, Mr. Connor?"

"I am, Captain. Oxygen levels are slightly lower than normal but well within the parameters. The temperature is a chilly fifty-two degrees. Obviously the environmental regulators are down."

"The lower oxygen levels could mean someone is breathing in there, though."

"Could be anything," Ridley said. "That's not a lot to go on."

He peered over Gravely's shoulder into the thick darkness beyond. He shuddered; it reminded him of the shadow walls. He wondered if this was all a trick, a ploy to get them to unwittingly pass beyond it and be sucked down into that dark oblivion. "Thank God for night vision."

"On that note . . . Alright, Mr. Connor. Switching to night vision."

No matter how dark, there could be no hiding from the cameras. With them on, even the blackest night would turn to day, the computers recalibrating the image so that the user could hardly tell the difference between the image they saw and a fully lit room. But when Gravely and Ridley engaged their night vision, something went wrong.

They both cried out in pain. On the bridge, Aidan watched as the screen went from pitch black to blinding white and then back to black as the two of them disengaged.

"We've got a problem, Mr. Connor," Gravely said. "I don't know what that was, but it was like staring into the sun."

"We got nothing on the screens, Captain. Just a flash of light."

"Same. Give us a moment. I can barely see."

"I ran a diagnostic. Everything should be fine."

"Yes, Aidan. I'm beginning to wonder about our computers. We are going to switch to full spectrum. But I think for the good of us both, we'll keep our eyes closed."

The full spectrum cameras were a poor man's night vision. The cameras flooded the room with infrared light, invisible to the human eye. It then collected it back, converting the data to an image the human eye could see. While not as good as night vision, it was better than walking in the dark. Except when Gravely engaged her infrared, the blinding white light returned.

"Still no good, Captain."

Gravely cursed under her breath. "Guess we'll have to do this the old-fashioned way. Lights it is."

"Captain," Aidan said, "maybe we should reconsider all this."

"This was your idea, Mr. Connor."

"Yes ma'am, and I am beginning to think it was a bad one. Maybe we could send in a Charlotte."

"We're already here, Aidan. We need to get this done. Fast."

Gravely tapped her left wrist and a computer screen appeared. Another tap activated her external speaker. She hooked her computer into the universal computer port and hoped that there was enough power in the ship's batteries to broadcast.

"Passengers and crew of the *Singularity*," she said. "My name is Captain Caroline Gravely of the American Merchant Marine ship *Chronos*. We intersected with you twelve hours ago, but despite our repeated hails, we have failed to make contact. You are adrift in a warp channel and your current trajectory takes you into a gravity well. If you can hear my voice, please respond."

Her words thundered into the blackness. To Ridley this was an utterly useless gesture. There was no one there and he had a feeling that even if there was, it wasn't someone they would want to find. When no one answered back, Gravely turned and looked at him. He just shook his head.

"Pursuant to Article 4-7 of Spacing Guild Regulations governing ships in the trade," she continued, facing the darkness once again, "we are coming aboard on a rescue mission. If you are injured, stay where you are. We will find you."

Gravely reached up and tapped the side of her helmet. Ridley did the same. Two beams of light erupted, and together they cut deeply into the darkness ahead. Yet still, it was the darkness, not the light, that held sway.

Gravely took a cautious step over the threshold of the airlock door. The absence of light was oppressive, and she found herself jerking her head from side to side, trying to illuminate as much of the room as possible with the beams from her helmet. She was in the antechamber of the airlock. Suits hung from hooks on the side of the wall, an American flag stitched on the chest of each.

"Definitely one of ours," Gravely said.

Back on the *Chronos*, Aidan was staring at the screen, trying to straighten out in his head what was wrong with this picture. It didn't take long.

"Those are the old Raytex suits, Captain."

Gravely rubbed the fabric between her fingers and even through her own suit's second skin, she could feel that he was right.

"Strange that they would have outdated equipment," Ridley said. "Maybe these suits weren't high on their priority list."

Gravely frowned. "Maybe."

Outdated, maybe. But in pristine condition. Suits hung neatly on their racks. Boots were lined up in straight lines beneath them. Whatever had come to this place, it never made it to the airlock.

Ridley shined his light on the inner door of the airlock. It was their entrance to the rest of the ship. Gravely approached it and was about to engage the manual release when the door swung open with a bang. Normally, with the roaring of engines and the noise of a ship, they wouldn't have even noticed. But in that silence, the opening of the door boomed into the darkness of the corridors beyond, echoing up and down the hallways.

Their lights cut through the glowering black air. In the swirling dust, they saw many things. People, animals, amorphous shapes that they hoped never existed in the world they knew. But it was simply an illusion. Just falling dust in the silence.

Gravely went first, stepping gingerly through the open portal, shining her light down both hallways as she did. There was nothing, just emptiness.

"Right or left?" Ridley asked.

"Right," Gravely said, taking a step. "Always right."

They inched down the corridor, Gravely with her hand on the sidearm she never left the ship without. The hallway was empty, the blank holoscreens that lined them mocking technology. The light from their helmets gave some illumination, but not as much as they should have. It was as if the darkness and swirling dust were thicker than they should be, blocking the feeble beams.

On the bridge of the *Chronos*, Rebecca and Jack stood next to Aidan. Every step that Gravely and Ridley took was broadcast on the great screens above them. Rebecca was watching their progress. Jack was watching Aidan. Ever since Gravely and Ridley had entered those black tunnels, Aidan had not stopped shaking. Now beads of sweet were starting to trickle down his face. Jack wasn't often nervous, but Aidan was starting to bother him.

Since he was watching Aidan, Jack didn't see the shadow that seemed to race across the screen above him, just at the edge of Gravely's light. He just heard Rebecca gasp.

"Did you see that?"

It was Gravely, though Ridley had never heard her like that. He would have taken mental note, but he had seen something too, and it had shaken him. It was no shadow, but a figure. A woman, he would swear. In a long, flowing dress of white fabric that shimmered in the darkness.

"How . . ." he murmured.

No one heard him. Gravely simply stared, wondering if her eyes had deceived her or if she had really seen him. An old man, with back stooped low from the pain of years and the burden of hard work. One who bore the image of her face long before she was even dreamt of by her parents or theirs.

Rebecca saw it too, back on the bridge. Saw a little girl on a bicycle, an impossible image drenched in shadow but real nonetheless. And then there was Aidan, his shaking hand covering his mouth as he stared up at the screen where he had seen himself only a few seconds before, walking through corridors that were all too familiar, even if his sane mind cried out that he had never seen them before. Not in life, that was. Not in his waking hours.

"Aidan," Gravely said, her voice shaking almost as badly as the hand that held the pistol in front of her, as if anything in this world could protect her from that image, "rewind please. Tell us what you see."

Aidan sat in his chair on the bridge, staring down at the command on his computer screen, the one that he need only tap to rewind the video and see what had passed only a few moments prior. His entire being rebelled. He did not want to see. He did not want to know. He felt Rebecca place her hand on his shoulder, looked up at her and saw the same fear in her eyes. But she needed to know, too. He looked back down at the computer screen and tapped it once.

The video flashed, and then the feeling of déjà vu hit them all as they watched a scene they had already witnessed. Aidan held his breath as Ridley and Gravely approached the point where the figure had been. He felt Rebecca's hand squeeze his shoulder. Then the moment came . . . and nothing happened.

"Did you see that?" They heard Gravely ask, once again. This time, their answer was different. They had seen nothing.

"That's not possible." Aidan rewound the video again. It was no use. The same blank emptiness met their eyes. "There was something there!" Aidan said, looking up at Rebecca. Now there was doubt in her eyes where fear had been.

"What did you see?" Jack asked.

"I saw . . ." Aidan began. Even as he started he knew he couldn't finish. What had he seen? And how to explain it?

Jack sighed. "What about you?" he asked Rebecca. "What did you see?"

She hesitated. "Nothing," she said finally. "Just a trick of the light I guess."

"Aidan. Aidan, what's on the tape?" It was Gravely.

Aidan looked up at Jack but he simply shrugged. Rebecca shook her head.

"We don't see anything, Captain. Nothing on the screen.

Nothing on the tape. It's just you and Dr. Ridley and the dust."

Gravely heard Aidan but didn't believe him. Neither did Ridley, who stood peering into the darkness as if staring long enough into it would reveal its secrets.

"It can't be," he said. "I know I saw something. I know I did. You saw it too, right? I saw how you reacted."

She had seen or thought she had. She also remembered what Ridley had said about tricks the mind might play. Now, here, staring through that black shroud, lit only by the feeble light of their helmets, she began to believe that their minds saw what they wanted, whether it was there or not.

"There was nothing there, Doctor. You heard them. They looked at the film."

"Maybe . . ." Ridley replied, "maybe what we saw can't be recorded on a camera or captured on film."

Gravely didn't respond to that. Rather, she took another step forward, motioning for him to follow. He shook his head but followed nonetheless. There was no use resisting.

The corridor opened into another, this one with doors along both sides.

"Crew quarters, maybe?" Ridley offered.

Gravely tried the door nearest them, ready for whatever might emerge from the room beyond when it opened. But it didn't budge and attaching the battery pack didn't help.

"Locked. Once we get the power back on, we can have the computer override their security measures. For now, let's move on."

At its end, the corridor split in half, leading off to the left and right.

"Right, I assume?"

"Always right," Gravely answered.

She attached the battery pack, and the door slid open.

It was then they found the body.

Ridley stumbled backward and would have fallen over had the other door not caught him. Gravely pointed her pistol at the dead thing, as if it might rise up at any moment to attack her.

"Mr. Connor," she said, "are you getting this?"

"Yes, Captain," Aidan answered. "We are."

It took only a moment for Ridley to regain his composure, his fear masking whatever embarrassment he might have felt. He knelt down next to the body. It was slumped over on its side, long blond hair falling down around its shoulders. He presumed this was a woman. He put his hand on the shoulder and rolled it onto its back. Gravely gasped and on the bridge, Aidan and Rebecca both turned away. Only Jack showed no reaction.

"Who could do this?" Ridley whispered. As he said it, he realized the true horror contained in that simple statement, for someone *had* done this. They had done it with their bare hands.

Ridley had been right. It was a woman, though it would have been difficult to tell from the face alone—or what was left of it. The face was shredded, covered in deep gashes that ran from the scalp to the throat, chunks of flesh having been ripped from her cheeks and neck.

"Claw marks," Ridley thought. If only they had been from an animal, that would have been so much better. But no, the thick red trenches spaced awkwardly across her skin could only come from human fingers.

There were empty black holes where her eyes should have been. Ridley felt a wave of nausea pass over him when he involuntarily thought of Cyrus. What was left of her skin was a chalky white, with spider webs of pale blue lines that crisscrossed its surface. What was left of her mouth was locked open in a scream, the last sound she had ever made.

"What happened here, Doctor? Could she have done this herself?"

"No, there's no skin under her fingernails," Ridley said, holding up one of her hands. "And the scratches didn't kill her. Her throat was crushed. No, Captain, this was murder. Judging by the state of the body, this happened a week ago, maybe. Week and a half, tops."

"So she's been lying here for a week?"

"I'd say so. That tells me a couple of things. One, we've got a madman on board. Two . . . whatever struggle followed, he won."

"How do you know that?"

"Well, you tell me. If the rest of the crew had taken care of whoever did this, would they have left her body here?"

"No," Gravely said, tightening her grip on her gun, "I guess you're right."

"We have to get off of this ship, Captain. There's no one here worth saving."

"I tend to agree."

The words had barely left her mouth when they heard the sound. It was the sound of metal on metal, a grinding . . .

*sssshhhhhrrrrrriiiiiieeeeekkkkk*

. . . that rippled up Gravely's spine and made every hair on her body stand on end.

"What the hell was that?" As if anyone would answer. As if Ridley wanted to know the answer.

They backed away from the body, Gravely keeping her gun pointed at the darkness, but finding scarce comfort there. They inched themselves backward down the corridor, unwilling to turn away from the noise. Ridley would have sworn there was something watching them. Just beyond their beams of light. Matching them step for step, but making no sound. Stalking them. Like prey.

They made their way back to the airlock, closing the door behind them. Ridley had never been happier to step into the void. They latched themselves to the line of the grappling hook and swung into space, their momentum carrying their weightless bodies down the thick wire to the waiting ship. In the instant before Ridley pushed himself from the metal floor of the ship, he heard another sound, that of a woman's voice.

She whispered only one word.

"David."

# CHAPTER
# 16

The door to the bridge slid open and Captain Gravely marched in, removing her gloves and throwing them down on one of the consoles. Ridley was right behind her.

"Mr. Connor, I've seen enough here. If you'll withdraw the grappling hooks and call back the Charlottes. Then take us a safe distance out. We've done all we can. There's no one left to save on that ship."

"Yes, ma'am." In seconds, the engines of the ship fired and the *Chronos* began to back away. From the other side of the *Singularity* came two whirling balls of metal, thrusters on either side, guiding the two Charlottes back into the ship.

"Captain."

Rebecca turned and looked at Jack. He had been hovering in the background, but now he had stepped to the middle of the bridge. She felt her stomach drop. So it would come to this.

"Just a second, Mr. Crawford. I'd like to put some distance between us and that other ship."

"Captain, are you sure that's a good idea? Those people might need our help."

Aidan glanced at Rebecca, but she was looking at her feet. Jack had said so little up to this point. Why now?

Ridley coughed out a laugh. "You can't be serious," he said rather than asked. "You were watching, right? You saw what we found on that ship? There are no people left. And if there are, they're mad. Or worse. No, we should never have stayed here as long as we have."

"But we don't know what happened," Jack said. "For all we

know, there could be survivors holed up over there somewhere. All I'm saying is that we should give them a chance. Aidan, here, says we've got another twenty-four hours. Why not take one more look? We can arm ourselves. I'll even go with you."

"Oh, this is insane. Captain, you can't be considering this?"

"I tend to agree with Dr. Ridley," Aidan said. "I think we've done our duty. Anything more is just risking more innocent lives."

"I'm sorry, Mr. Crawford. We can't stay."

Gravely turned back to Aidan while he called up jump routes that would avoid the *Singularity*. Jack Crawford stood in the center of the bridge, his jaw set. He looked over at Rebecca and she knew the question without being asked. She sighed deeply, but nodded once in agreement nevertheless.

"Captain," Crawford said flatly.

"Mr. Crawford," Gravely said, not bothering to hide her frustration, "perhaps you and Ms. Kensington would be better served waiting in the passengers' quarters. We can discuss this later."

"No, Captain, we will discuss it now."

In that moment, a chill fell over the bridge. Everyone in the room turned and gaped at Jack. He saw the confusion on each of their faces. Fear too. It lasted only a second for Gravely required only a moment for her to realize what was happening. For the first time, she truly took measure of this man before her and cursed herself for her stupidity. She was getting sloppy and she had let him slide right past her without question.

"Who are you, Mr. Crawford? Who are you really?"

"That's not important," he said. "The only thing that matters is that you understand the situation. I'm not asking."

"No, I think it does matter. People don't give me orders on my own ship, Mr. Crawford. No matter who they think they are."

Jack ignored her and turned to Aidan. "Mr. Connor, take the ship back to our previous position above the *Singularity* and reengage the grappling hooks."

"Captain," Aidan said quietly, "what is this all about?"

"I believe, Mr. Connor," she said, never taking her eyes off Jack, "that this is what you might call a mutiny."

Crawford laughed once. "Not a mutiny, Captain. I outrank

you."

"Oh damn it all," Ridley said, slumping down into a chair. "You're ISS, aren't you? You knew this would happen, didn't you? You knew about the ship. You knew we'd find it here. You've known all along."

The Internal Security Service was often whispered of and much feared, but rarely seen in action. Their agents were not to be trifled with, and if Crawford was truly one of them, then the ship that Ridley had hoped to never see again was probably even more terrible than he suspected.

"Look," Crawford said, "what I knew or didn't know is neither relevant nor important to what we must do here. Nor is my affiliation. All that's important is that we finish this. I gave you an order, Mr. Connor."

Aidan looked up at Gravely and she nodded. He turned back to Jack and tried to give him the worst look his face could manage.

"I don't take orders from you," he said.

"That's right, Mr. Connor," Gravely said. "And, Mr. Crawford, I think you're on the wrong ship. I don't know if you heard, but I'm retired. If you want to file charges against me when we reach Riley, then you feel free. But I'm taking the *Chronos* out of this place and there's not a damn thing you can say to stop me."

"Enough!" Crawford shouted. He reached behind his back and pulled out a pistol that he pointed directly at Aidan. "Mr. Connor, you will do as I say or I will eliminate you and find someone who will."

"How did you . . ."

"Please, Captain," Jack said before she could finish. "I don't know what kind of half-assed operation you think we're running here, but your stubbornness is not going to cost me that ship. Now if you don't mind, please tell your navigator here to do as I say before I have to kill him."

"Do it, Aidan."

Aidan looked up at Gravely and she saw the defiance in his eyes. "Do it. Please."

Aidan glanced back at Jack Crawford and both men were fully aware it was only the latter's gun that kept them apart. But only Jack knew the damage he could do to Aidan with his bare hands.

"Aye, aye, Captain."

Aidan maneuvered the ship back into position over the *Singularity*. He fired the grappling hooks, and the two ships were connected once again.

"Alright, we're here. For now at least," Aidan said, spinning around in his chair to face Jack. "But you can't watch us twenty-four hours a day."

"No," Crawford said, "that's true. I can't." Crawford smiled over his pistol and for a second, Aidan was afraid he was about to shoot him. "Computer," Crawford called out, "command protocol Crawford, Jack, 96367."

"What are you doing?" Aidan gasped.

But he knew, even before Gravely answered, "He's taking control of the ship."

The computer answered back, "Command protocol Crawford, Jack, activated. Mission parameters require a second authorization before protocol activation."

"Ha!" Ridley stood up and glared at Jack. "What now?"

Aidan smirked. "Yeah, Jack, now what? You can't seriously think anyone on this ship is going to help you do this."

When Rebecca spoke, Aidan felt a little bit of something inside of him break, something that to that point had somehow survived everything else he had seen.

"Computer," she said, "Kensington, Rebecca, authorization 57846." She faced Aidan and gave him a look that begged, pleaded with him to understand.

"I'm sorry, Aidan. I have my orders too."

# CHAPTER
# 17

Aidan sat slumped in a chair on the bridge, staring up at the monitors above him, the room silent except for the roar of the ship's engines. Even they were muffled now, their only job to keep the *Chronos* in stasis above that accursed derelict, the one Aidan wished he had never seen.

He considered turning off the monitors. It was one of the few things left on the *Chronos* he could control. But no, as long as he could, he wanted to keep an eye on that ship.

It had all happened fast after Rebecca turned on them. Aidan laughed to himself bitterly. She had not turned. She'd never been with them. With the computer under his command, Crawford had locked down the controls. The ship wasn't going anywhere.

"Not until we secure that ship," he had said. "Then you can have her back."

Ridley had stormed out of the room without a word. Gravely maintained her dignity, even if Aidan couldn't. Not that he made a scene. He was too angry to move. Too angry to speak. He simply glared at Rebecca, who had long since refused to match his gaze.

"What would you have us do?" Gravely asked.

"We're going back over to the *Singularity*. And when I say we, I mean all of us."

"Shouldn't someone stay with the ship?"

"Why?"

"It just seems prudent."

"We don't have time for prudence."

Crawford walked over to the console, standing uncomfortably close to Aidan. He pointed up to the image of the ship on the screen.

"That ship is our number one priority. It's obviously in worse shape than I had hoped and we don't have much time. The faster Dr. Kensington can bring her back online, the faster we will be out of your hair. That's what you want, right?"

Gravely didn't bother to answer.

"Good. You have fifteen minutes to get your minds right. Then we go back and this time we don't leave until we know what happened over there."

With that, Jack and Rebecca left together. Gravely followed behind them. She had said nothing else to Aidan and he appreciated that. He didn't feel like talking. So he sat there, staring up at the screens, occasionally tapping at the computer to see if he could regain control, the flashing red of an invalid command the only response he received.

The door opened and Rebecca walked in. She stopped just beyond the threshold. Aidan didn't give her the satisfaction of asking her to come any closer. In fact, when he did speak, he didn't even look up at her.

"Another message from your boss?" he said. "What does he want now?"

"Jack's not my boss," she said, crossing her hands across her chest. "And he didn't send me up here."

"Oh I see. So you only have yourself to blame."

"Aidan . . ."

She started to explain herself, to make an argument about why he should forgive her. But there was nothing to say and part of her didn't think she owed him an explanation anyway. She considered turning and leaving, but instead she walked across the bridge and sat down across from him. "Aidan, look at me."

"Rebecca," he said, slamming his computer down on the console and looking up at her, "I'm not exactly sure why you think I want to talk to you or why you think I care about anything you have to say. Yeah, I liked you, and I thought maybe there was something there between us, but whatever it was, whatever it might have been, it's gone. I don't even know why you're here. You don't owe me anything, right? I get it. You have your orders. You are doing what you have to do. That's great. But you've put this ship in danger. You lied to me, and you lied to Captain Gravely. Honestly, I don't care about your reasons. I don't care about your excuses. You made your choice. Now we all have to live with it."

Rebecca took a deep breath and sighed. She had expected this, even if she hoped things would be different.

"I know you're upset. I would be. But you need to understand something. I didn't know you or anything about you when I came on board. But I did know about the *Singularity*. I did know what it meant and I knew how important it was that we recover her if we could. You can judge me if you want to. You can sit here and pout about it. And you can be so pissed off at me that you won't even talk to me. Or you can help me finish what we started and get the hell out of here as soon as we can. That's your choice."

Aidan frowned and shook his head. When he looked up at her, she knew he was listening.

"And when this is all over," she continued, "you can be mad at me then. Or maybe you can think about forgiving me. All I'm asking is that we put that aside for now, if you can."

The two of them sat there, heads bent, both wondering how Aidan would react. Rebecca hadn't known him long enough to be sure, and in truth, Aidan had no idea himself. Finally, he leaned back in his chair and exhaled deeply. As he did, Aidan felt the anger and the frustration melt away. He looked over at Rebecca and suddenly knew that she was going to win this battle in the end. Letting his temper get the best of him would accomplish nothing.

"Who are you, Rebecca? Who are you really?" he asked. The exhaustion in his voice seemed almost desperate and she felt the regret she had tried to keep buried suddenly resurface.

She tried to smile. "I'm exactly who I said I was, Aidan. I'm a warp physicist, who always wanted to go to space. I work for the ISS, or I have, at least, for the last few years. But this is my last assignment. I don't want to do this, not anymore."

"Sounds like you are about to be unemployed," Aidan said flatly. Rebecca laughed.

"Yeah, I guess that's true."

"Well, you can sleep on my couch."

Rebecca grinned slyly. "I was hoping for better than that." It felt like a thousand pounds vanished from her shoulders when Aidan reached for her.

* * *

Ridley hadn't waited for Jack to finish giving orders before he stormed off the bridge. He had left the government to get away from people like Jack Crawford. Now here he was, once again under their thumb.

The *Chronos* was back in orbit above that accursed ship. He'd be going back. He knew that now. Crawford would require it and there was no denying a man like that. Ridley was angry—so angry that, as he walked into the infirmary, he almost didn't notice Cyrus. Almost.

The door to the infirmary opened and Ridley stumbled to a dead stop. Cyrus was standing at the edge of his cell, his nose so close to the force field containing him that it crackled under his breath. He was staring at Ridley, if it was possible for him to stare. And he was smiling. Between that smile and his eyeless gaze, Ridley couldn't say which was worse.

"How did you . . ."

Cyrus couldn't be awake. Ridley had pumped him so full of tranquilizers that he should be dead asleep. In fact, Ridley's only concern had been that he would accidentally kill him. Then Cyrus spoke and something deep within Ridley, something that defined him, something that kept him sane, snapped. And that's when Ridley truly knew fear.

"Hello, David," Cyrus said, almost lovingly. It was not his voice. It was higher than it should be, with an accent that was not and had never been Cyrus's. Ridley knew that voice. He knew it, even if it wasn't a perfect copy, even with a tinge of the gruffness and timbre that had been Cyrus's.

"No one calls me that," he whispered, swallowing deeply despite the dryness of his mouth. "No one, for a long time."

"I do. I always did."

To the world, his name was Malcolm Ridley. But his first name was David. He had hated it all his life. Most people had respected his request to be called Malcolm. But there was always one person who refused, one person who insisted on calling him by the name he was given at birth. Ridley had not heard her voice for a very, very long time. Not until now.

"Come here, David. Come closer so I can see you better."

Cyrus smiled and a mixture of pus and blood and black ichor pooled in the pits of his eyes. Ridley found himself pulled toward the cell, inexorably and involuntarily, as if he had no choice but to follow the commands of the voice.

"That's better. Now why don't you lower the force field? Let me out of this cell so I can give you a hug."

Ridley stood, his mouth open in a mixture of stupid amazement and fear.

"Who are you?" he said, his voice shaking.

The thing that was Cyrus cocked its head to the side, a look of confusion spreading across its broken face. "Who am I? David, surely you haven't forgotten your own mother."

"No . . ." Ridley whispered, stumbling backward into a tray of instruments. They fell to the floor with a crash, skittering along the cold, metal surface. But Ridley paid them no mind. Instead he stood, staring at what could not be.

"No," he repeated. "You're Cyrus McDonnell."

The thing started to laugh, the sound pounding on Ridley's aching brain, driving him closer to madness than he ever thought possible. He wanted to shut it out, to run from that place, but something kept him there, locked in that spot. Frozen.

"That's simply not true. Cyrus is dead, honey. You know that. You've known it all along. That's why you drugged his body. That's why you wanted it to sleep. You were afraid. But there's nothing to fear. Mommy's here now."

"But you died," Ridley whispered, to himself as much as the thing across from him.

"No, not dead," it said, almost soothingly. "Merely sleeping. Sleeping until, through sleep, I could come back to you. And now, I have returned. I'm sorry for how I left you, David. I'm sorry for what I did to you. I never meant to hurt you. But Mommy's mind wasn't right, you see? She needed help. But now I see things clearly."

"No!" Ridley screamed, finally backing away. "No! This is impossible. How do you know all that? How can you?"

"Because I'm your mother, son. Do your ears deceive you? Do your eyes not see? I know this is not what you expected. But it is a gift. Through this empty shell, I have returned to you. Now come to Mommy. Come let me go so we can be together. Forever."

"No!" And this time, Ridley did run, away from the thing with his mother's voice and another's face. Ran to anywhere, anywhere but that accursed infirmary.

The thing that had been Cyrus McDonnell stood in its cell, the smile it had plastered across its face beginning to fade away.

"Hmmm . . ." it murmured in a voice that was not Cyrus's, but wasn't that of Ridley's mother, either.

"How disappointing."

# CHAPTER
# 18

Rebecca, Aidan, Gravely and Ridley stood in the airlock, their skintight suits shimmering under the harsh lights above. They waited for Jack. Since the events on the bridge, Gravely had deferred to him. She didn't like it, but she liked having no control over her own ship even less. The sooner Jack found whatever he was looking for, the sooner things would be back to normal. Right now, she was more concerned with Dr. Ridley.

"You alright?" she whispered.

Ridley swallowed hard before he said, "Yeah. Of course." The way his hands shook and the sweat that beaded along his hairline said differently.

Ridley had run from the infirmary like a madman. In truth, he had been a little bit mad and if anyone had come upon him in those moments of insanity, he would be sharing the isolation cell with Cyrus.

He had calmed himself though, cowering in the corner of some dark corridor of the ship, repeating that it was all a hallucination brought on by the lingering effects of the warp sleep or the increasing distortions created by the black holes. Still, he didn't go back to the infirmary afterwards. He wondered if he ever would.

The door slid open and in stepped Jack. He was already wearing his suit. He carried a pulse rifle in each hand and had three more slung over his shoulder. He threw one to Aidan, handed another to Rebecca, and then Gravely and Ridley.

"I see you opened the arms locker," Gravely said.

"That's right," Jack answered. "Based on what you found last time, I didn't think you would mind."

"Of course not," Gravely said. "It just would have been nice if you had asked."

Jack almost grinned, but he stopped it at the last moment. He didn't have to ask, but there was no use rubbing it in.

"Right," he said, looking around the group, "this time we are doing this by the book. No more pussyfooting around. Our time is running short. We are going to hit the ship and hit it hard. We'll find whoever is responsible for that body and neutralize him by any means necessary. Remember, the ship is our primary objective. If we can save the crew, all the better. But assume anyone you meet is the enemy. Err on the side of putting them down."

Aidan couldn't say he was shocked by these "orders," but they bothered him nonetheless. He wondered what it was about the ship that was so valuable and questioned why those on board wouldn't be equally important. He had tried to pry some of the information out of Rebecca, but she wasn't talking. She apologized profusely and he knew that her guilt was such that he could probably force it out of her, but he hadn't pushed. Now he wished he had.

"It's not important to you to have them alive?" Aidan asked. "Won't they have information you need?"

Jack frowned. Thirty minutes before, Aidan and all the rest were ready to leave any survivors behind. Why the sudden concern?

"The information they may have is important, yes. But our orders are to recover the ship at all costs. Something tells me we won't have to worry about survivors. Maybe one, and we all know what he did. Now, if there are no more questions, let's go."

Jack didn't wait for them to respond. He pulled his helmet down over his head and walked to the airlock. He turned to the others and each gave him a reluctant thumbs-up. Jack engaged the vacuum pumps and opened the door to space.

He and Aidan went first, zipping down the lines to the ship below. Rebecca and Gravely followed, with Ridley bringing up the rear. Aidan looked up at the *Chronos* above them and he wished they were far from here. He thought how strange it would be when they returned, to ride the zip lines up to the ship instead of down. It was a silly thing; there was no up or down in space. But old habits died hard.

With Jack in the lead, things moved much more quickly than

they had earlier. Aidan realized the man's strength when he spun the manual release with hardly any effort. The same thick darkness Gravely and Ridley had experienced met them again.

Jack switched on his helmet lamps. The others did the same without having to be told. Gravely thought it was strange; even with three more people and their lights, the room seemed as dark as ever, the blackness beyond as impenetrable as when she and Ridley had stood alone.

Jack took the point, stepping first into the empty airlock and opening the door beyond. He peered around the corner, shining his light left and then right. When he was sure their path was clear, he motioned with his hand and they followed.

Ridley was shaking. Even with the others, even with a rifle in his hands, he found no comfort. He had felt something, back in the infirmary with Cyrus. A presence, one beyond himself and the insane man just behind the force field wall.

He hadn't so much noticed it at the time. How could he with everything else? But it was there. Now in the silence and the blackness, with the same dark feeling bearing down upon him, he remembered. And remembering was the worst thing of all, for that presence was with him still.

Jack didn't bother to try the doors in the next corridor. He made a mental note to scour them later, when the power was back on and he was sure no one was hiding within. On they pressed, their feeble lights barely illuminating their path, until they came to the next door. They knew the body was lying beyond it. From here on was unexplored territory.

The door slid open and Jack stepped through. Then he stopped dead. He turned and looked at the four behind him. Aidan saw it first. The look of doubt, one he did not expect from Crawford. When Jack stepped to the side, Aidan knew why. The body was gone.

Gravely cursed under her breath. Ridley just stared. Rebecca glanced at Aidan and he tried to reassure her with his eyes. He wasn't sure he succeeded.

"So there *is* someone left on the ship," Jack said. The doubt that had been in his eyes before was not mirrored in his voice. Instead, Aidan heard a steely resolve, the cold timbre of a man who was ready for action. "Stay close."

Jack turned and raised his rifle to his shoulder. The others did the same, though only Captain Gravely looked comfortable doing it. They advanced down the hallway in the shape of a triangle, Jack at the point and oblivious to the rest of them. That was probably for the best. The others were scared and it showed. In every shadow, in every falling particle of dust, they saw movement. Enemies lurking in the darkness.

Aidan stopped and only started walking again when Ridley stumbled into him. It had been there, in the back of his mind, what all of this reminded him of. It was the shadow wall that he saw, the one from the dreams. It was ever before them, retreating from their lights, hiding unknown evils.

They pressed forward. Aidan noticed Jack was holding a computer pad in his free hand on which a map was displayed. So they weren't wandering aimlessly. He glanced over at Rebecca and felt a spark of anger. She still wasn't being completely forthright with him, whatever her reasons might be, and he didn't like it. He didn't think on it long, however, as Jack threw up his hand and they all came to a stop.

Jack slipped his computer into his pocket and raised his gun, pointing it at something that none of them could see. They stood in silence, peering into the emptiness. Aidan opened his mouth to speak, but before he could break the silence, something else did.

It was a small sound; one he couldn't describe at first. How Jack had even noticed it, he couldn't say. It was a shuffling sound, a *whoosh whoosh whoosh* in three quick beats, followed by a pause, and then *whoosh, whoosh, whoosh* again. It sounded like cloth against metal, a dragging sound. A chill rippled across Aidan's skin. Yes, definitely dragging.

Gravely put a hand on Aidan's arm and looked up at him. He could see in her eyes that she had come to the same conclusion. Jack took a cautious step forward and they all matched it, inching along the hallway, their lights feebly picking at the darkness, failing to reveal what was beyond.

Aidan's eyes deceived him, and he saw demons dancing in the abyss. Then something else appeared—something more concrete. At first, he thought he was imagining it, the thing, dragging a body behind it. Pulling it along by one leg, as the arms hung limply behind.

"God," Rebecca gasped.

Dr. Ridley raised his gun, his finger on the trigger. He didn't pull. "Shoot it," he whispered.

Jack put his hand on the barrel of the rifle and pushed it down. "Not yet," he said. "Follow him."

They did, trailing behind, keeping the same distance. It was gruesome work, there in the shadows. Aidan had a nearly irresistible urge to fire his weapon, to end this slow motion pursuit once and for all. Whatever Jack was seeking, this thing did not possess it. Then it stopped walking.

The five of them stopped with it, the space that separated them seeming all too small. Aidan imagined it turning, dropping its carrion cargo and charging them. Blood-soaked body and face filled with insanity and rage. When it did turn, it was only ninety degrees. It pulled the body behind, disappearing into another room.

Jack turned to them and said, "Be ready."

Aidan tightened his grip on the rifle. He didn't like Jack. In fact, he hated him. He cursed himself, for in that moment, he was glad Jack was there. The group crept forward, not saying a word as they approached the door, as if maybe they would surprise whatever was behind it. But how could it not already know of their presence with their beams of light the only illumination in this place?

In truth, the door was already open, someone having slid it back into the wall at some point earlier. Thus it came as a shock to Aidan when they turned and gazed into the open room. That shock did not last long before it was replaced by a newer and more terrible one.

The door was open, and the crews' beams of light seemed to converge into one, illuminating the room beyond. Aidan noticed that the light seemed to finally have the effect one would expect. It was able to fully light the chamber while also casting grotesque shadows over the scene that met their eyes.

Dr. Ridley knew that he would not try and describe it later in the detailed record he had a habit of keeping about everything that transpired on the ship, for he had no words. Not for this.

What did they see? They stared into the pit that day and Satan was on his throne.

The room beyond was an observation deck of sorts, but much more majestic and—at some other time at least—beautiful than the one on the *Chronos*. The far wall was made entirely of glass, tempered, no doubt, against the dangers of space but still open to their wonder. They would notice it later, but not then. Their eyes were not on the heavens.

The room was bare. Empty, save for a single chair. A massive cathedra that sat in the center. A piece of furniture from an older time. A captain's chair, one that had been brought aboard by the master of this ship. The man who, by all accounts, was seated in it even now.

He stared at them. His eyes flashing coal black in the glare of their lights, his nostrils flaring, two strong hands gripping the sides of the chair so tightly the bones of his knuckles shone through his skin.

He still wore his regulation blues, the uniform of a naval officer, but they were torn in places. Ripped, cut, even gnashed by the teeth of those who would be his victims. The blood of those same had turned the cloth from blue to an unnatural reddish-black.

Perhaps he alone would have been a figure malevolent enough to send them all screaming into the darkness, even Jack. That there was more horror to see kept them rooted in place.

The captain, the king of this ship, sat on his throne amidst his subjects. They were there, spread out before him. Seven of them. Kneeled. Bowed. Like penitents at prayer. Or perhaps slaves, kowtowing before their emperor.

There was no mystery as to where the blood that covered the captain's clothes had come from. The bodies of those who lay before him were shredded, large chunks of flesh ripped from them, their stomachs disemboweled, their throats cut. And the stench, that awful smell.

They had died in horrible ways, only to be dragged here. To become part of this macabre scene. One the captain presided over in silence. Waiting for someone. Waiting for them. He glared at each of the crew of the *Chronos*, his eyes moving over the group, stopping only when they fell upon Captain Gravely.

His mouth moved and one word slipped out in a tortured whisper: "Caroline."

A shot rang out, the bullet catching him right above his left eye, splattering the mad captain's blood and brains all over the great window behind him. Gravely's rifle clattered along the floor. Her knees buckled and she fell to them, letting out a howl of pain and anger and grief. Jack glanced at her as he removed his computer from his pocket, his fingers dancing across its surface.

"That's eight," he said to Rebecca. "The captain and seven crew. Should be all of them."

Rebecca nodded as he stuffed the computer back in his pocket, though her eyes were on Aidan. He had taken Gravely into his arms, her uncontrolled sobs shaking his body as they rolled through hers. He looked up at Rebecca and Jack. "How did he know her name?" he shouted. "How could he know?"

Jack looked down at them. There was no emotion there. Not anger or pity or empathy. Just indifference. Almost boredom.

"Because," Jack said, "he's her father."

\* \* \*

It moved through the *Chronos*, walking—if such a thing could walk—in shadow and shade, though in truth, the darkness walked with it.

Reality seemed to shutter as it passed, to shift in and out of focus.

It came to the door of the infirmary, passing through without opening it.

Cyrus stood, watching as it entered. The chaos—shaped like a man, but taller and thinner—came to stand before him.

When it spoke, Cyrus heard it in his mind.

"The vessel is shattered."

"Release me and I will finish it."

"No, we wait," it said, before vanishing. "Another remains."

# CHAPTER
# 19

Jack stood over one of the bodies, pressing its flesh against his computer, checking the DNA just to be sure that the crew of the *Singularity* were all accounted for. Aidan still held Gravely and she made no effort to break away from him, though he was fairly certain she was no longer crying.

Aidan looked up and caught Rebecca's gaze. He wanted to grab her, to pull her aside and demand an explanation. She must have seen it in his eyes. Rebecca shook her head, almost imperceptibly, and mouthed, "Not here." Aidan let it go, but in his mind, that was a promise he intended to enforce.

"That's all of them," Jack said, as he let the hand of the last victim thud against the metal floor. "Captain and crew accounted for. At least we know there's no one else on the ship." He sounded almost cheery.

"I think I should take the captain back," Aidan said.

Jack frowned and shook his head. "No, no, no. We don't have time for that. Look, we get the ship back online and you can do whatever you want. Fact is, I need you."

"Be that as it may. . ." Aidan began. Captain Gravely stopped him.

"I'm fine," she said. Aidan looked at her and she saw his mounting protest on the verge of becoming vocal. "I'm fine," she repeated, this time more forcefully. "Let's just get this over with." She stood up, straightening her suit as she did. "But, Mr. Crawford, at some point I expect some answers."

Jack simply looked at her and Aidan felt sure she would get none from him.

"Yes," Aidan said, "if you know what happened here, I think we all deserve an explanation."

"Why would I know anything?" Jack said. "I'm just here to recover the ship. If you want some explanations, maybe you should ask him." He pointed to Ridley, who at that moment looked terrified.

"Well . . . " he stuttered. "It's the sickness, obviously. The worst possible case, I'd say. What else could it be?"

Aidan watched Jack and Rebecca. Jack showed nothing, as he expected. But Rebecca couldn't help but cast a furtive glance in his direction. Aidan knew then; whatever this was, it had nothing to do with the dreams.

Jack rubbed his fingers along the bridge of his nose. "Let's just get to the bridge."

No one offered any objection. They backed away from the carnage into the darkened corridors of the ship. Captain Gravely cast one last glance at the man who, in a different world and a different time, had been her father. It was all too much. How he had come to be here? How he had turned into the monster they had found? Where had he and his ship been for the last decade? For now, she felt only sadness and pain.

They walked down the corridors, the darkness as thick as ever, but not as oppressive. Not as ominous. They felt relief that at least they were alone, or that was the lie they told themselves. For they all felt it, the tickle in the back of their brains, the warm breeze caressing their necks like the breath of a lover. The eyes upon them. There was *something* whether they could describe it or not, no longer somewhere in the distance but all around.

Aidan followed Jack. Not that he had to. The vague sense of déjà vu had been replaced with certainty. He knew he had been here before. He knew the bridge was up ahead, around a corner and through a door. Sure enough, they found it. When they entered, the others gasped. Only Aidan wasn't surprised.

The bridge was like any other. Consoles, terminals, video screens. But it was the ceiling that they all stared up at. The entirety was made of glass, or something like it, clear and transparent, the darkness of space shining down upon them from every inch of it. Aidan could almost see the black hole.

"Alright," Jack said, "let's see what we've got."

Jack removed his helmet and the others followed. As he did, the lamps built into the shoulders of the suits came on, though they provided no more illumination than those on the helmets. Jack plugged the portable power unit into the console. The lights flickered once and Aidan almost raised his rifle as the shadows of a dozen different creatures momentarily danced long the walls. Then there was a whirring sound as the computers powered up.

"Excellent," Jack said, gesturing to the console in front of him. "Dr. Kensington, if you would."

Rebecca sat down and ran her fingers along the screen. The portable unit wasn't large enough to run the entire ship, but it could power the computer system.

"Running diagnostic," she said.

The computer screens flashed red and Rebecca sighed. "Looks like the engines were fried from the . . ." She trailed off, and Aidan didn't think it was because she couldn't find the right word.

"The jump," Jack finished.

"Yes, the jump." Rebecca swallowed deeply and Aidan chuckled to himself. She was a terrible liar. "It looks like somebody tried to re-initialize it and only made it worse."

Now Aidan was legitimately confused. "Really? How's that possible? It's a relatively easy process."

"Unless you don't know what you're doing."

"But every member of the crew would have known. Especially the captain."

"Well, he *was* out of his mind," Ridley offered.

Aidan eyed Gravely, but she showed no emotion. "Yes," he said, "that must be it." Aidan leaned over Rebecca's shoulder. "What's that?" He pointed down to a flashing icon on the left side of the screen. He had a feeling he knew, but he wanted to hear Rebecca say it.

She looked up, glancing from Jack to Aidan. Jack shook his head, but she ignored him. "It's the captain's log. His last entry."

"Well that seems pretty important, doesn't it? Maybe something we should listen to? Might save us some time and we don't have much of that, right, Mr. Crawford?"

"I don't think . . ."

Aidan didn't wait for Jack to finish. Instead, he reached down and tapped the blinking icon. Gravely gasped as her father appeared on the screens above them. It was not the same man they had seen only minutes before. No, this man was exactly as she remembered him. The same kind, sad eyes. The type of face you would call fatherly, whether he was related to you or not. The date flashed on the screen – June 18, 2159.

"God," Aidan said, "that's ten years ago. How . . ."

He looked at Rebecca and in her eyes he saw that she had expected this. That she had known it all along.

"Aidan . . ." she began, but before she could even begin to explain, she was interrupted by the voice from the screen.

"The dreams will stop," it said. "That's what they tell us will happen, if we succeed at least. And that was enough for me, for all of us. Sometimes, I think everything in my life comes down to those impossible dreams. They never were dreams, though. Not really. Not to me. I call them that only because that's what the lab guys, the scientists and the psychologists called them. Just 'resonance in neural circuits.' I guess that is why I am making this entry in my log. I hope they end, but I do not want to forget. I do not want to believe the lies. They have not seen. They do not know."

"The dreams?" Ridley whispered. "How will they stop? What does he mean?"

Jack simply stood, on the verge of rage, but with growing resignation. "He could try and stop this, he thought. But they would never let him. Their desire to know was too great now. Who knew what they might do? Then the other Captain Gravely continued.

"The last one was the same as the first. It was the same as them all. A valley opens up before me. But it is unlike anything I have ever seen. There are no majestic cliffs, no free-flowing waters or forests clinging to its sides. No. Hell has come to this place. The ground is scorched and barren. There is no life there, nor will there ever be.

"I can see dimly; the pallid yellow of the cloudless sky bears down on me like coming twilight. Even though there is no sun. Even though this place lies between the darkness and the light. In shadow. Though what casts that shadow, I cannot know, nor do I wish to. But the light is enough that as I walk down that valley toward its end, toward *the* end, as it narrows to a point where I do not know if I can go on, I can see *them*.

"They stand along the valley's edge on both sides. High above me. Silent and unmoving. Figures, black. Hooded and cloaked, perhaps. But I think not. They are the shadow itself. Their eyes are ever upon me, though they do not move. For they do have eyes. Great pools of emptiness where their faces should be. And they speak to me. In whispered words and phrases. In wisps of cool breeze that seem to surround me, though the air is still and hot. What do they say? Can I know? Somehow I do. But whatever that truth may be, I cannot bear to repeat it here. I cannot tell what cannot be denied.

"For ten years I have walked down that valley. Every endless night I have seen them. And they have haunted me, even in waking. I have told no one, and neither will I. Wouldn't they think me mad? If I told them how the shadow figures watch me? How I see them sometimes, reposing under the streetlight beside my home? How they stand and do not move? Their cold, never-blinking eyes? How I have found them in photographs, even those from my childhood? Lurking in the distance?

"Nameless sentries on the edge of existence and the frame? How I can feel them, standing behind me, even now? Their cold breath on my neck? And if I turn? How I catch them in the corner of my eye, even if they vanish by the time I look fully upon them? Yes, they would think me mad. And a mad man is most unwelcome in the void."

The screen went blank. There was nothing else to see.

"My father wrote me a letter," Gravely said, her resolve unable to keep out the quiver in her voice, "before he left on his last mission. He told me that he wasn't sure if he would ever come back, that the dreams had become too much, but he planned on doing something about them. He said that if he succeeded, the nightmares would go away. That he would be free of them. I didn't find the letter until after his ship had departed. Two weeks later, we received notification that his ship was lost, presumed destroyed. They assured us it was an accident, but I always knew better."

"I'm so sorry, Captain," Rebecca said. It was a clumsy attempt, empty words that did nothing to salve the pain.

"Why did you bring me here?" Gravely's voice was a whisper of barely constrained rage. "Why me? Why us?"

"It was a coincidence," Rebecca answered. "We knew the ship was here, and yours was the only one going to Riley any time soon. A private shuttle or a military ship might have aroused suspicion. It simply made sense."

"But you knew," Gravely almost pleaded. "You knew this was his ship and you brought me out here anyway."

"We didn't know," Rebecca said, but Aidan could hear in her desperate voice, the way it seemed to float up an octave higher than usual, that not even she believed that. "Not for sure. We had an idea, of course."

"Enough. Enough of this," Jack said, standing up. "I'm sorry, Captain, but this was bigger than you. Besides, haven't you always wondered what happened to your father? Now you know."

"I know nothing!" Gravely cried. "I know less than I knew before! And what I do know is so much worse than not knowing."

"Look," Jack said, and Aidan knew he was reaching his limit, "you've all learned more than you should have. Now, we need to get to work. Aidan, Rebecca, get down to the engine room and see if you can get it straightened out. Dr. Ridley, Captain Gravely, why don't you explore the crew cabin? Maybe you can find something. Answer some of your questions. More than you probably should, no doubt. But I'm shorthanded and can't afford secrecy."

The others didn't bother to answer before leaving Crawford behind. Aidan grabbed Rebecca's arm, virtually dragging her off the bridge before Jack could change his mind. The captain and Dr. Ridley left as well, the latter just glad he didn't have to go anywhere by himself.

Jack breathed deep and exhaled slowly. Finally, blessedly, he was alone. But somewhere, in the deepest recesses of his mind, he knew that was a lie. The shadows were there to keep him company.

# CHAPTER
# 20

"Alright," Aidan said, as he rushed out of the bridge, Rebecca on his heels, "I think the time for secrets is over, don't you?"

"Aidan . . ."

She followed close behind, though she had to jog to keep up. She held the map of the ship in her hand, but Aidan didn't seem to need it. He rushed ahead, not paying attention, turning down what she would have thought were random corridors, but each one was the right decision, leading her down the path her map dictated, as if he knew the way.

"No," he said, turning on her. He didn't really trust her, not after everything that had happened. But he needed to hear something from her, even if it provided only a glimmer of the truth. "Don't Aidan me. You saw what happened here. I don't think I have to explain. Nothing about this ship makes sense. Captain Gravely's father? Last time I checked, he was killed in action a decade ago. So why was he walking around on this ship?"

"Aidan, I don't know what you want me to say."

"Yeah, usually when people say that, they know exactly what to say," he said, turning away from her. "You know," he said, "in the old days, when you found a ship adrift on the seas, the sailors would claim it was cursed. That whatever bad luck had befallen the ship would follow anyone who tried to take it for themselves." He looked back over his shoulder at Rebecca. "You believe any of that?"

"Maybe some of it."

Aidan turned and walked back to where Rebecca still stood and put his hands on her shoulders. "Tell me what happened here, Rebecca. Why is everything obsolete? Why is the captain's last log entry from a decade ago? I know you know. Just tell me. Don't you think it's time?"

Rebecca looked up at Aidan. "Why not," she thought. Why not?

"You don't speak of this to Jack. Or anyone else either. Not unless it is absolutely necessary. Do you understand?"

Aidan nodded. "Of course."

She fixed him with her eyes for another second, hoping to seal that promise. But she knew that there was no need. "I'm only telling you this because I think it will help us finish what we need to do here. Anyway, it should be obvious by now," she said. "Honestly, you shouldn't need much explanation."

"I'd like to hear it from you anyway."

"Officially," she began, now walking ahead of Aidan as they talked, "Captain Alexander Gravely and his crew of seven men and women were killed in an accident, tragic and unexpected, of course, involving a core breach that occurred while the ship was in warp."

"No debris left behind, no evidence."

"Exactly."

"The perfect cover."

"You have to understand, Captain Gravely wasn't the sort of man who could just disappear."

"I know," Aidan said, "I remember when it happened."

"That's why he was on this ship. We needed a man like him, an experienced and respected commander. What we were trying was extraordinary. An entirely new form of travel."

"What's wrong with the old way?"

Rebecca stopped walking. She turned to Aidan, "You know the answer to that."

"The dreams."

She nodded. They were walking again, through the darkness that should frighten them. But familiarity breeds contempt and so they ignored it, almost sauntering along, no longer hearing the whispers that grew louder at the mention of the dreams.

"Yes, always the dreams. Here's the real truth, Aidan," she said, stopping in front of the door that lead to the engine room. "The one that could get me in a lot of trouble if it ever got out. The dreams are much worse than you've been lead to believe."

"What does that mean?" Aidan asked. He had lived the dreams for a decade. He knew exactly how bad they could be.

"Their effects, I should say. The official position of the Spacing Guild is that less than one hundredth of one percent of sailors will experience Braddock's Syndrome, sleep-madness. One in ten thousand. You tell me, Aidan, in your experience, does that sound right to you?"

Aidan frowned. It did not. He had known too many men who had lost it, seen too many pairs of insane eyes, heard too many mad shouts, given his condolences to too many widows—widows in mind, if not in body. "No," he said softly. "It doesn't."

"That's because it's a lie. The number is a hundred times higher than that, worse even. Current estimates are closer to one in seventy-five."

Aidan gasped. "God in Heaven." He had believed it to be higher, but not that high.

"And it creeps up every year. The testing for the Navy? When I took the tests, the standard was much harsher than it is now. The fact is, if they bounced everyone that falls within our most recent parameters for Braddock's, we wouldn't be able to staff the fleet. It's particularly bad among the merchant guild. The number of ships that are lost every year in hyperspace is staggering."

"And the Guild needed an answer."

"The whole government did. And this was ten years ago, remember? Things have only gotten worse."

"And you've been covering this up for that long?"

Rebecca shook her head. "What was the alternative?" she asked, throwing up her hands. "The whole system depends on deep-space commerce. End the warp system? Close the warp channels? Then all of these worlds become tiny little outposts. God, half of them can't even support themselves. Not without the trade. No, if the data got out there would be a panic.

"It was bad enough with the Guilds. They don't believe the

official numbers anyway. Why do you think the freight rates have skyrocketed the last decade?" Rebecca rubbed her hands
through her hair and she felt the pressure of the mission on her again, the responsibility that had led her to deceive Aidan in the first place. "You can see why this ship is so important. Things are getting critical, Aidan. If it gets much worse, I don't know how much longer the system can take the strain."

"So that's what they were doing these past ten years? This ship? Conducting experiments? Looking for some new technology?"

"No, no," Rebecca said. She almost laughed, not that any of this was funny. "Nothing like that. I wish that were true. The *Singularity* wasn't researching anything. The *Singularity* is a test ship. She carries a new drive, a new design. One specifically built to handle the stresses of high gravitation."

"High gravitation?"

Rebecca nodded. "The *Singularity* bears her name for a reason. As long as we've known about the black holes, there's been a theory. The singularity in a black hole is a myth, a fiction. It doesn't really exist. It can't exist.

"It is the ultimate flaw in our mathematics. The singularity is like dividing by zero—it can't be done. There must be something else there. Some people have speculated that what goes into a black hole must come out somewhere. Our theory is that every black hole has a sister, a twin. And that if you map these twins, you can find pathways through the stars."

"Wormholes?" Aidan asked.

"Something akin to them, yes."

"But that's absurd. Even if the theory was right, nothing can go into a black hole and come out of it."

Rebecca smiled. She held up both hands, gesturing to the walls around them.

"Wait," Aidan said, "you mean this ship . . ."

"Yes, this ship."

"But how?"

"The key was," Rebecca said, "to change the way we thought about the gravity wells. You're right; whatever goes in is destroyed. There's no construction technique that can survive the black hole. But we could do some things to lessen their effect. We made it elongated, like an arrow.

"The gravitational forces of the black hole tend to stretch objects as they enter. The shape helps mitigate that. Liberal use of tempered glass. Solid, but able to flow, expand somewhat amidst the heat and gravitation. But those were merely design choices to soften the blow, as it were. They were not the key. The key was to combine warp technology with the black hole."

"What good would that do?" Aidan asked. "Wasn't warp the problem in the first place?"

"Warp yes, but there are two phases to the warp process. First, creation of the warp bubble," she said, holding out the palm of her hand and demonstrating with the other. "To separate the ship, to move it between realities—our reality and the other. Then, when the warp drive engages, the jump begins.

"That's when the dreams start. The *Singularity* was designed to do something different. To engage the bubble, yes. But then, rather than engaging the warp drive, to use the standard engines to move it through space. Specifically, into a black hole. The gravitational effects are minimal. The warp bubble protects the ship, and the ship is able to travel, through regular space, into the heart of the black hole."

"So that's what they did."

"Yes, it is. On June 17, 2159, the *Singularity* warped from Earth space and arrived at Sigma-1, the nearest black hole."

"But wait, why warp at all?"

"We still have to get to the black holes. It's a limited solution. Some warping will always be necessary. But we could dramatically cut down on its use with this technology, hopefully enough to eliminate its ill effects altogether. At least that's the hope. In any event, on June 18, 2159, the *Singularity* engaged her warp bubble and passed beyond the event horizon of Sigma-1. That was the last anyone ever heard of her."

"She disappeared?"

"Completely. We expected to lose communication once she went beyond the event horizon. But all of our projections, our calculations, our theories, pointed to her arriving here, at this spot, just beyond Anubis, the farthest colony at the time. It was the perfect location. This was deserted space. No trade ships, no warp traffic, no danger of espionage or accidental witnesses.

"Unfortunately, the science vessels waiting here for her to reappear did so in vain. She never returned. You can imagine what happened next. Scouring every known black hole. Accusations and recriminations. Assumptions that our calculations were wrong, followed by a belief that the test had merely failed. The ship had gone in and been destroyed. The story was put out that Captain Gravely, and his crew, were lost in an accident."

"So they found nothing?" Aidan asked.

"Nothing, until a week ago. Listening satellites circling Anubis detected a ship in normal space where no ship should be. High resolution scans returned images of a vessel, one matching the general specifications of the *Singularity*.

"I was given the task of making contact with the *Singularity*, establishing the whereabouts of the crew. Salvaging her if possible. But collecting the data gathered by the crew was our number one priority. Jack Crawford was tasked with assisting me. It is a testament to the seriousness of this mission that he was chosen. His reputation precedes him."

"But wait," Aidan said, "what happened these last ten years?"

"You already know," she said. "I mean, there's only one answer, right? Judging by what we found so far, I would say that the *Singularity* went in to the black hole ten years ago. For those on the ship, ten years passed"—Rebecca snapped her fingers—"in the blink of an eye. They arrived here. The captain went crazy. Murdered the crew. A week passed, and we found them."

"But how could a ship lose ten years?"

"The truth is, we know so little, so very little, about these things. All we know for sure now is it seems that the ship came through relatively unchanged. No worse for the wear."

"Are you so sure?" Aidan asked.

Rebecca hesitated. "What do you mean?"

"Nothing. It's just . . . the air feels different here, if that makes any sense."

She smiled. "After all we've been through, I can see why you would say that. But no ,Aidan, the worst for this ship has passed."

Rebecca inserted the portable battery into the terminal and

opened the door to the engine room. She and Aidan stepped inside. As their lights illuminated the room within, Rebecca gasped. Aidan's initial thought had been that the engine was unlike any he had ever seen and he was glad Rebecca was with him.

Without her, he would have had no hope of fixing it. But when he saw what had startled her so, he knew that it probably didn't matter who they had with them. The ship wasn't going anywhere.

"What happened here?" Rebecca whispered.

The computer consoles were smashed, along with the lower half of the engine itself. Bits of silicone and computer chips were scattered about the floor, broken into a thousand pieces. The culprit sat discarded at the bottom of one of the terminals—a bright red ax.

"Look," Aidan said, pointing. "Fire control."

It had amused him, on occasion, that ships still carried them. The bright red axes from a time long ago, labeled as part of the fire-control equipment of the ship. Though if the automated flame suppressant systems failed, what purpose could an ax really serve? In truth, he had never known them used for good. For murder and mayhem, though? They were the perfect choice.

"I have to talk to Jack about this. I knew we had some problems, but nothing like this."

"I don't know if this is salvageable, Rebecca."

"Look, you stay here. See what you can do."

"I don't know how to fix a machine like this!"

"Don't worry about fixing the machine," Rebecca said, "but if you can at least get the computers online, that would help."

Aidan started to protest, but she held up a hand. "Aidan, please, just do this for me, okay?"

He suddenly was angry, but only with himself. He had no resolve when it came to her and he hated it. "Alright," he relented.

"Be back soon." Rebecca reached up and kissed him quickly on the lips. "I promise."

As the door closed behind her, Aidan looked up at the broken monstrosity before him. The room suddenly grew darker, as rooms and corridors seemingly had at regular intervals the entire time they had been on the ship.

"Computer," Aidan said to himself, "how about some lights?"

He sat down behind the console and had an almost irresistible desire to laugh. "Where to even begin."

# CHAPTER
# 21

The *Singularity* and the *Chronos* hung in space, two silver mirrors reflecting each other's light. In emptiness they waited. In silence they remained. To the observer—if there had been one—they seemed utterly at peace, floating in the nothingness, but to believe that would be folly, for giants surrounded them. Beasts that sought to feed, with hungers that were never sated. The greatest of them sat just beyond the two ships that  slowly, inexorably, drifted toward the mouth of doom.

There was silence in the depths of the *Singularity*, in the engine room where Aidan tinkered with broken consoles and cursed smashed computer chips, in the darkened hallways where Rebecca's feeble light bobbed up and down as she walked back to the bridge, in the crew quarters that Dr. Ridley and Gravely had decided to divide between them and investigate. And silence on the bridge, where Jack Crawford sat staring at diagnostic reports and crew logs from the *Singularity*'s last mission. In that silence, they stood alone. Or at least, that's what they believed.

But the men and women aboard the *Singularity* were not alone, for there was nowhere onboard that ship where *they* were not. They mingled in the shadows. They waited in the darkness. They walked in the black corners and darkened hallways of the ship. Always watching. Holding the feeble minds of the crew in their hands. Seeking which ones to devour. And then their gazes fell upon those who had the most to lose.

The smell started as a tingle, a hint of something acidic, something that bit at the back of Jack's throat and burned the hairs of his nose. Then it grew stronger, thicker, until it filled his nostrils so thoroughly that he thought he might never escape it. It was the scent of his childhood, a certain type of cologne that in all his life, he had only known one man to wear: his father. When he spoke, Jack wasn't even surprised. He simply turned to the sound of the voice.

"I never took you for a desk job."

His father was leaning against the bulkhead, still dressed in his tuxedo, hands jammed into his pockets.

"I do what the job requires," Jack said dryly.

"Of course you do."

Austin Crawford pushed himself away from the wall and ambled around the bridge, almost sauntering, as if he was visiting a museum and perusing the art.

"Why are you here?"

Austin grinned. "Me? I'm here for you, son. Just like I always was."

"You were never here for me," Jack said flatly. "Never."

Austin stopped and took measure of his son. Austin's face was implacable, just as it always was. But Jack thought he saw a quiver of emotion pulse across it, though what feeling it was—anger? sadness? pain?—remained hidden.

"That's not true," he whispered. "That's not true at all. I gave you everything I had. I made you the man you are, for better or worse. And you never hated what you became. When you wake up in the morning and look in the mirror, what do you see? That's me, son. I've always been with you. I always will be."

The two men stood now, glaring at each other over the space of a few short feet. It seemed like the gulf of eternity. The distance between them shimmered, like vibrant air on a hot day over black pavement.

"Then tell me, Father, why are you here, now?"

"To help you finish your job," Austin said. "To help you see it through to the end."

Jack could feel the veins in his head shrink, the pounding of blood against his temples, new pain with every heartbeat. Should he have been afraid in that moment? Terrified of the specter that stood before him? His dead father, killed by his own hands? Perhaps, but he was simply bone tired. Spent, like an empty shotgun shell.

"We have what we came for. I don't need you."

"But you don't have it, son. Not yet. This ship must be saved. It's special, you know?"

He did know. He had known all along.

"We have the ship. She's ours now."

Austin shook his head slowly. "They are working against you. They want to destroy it. To let it slip back into the void. You cannot allow that."

"Who? Who wants to destroy it?"

"The others," Austin growled, and the acid that dripped off his tongue when he spoke the words seemed strong enough to burn a man, as if there were none to be hated more than them. "Traitors. Subverters. Enemies. They will oppose you at every turn. They are in it together."

"Maybe I don't want to save it," Jack said. "Maybe I want to see it destroyed. All it's brought me is you."

Austin smirked. "Don't be a fool." He coughed. "You really don't get it, do you? They are coming for you."

"I think I can handle Connor," Jack said.

The smirk turned into a laugh. "Not Aidan. No, you can handle the living. But can you overcome the dead?" Jack turned pale. "Ah, so there is something you fear. And fear it you should. They have waited for you, son, all this time to take their revenge. The dreams gave them a portal, purchase in this world. A foothold from which to invade your mind. They are close, my son, and they will have you soon. But this ship has seen wonders that you cannot imagine. It is their prison, you see? Our prison. As long as it exists, they cannot touch you."

"And if I should fail?"

"If you should fail, then they will haunt you all the days that remain to you, until, screaming in insanity, you take your own life and become theirs forever. That is your fate, if you should fail now."

Jack had been inclined to disbelieve his father, to assume that this was a ruse, a trick. But then he saw them. The teeming mass, the dead returned for their vengeance. He saw Elizabeth, her face soft at first, then stricken with the poison coursing through her veins, and finally melting and twisting with hatred.

Robert lurked behind her, more animal than man. So many of

them, mere shades of their former selves, all lacking some basic piece of humanity. They were hunters now. Haunters of the dark, seeking to devour their one enemy, mortal in every sense of the word.

As he watched them, just beyond the wall of sleep, the wall of shadow that had come from his dream and into the real world, something inside of Jack cracked. A dam split. The black, lightning strike line snaking down its shell until it gave way in one great crash. Behind it, the flood. The totality of a lifetime of fears hidden and ignored, suppressed below a thin sheen of training and self-denial. His rational mind drowned, replaced by one overarching imperative. Protect the ship at all costs.

Jack did not notice his father studying him and missed the look of triumph that passed briefly over his face.

"You will do what is needed, I trust?"

Jack barely heard him over the thunder of his own fears, over the howls of rage that he and he alone discerned from the spirits who darted in and out of existence somewhere behind Austin. He nodded once and Austin had all he needed.

"I'll be with you, son," he said, backing away into the swirling darkness. "I will never leave you."

Then he was gone, vanished along with the rest of Jack's phantoms. Jack stood alone. In that silence and emptiness and loneliness, another wall came tumbling down. For the first time that he could recall, Jack wept until he collapsed to the floor.

Somewhere in the darkness, the thing that had been Austin watched Jack through empty eyes. As his form melted back into a thin, black wisp of shadow, he felt the power of Jack's fear and fed upon it. And, were such a thing not so entirely foreign to its true constitution, it would have smiled. Instead, it merely melded into those that surrounded it, awaiting its day of liberation.

\* \* \*

Rebecca was starting to worry. She had left Aidan behind in the engine room fifteen minutes before, but she still hadn't reached the bridge. She had followed the map on the computer screen, tracing her way through the oppressive darkness of the ship, cursing herself for not having Aidan focus on fixing the emergency lighting. She removed a pair of night-vision goggles from her breast pocket and held them up to her eyes, keeping them a few inches away from her face. The same blinding white glare as before.

Somehow, in the rush to explore the ship, she had been so concerned with maintaining her cover and achieving their objectives that she had not stopped to think about their night-vision's universal failure. A malfunction was not out of the question, even if she had never known one to occur. But on both Gravely and Ridley's suits? Even if it was some bug in the computer system of the *Chronos*, her goggles were independent. Yet, they didn't work, either.

Standing in the darkness, she considered what it could mean. Radiation? Maybe, but she figured enough radiation to fry all their systems would have killed everyone on board. Or at least ruined their computers. She looked down at the computer pad in her hand, the one that had led her in circles for the last fifteen minutes and smirked; maybe it had.

She glanced back up at the night vision goggles again. For the first time, she noticed that it wasn't simply blinding light she saw. There were gradations, slight though they might be, and some areas shone brighter than others. She squinted, thinking that if she concentrated enough, she could almost make out the hallway. Then something moved in the light.

It was a small movement, but one that Rebecca couldn't chalk up to mistake or hallucination. She dropped the goggles. They skittered across the ground as she fumbled with her rifle, finally raising it to her shoulder and pointing it at her unseen adversary.

"Who's there?" she shouted, swinging the gun wildly from side to side. Nothing answered back. Only the black night, her lights vainly fighting a losing battle against its completeness.

Rebecca kept her gun pointed at the nothingness, looking down only to see the next turn on her map. She'd had enough of standing in the dark. Her heart missed a beat as the screen flickered for a second and then faded to black.

"Oh shit. No. No, no, no!"

She slapped the side of the pad—vainly she knew—in the hopes that it would fix itself as quickly as it had died. When nothing happened, she rolled the pad up tightly and stuck it in her pocket. She backed away, pointing the rifle in the direction of the movement she had seen. She kept on until she backed into a wall.

She slid her body to the right, hoping to retrace her steps to the engine room. But she had come so far and the computer had turned her around so completely that the hope of finding Aidan again seemed a slim one at best.

Rebecca felt the first fingers of panic start to tighten around her throat. Tears stung her eyes, but she knew to lose it now might be the end of her. She couldn't say what it was that she believed lurked in that darkness just beyond her sight. Whatever it was, she didn't want to meet it.

Then came a sound, not from the direction she faced, but from somewhere to her right. She spun around, pointing her rifle right and then left. First in the direction of the movement, then in the direction of the sound and back again.

The sound came again, this time louder and more distinct. Her mouth fell open and the gun dropped to her side. She could no longer lie to herself about what she heard. Not like at first, when it was but a tinkle in the distance. It came again, a ringing, chiming sound, the *ding ding* of a bell on a child's bike. Then the physical embodiment of that sound emerged from the shadows into the feeble light, though it might as well have come from the deepest recesses of her mind.

The girl stopped in front of her, putting one white sneaker-clad foot on the deck. She looked up at Rebecca and smiled.

"You're gonna miss the festival, silly."

Whatever reserve Rebecca had maintained fell to the ground along with her rifle and shattered. She broke and ran away from the girl, away from whatever lurked in the shadows, not knowing or caring where the winding corridors were taking her.

She didn't stop until she ran headlong into a door, one of the only ones on the ship, which now had power. It slid open and she found herself in the engine room, just in time to hear Aidan scream,

"You're a liar!"

to no one in particular.

* * *

While Rebecca wandered in circles, Aidan sat in the engine room staring down at a broken motherboard.

"What I wouldn't give," he said, "for a Charlotte about now."

He discovered a tool chest in one of the compartments that normally would have supplied everything he needed. Unfortunately, it wasn't tools he lacked, it was parts. Whoever had gone after the engine had done an effective, if not thorough, job. The warp core was intact. That had been the first thing he checked. If they had tried to run up the engines with a warp core breach, there wouldn't have been anything left for the search teams to find.

That was the good news, but it was completely undermined by the bad. The damage to the ship's standard drive was extensive, and they were in the one place where that mattered. Normally, they could have warped the ship to habitable space and then had her towed in the rest of the way. But this close to a black hole, going into warp would be suicidal. The gravitational forces would tear the ship apart. They could surrender to gravity and warp *in* to the black hole, but that was about it. Aidan didn't feel like that was a viable option.

"Maybe for Jack," he mumbled.

It was rather simple then. If Aidan couldn't repair the standard drive, the *Singularity* wasn't going anywhere. Since the drive also powered the ship's electrical grid, he couldn't even turn on the lights. He managed to access one of the ship's emergency batteries, but there was only enough juice left to power some of the ship's doors. At least they wouldn't have to use the manual releases, he thought. But the sinking feeling that the damage was beyond his ability to repair was growing by the minute. His only hope was that Rebecca could be of some help.

"What I really need," he said to himself, "is Cyrus."

The words had no sooner left his mouth than he regretted them. Even though this had been their first job together, he'd known Cyrus through the trade for several years. While they had never been particularly close, he'd always liked him. He'd also met his wife once, daughter too.

He did not relish the thought of their next meeting. It had been the spacing guild's tradition for as long as it had existed that a dead crewman's fellow guildsman, and not the captain, was responsible for notifying the next of kin. And while Cyrus wasn't dead, he might as well have been.

Aidan didn't turn when he heard the door slide open behind him. "Back so soon?" he asked over his shoulder, his attention focused on a micro screwdriver he had jammed into a broken motherboard.

"But, my friend," he heard his own voice say, "I never left."

"I should be surprised," Aidan thought. He wasn't. Not at all. He had expected this, somewhere, deep inside. Had known it must come, from the first instant he looked up at the familiar corridors of the derelict *Singularity* on Captain Gravely's video feed, since the moment that the captain and Dr. Ridley had walked down hallways that he had also trod in dreams he wished he had never seen.

Even before then, really. When he stood on the deck of his old ship, in the most recent dream, and watched the image of his past self do things he could not recall and hoped never really happened. Yes, he had expected this. In fact, he had hoped for it. Needed it, really. He needed answers.

He turned in his chair and looked upon the image of himself, dressed in the blue jumpsuit he often wore, his hands crossed across his chest. He was as Aidan had seen him in the dream. Younger, less worn, as if years had passed between them.

"You're not surprised to see me, I take it?"

"How could I be?" Aidan said. "I know you so well."

His doppelgänger snorted. "Do you? Or am I the one person you don't know at all?"

"I know you're not real," Aidan said. "I know you're an illusion, a figment of my own imagination. Some combination of the effects of the dreams and the gravitational forces of the black hole. That's all you are. And I don't have time for you."

Aidan spun his chair around, turning his back on the phantasm that stood nonchalantly just beyond the filaments of darkness in the engine room.

"That won't work, Aidan," the voice behind him said. "I'm not going anywhere."

Aidan turned back, and sure enough, the other was still there. The perfect copy of Aidan, sandy-brown hair and a small scar beneath his left eye from a high school fight over a basketball game.

He didn't feel any of the things he should have. No terror. Not even confusion. His rational mind kicked in at that moment. He evaluated the situation, took stock of what was happening to him. Perhaps he was standing in the presence of a demon, a shape-shifting beast intent on driving him insane. Or an alien maybe, one that had come aboard the ship and now sought the undoing of its newest possessors. For what purpose, only it knew. Or maybe—and was this better or worse?—this was all within his mind, brought on by stress and creeping madness.

"The latter is more accurate," the thing said.

Aidan rubbed his tired eyes. He was slipping now, slipping away. His mind was breaking and if he didn't get a hold of himself, he was afraid he might never recover.

"You're finally beginning to see things as they truly are."

Aidan looked up at the doppelgänger, his head cocked to the side. The image of what could best be described as pity on his face.

"I'm here to help you, Aidan. I'm here to help you see."

"See what?" Aidan said, putting aside the absurdity of all of this, accepting, for the time being at least, that it was real. "If you wished to help me, you'd go away."

"I can't do that," he said, a flat implacable look spreading across his face. "There is a hole in your mind."

Now all of the things that should have happened from the very beginning did. Aidan felt a chill ripple down his spine as his blood went cold and his hair stood on end. Fear came into his heart as he thought back on Lieutenant Felix, a mere boy who had murdered his shipmate on the *Alabama*, and the words he had spoken from his cell. "There is a hole in your mind," Felix had said. "A time will come where you will be called upon. And in your hands will rest the fate of many. Perhaps then you can redeem your lost soul."

"Have you come to fill it?" Aidan asked the spirit of his past.

"I can do nothing alone. You must see for yourself. You must remember, if you are to keep your mind from shattering like a thousand pieces of glass."

"I don't understand," Aidan said, almost desperately.

The other Aidan walked down the steps, into the well of the engine room. It ran its hands along the console, picking up the ax that had been used to destroy it, all while Aidan wondered how much of this was real and how much a mere illusion.

"Oh what violence man can do to his own creations," it said. "Damage them at times. Destroy them at others. Wouldn't you agree?"

Aidan said nothing, and the thing frowned.

"Your dream, Aidan, the one you had aboard the *Chronos*. Have you not wondered about what you saw?"

"I saw you," Aidan said.

"No. You saw yourself. You saw the thing you won't let yourself remember. The thing you did. The thing that haunts your unconscious mind even now."

"I did nothing," Aidan said. "It was an accident."

"How can you be so sure? After all, you don't remember it. Do you? You only remember the dream."

Spawn of Hell or the making of his own mind, the thing knew him too well. Aidan didn't know what happened that day on the *Vespa*. But he could not shake this sinking suspicion that it was his fault. Not in some trivial way. Not the result of some misplaced sense of responsibility, spun from the guilt of a survivor. No, something far more tangible than that. He did remember the dream all too well. What he had seen himself do, just before the scream woke him.

It was a simple thing to destroy a starship. Far too simple, really. Aidan had thought on it often, wondered why the engineers never fixed the problem. It was a trade-off. On the one hand, people didn't trust the computers, the machines. No matter how advanced or sophisticated they were, even if they were far less prone to error than the men who ran the ships.

So there were always mechanisms, manual overrides. One of those involved the power allocation to the warp drive. Overload it, and the core would breach. At that point, the destruction of the ship was inevitable.

And that's exactly what the dream had shown him. His hands, typing in the commands to direct far too much power to the warp core. It would have been simple after that. Fire the standard engines, move the ship out to trans-Plutonian space. Send out a false emergency broadcast. Get into an escape pod and wait. Till breach was imminent, till there was nothing more that could be done to stop it and save the ship.

Then launch. Launch and watch the ship as it drifted away, growing smaller and smaller until replaced by a fireball ten times its size, one fed by the oxygen in the ship before it suffocated in the vacuum of space. Then nothing but debris and wreckage. And the bodies of the dead.

"But that's not possible," Aidan said, looking up at the other with confusion written on his face, arguing with his own thoughts. "I was injured. Burned." He was on the ship when the disaster started. That was the only explanation. "If it had happened the other way, if I was the cause, then I would have been fine."

"Oh, Aidan," the doppelgänger said with real pity in his voice, "what a web of lies you have created. And how tangled in them you are. I don't even know how to begin to free you."

"No more games!" Aidan shrieked. "Show me why you're here!"

"Why was the last dream different, Aidan?" he said, stepping around the table between them and facing Aidan, close enough that the two men could touch if they dared. "Why did it change? Why did you see something new?"

"What does this have to do with anything?"

"Answer the question, Aidan, if you can."

"I don't know. I'd seen all there was to see. I'd reached the end of the dream."

The other laughed.

"Men see the same dreams for fifty years, Aidan. Have you ever heard differently? Can you name one other case like yours? Any other who has not lived the same nightmare over and over and over again? Yet you were different. Something happened, Aidan. Something happened in the dream. Think back to the last time you stood on this ship, before you had your breakdown. What did you see? And what have you forgotten?"

Aidan did think back. Back to the last warp jump he had taken on the *Vespa*, before the doctors told him that a combination of exhaustion and hysteria had kept him confined to the infirmary. For rest, they said. He had been here, on this ship. Standing on the bridge. Staring up at the endless darkness of empty space.

That inevitable future, fifty billion years hence. When every star was dead and all life extinguished. Nothing but vacant black holes remained to mark the passage of what had been the bright wonder of the universe. What had he done then, when faced with such an inevitable fate, such an awful truth?

He had believed since that moment that he simply woke up to a world where the sun still shone, where the stars still beckoned in the night sky. But now, as he stood in the engine room, and as the other Aidan stared at him with unblinking eyes, he realized none of that was the truth. Something else had happened.

Aidan glanced up at his doppelgänger, at that demon from his own mind. His mouth fell open. In shock, maybe. Or in hope that he was wrong. Hope that the other would disabuse him of the truth that had come tumbling forth in his mind.

He had not woken from the dream in that one instant of crushing truth. Instead, he had turned to find that the shadow wall stood behind him. It had always been a part of his dream, of course. But never like this. Never simply appearing. Never beckoning, as this one seemed to do. Promising an escape from the end of time.

He had two choices, it seemed. He could stand and witness the end of all things, be in the presence of an emptiness so vast, so complete, that it threatened to swallow him whole. Or he could do something that heretofore he would have called truly insane. To pass through the wall of shadow and witness what lay beyond.

In one moment of pure impulse, Aidan made a decision and dove, head first, through the shroud.

It was not until Aidan left his feet that he asked himself why he was doing this. It wasn't until the die was cast, the Rubicon crossed, that Aidan's rational mind questioned the wisdom of his actions. After all, it was only a matter of time until he would wake and emerge from the dream, away from that place.

It was too late for regret. When Aidan passed through the shadow wall, he knew what regret truly was. What lay in the spaces between space and what was the substance of shadow. The fall did not end quickly has he had expected, sprawled on the ship floor just beyond the wall of night through which he had passed. No, the shadow divided more than the dimensions of a room. It split space and time and distance. It was the seam where our world connected with some unknown other.

Aidan fell headlong into that world. He did not fall freely. Rather it was as if the air—if it was air—of that great labyrinthine blackness had substance of its own, thickness and viscosity, like oil more than air. Aidan slipped through, floating as much as falling, until he landed with a thud upon an obsidian beach on the shores of a putrid, dead sea.

How many times did his mind break in those next few moments? How many ways was it twisted and torn? Was it the sky? That purple dark dome that pulsated and undulated, echoing the living membrane of an ungodly organ? Was it the great, black sun that shone darkness down upon him, like the pupil of a massive eye? An inversion of the sun's gift of light and warmth?

Perhaps it would have been those things, were it not for what he saw as he crawled up the obsidian beaches to their very crests. There he looked down on a city of febrile darkness and the Stygian-spired mountains that surrounded it, their tooth-like peaks piercing into the sky like a beast ready to devour, more maddeningly high than any ever known on Earth.

Those who dwelt within that city had come for him. These he had seen before, he guessed, if only the barest image of them, the slightest vision. How would he ever describe such beings? They were the darkness made manifest. Tall and thin, and made in the image of man it seemed, if only his outline. Two legs, two arms. A torso and a head.

But there the similarities ended. They walked in a halting fashion, like their bodies were struck with palsy, as if walking was foreign to them. They seemed to shake and jerk with every step they took. Their backs and their arms and their legs seemed permanently, if ever so slightly, bent, adding to the grotesqueness of their movement. They held their hands in front of them, their long, thin, snake-like fingers reaching for Aidan.

Their faces were the worst. Their skull-like visages, without the shimmering whiteness, but all the blank emptiness where the nose, the eyes and the mouth should be. Yet they saw Aidan as they stumbled toward him. And the darkness seemed to move with them.

They whispered, voicelessly perhaps, if all of this was truly in his brain. Whispered his name. Aidan screamed. He screamed like so many others who had come before him to those Plutonian shores. Screamed until the darkness closed in upon him and he remembered no more.

"So you see now," the other said. "You see the truth. You see what happened to you on the *Vespa*."

Aidan did see. But still, he did not know the whole truth. He could not remember what happened after the folding darkness had enveloped him. He could not say where he had gone from there or what had happened when he woke.

"I went to the infirmary," he said out loud. "They said I was fine. They said it was just fatigue."

"Did they? Is that what they told you? Is that what you truly remember?"

Aidan looked into the mirror of himself and was confused. None of this made sense. Then suddenly, a moment of clarity.

"You're saying none of this is real."

The other grinned. "Who can say what is real and what is not? You tell me, Aidan. How many do you know who have seen beyond the wall of sleep and returned to tell the tale? And who knows what dreams may come to the minds of those so afflicted? Who knows what they see with the third eye? What worlds they may form? What visions? What scenarios? What epics their insane minds might conjure to prevent the mad from knowing the truth?

"It seems to me that two possibilities lay before us. The first is that you sit now in an insane asylum in some secret location on the North American continent. A vegetable, hidden away within. Mad. Living a figment of your imagination, and that none of this," he said, gesturing around the room, "is real."

"And the other?" Aidan whispered.

"The other is that you woke that day on the *Vespa* the most dangerous of insane men—the one who wears the mask of sanity, one unrecognized either by himself or those around him. Misdiagnosed by careless doctors, you were allowed to return to your position where, mad with fear of what might happen if you reentered the dream, you destroyed your ship, its captain, and the crew.

"You then escaped in a life pod, where you remain in stasis to this day. Your brain passes the time by creating all of this, a world for you to conquer. To give you a way to save your own sanity. Perhaps if you find a way to save this ship, you will find salvation for yourself as well. Maybe that's why you are here. But either way, none of this is real."

The other watched with smug satisfaction as Aidan's jaw fell open. "That can't be. That makes no sense," he said, even as he knew that it did.

"Ask yourself, Mr. Connor. What makes more sense? What I just told you? Or that you were a crew member on a ship that was destroyed. You, the sole survivor. Injured, mysteriously, but nevertheless escaping a warp core breach that should have destroyed everything in the vicinity, including your escape pod. And then, despite the fact the ship was deep within the warp zone, your capsule just happened to float into well-traveled space where you were rescued by a ship, one captained by a woman close to retirement.

"That she, despite your recent incident, hired you immediately as navigator of the *Chronos*. Where you met a girl and discovered a mystery to be solved, one that just so happened to involve a derelict, the same ship you had walked upon in your dreams of old. One that so conveniently was once under the command of your captain's father. A ship in distress, one you could save, perhaps redeeming yourself and fulfilling a prophecy given to you by an insane man. And now, you are talking to the physical manifestation of your own psyche. You tell me, Mr. Connor. Which is more insane?"

The doppelgänger took two more steps toward Aidan, and now they stood mere inches apart. "Either way, this I tell you. All of this is a fiction. And no matter what you choose to believe, what you must do remains the same. You must save this ship. It is the only way you might fix your mind and recover your lost soul."

"No," Aidan murmured, his voice shaking. "You're a liar!"

At that moment the door slid open and Rebecca stumbled

inside, falling to her knees. Aidan spun around to the noise and saw it was her. He turned back to where his mirror image had stood. He was gone, vanished.

For a long awkward moment, it stayed like that. Aidan, staring, pale and open mouthed, at seeming nothingness. Rebecca, doubled over on her knees, sobbing on the floor, thankful to God that she had made it here, but also with a creeping uneasiness that Aidan wasn't coming to her aid. But it lasted only a second before Aidan, regaining his senses, raced across the room and slid down on his knees beside Rebecca.

"Rebecca," he said, grabbing her by the arms, "what's wrong?"

She pointed toward the door, but then she didn't know what to say, how to explain what she had seen without sounding crazy.

"There's something out there," she said finally, settling on the vaguest possible explanation.

"Something?"

"I saw something."

"Something from your dreams," Aidan stated more than asked.

She looked up at him and felt an almost over-weaning relief that maybe she wasn't crazy after all. "Yes."

"Where's your rifle?"

"I dropped it back there."

"That's alright," he said. "Whatever it was, I don't think it uses guns."

Aidan and Rebecca both jumped when the door slid open again. In stepped Gravely, and she held her rifle in her hands.

"Come on," she said, without bothering to ask why they were on the floor. "Dr. Ridley's gone missing."

# CHAPTER
# 22

"I'm not so sure we should split up," Ridley said. "Not with everything that's happened."

Gravely and Ridley stood at the entrance of the corridors that housed the crew compartment of the *Singularity*. Since Jack had a complete list of the ship's computer codes, he was able to override the security procedures that had kept the doors locked.

"There's nobody left on this ship, Malcolm."

"Yes, but after everything you've been through are you sure you want to be . . ."

Ridley stopped in mid-sentence, cut off by the way the captain squinted her eyes and set her jaw. He immediately felt shame. The truth was, he didn't want to be alone. That was bad enough. Seeing how the captain knew it also, well, that was intolerable.

"You're right," he said. "The faster we get this done the better."

"And the sooner we can get home," she said.

It was the first time Ridley had heard her mention home. He knew something about the captain's past and he knew that she had no home. Not really. He wondered if she meant Earth or the *Chronos*.

"I don't like it," she said, glancing around. "It's strange. Something's off."

"The gravitational effects . . . " Ridley began.

"No, no it's something else. I don't know. Maybe nothing. Look," she said, turning to him, "we probably won't find anything here. Take fifteen minutes. You go left. I'll go right. Go through the quarters and if you find anything that looks official, just take it with you. If Aidan and Dr. Kensington can't get the engines going, we'll need all the information from the ship that we can get."

"Jack will, you mean."

"Right," Gravely said. "The simple fact of the matter is his mission is our mission, at least until we can go our separate ways."

"Understood."

"Fifteen minutes. Then we meet back here."

Ridley watched Gravely disappear into the corridor beyond. He was amazed out how quickly she seemed to be swallowed.

Ridley shivered. It wasn't that he was a coward, far from it. But most people who use words like "coward" have never really tasted fear, never known its weight. Have never had to stand in its midst, and feel its hot breath on the nape of their neck. Ridley never had. Only in the dreams when he faced his mother.

Maybe that was why he found so much terror in this place. Why he hated every inch of it. This felt like them, the dreams. Not in a simple way. Not in the smell of decay or the cold kiss of the air. In the sights you saw or the things you heard. Something deeper than that. A sixth sense maybe. The cold chill of a premonition. Like the feeling you were being watched. Yes, those feelings all came with the dream. He had felt them since he had stepped onboard this ship.

The first room he came to was that of an Ensign Robertson. He knew the name only because of the pair of discarded fatigues he found on the floor. There was a blood on them, Ensign Robertson's or someone else's. Maybe both.

What struggle had gone on here, he wondered. He questioned whether the captain could have done it all himself, or whether some others in the crew had initially sided with him, only to be betrayed in the end. Or maybe it was simpler still to assume the captain had surprised them, killing a large number before facing resistance from those who had remained. But why had it happened? That was the greatest mystery of them all.

They knew so little about the ship, so little about its mission. Jack knew, of course. Rebecca too. If Dr. Ridley had any skill at figuring the yin and yang of humanity left, he was sure Aidan knew by now as well.

There was much that was obvious from the captain's final log, however. An experiment had taken place on this ship and those upon it were the test subjects. That experiment had been to avoid the effects of the dreams, perhaps to circumvent the sleep altogether. To provide a new way to travel that did not come with its burden. Oh, how they had failed.

"No," Ridley said to himself. "Not failure."

When the guinea pigs all die, the test is merely completed. With results unsatisfactory, yes, but results nonetheless.

He left Robinson's room behind, having found nothing but personal logs. Holos of family and friends back home. He entered the next room and couldn't stifle a gasp. It was just like Ensign Robertson's, save for the fact he recognized the woman in the picture sitting on the bedside table.

She had an arm around a man no older than she, her head tilted against his, the kind of smile that couldn't be forced. She wore a yellow summer dress, he a shirt with NAVY emblazoned across the chest. A fiancé, husband maybe. He preferred that, somehow, to boyfriend. For when she disappeared, a boyfriend would have simply moved on. Forgetting her. Finding another to take her place. But a husband, a fiancé, he would remember.

Even if he did marry again, that woman would know her story. Know that she had been someone of surpassing importance to her husband. The first love of his life. And she would think, what a woman she must have been for a man like my husband to love her. Somehow, that made Dr. Ridley feel better.

Yes, he had seen her face before, though it had looked nowhere near as lovely as the image he now looked upon. He had seen her as she had died, her face cut to ribbons, her body left to molder on the cold, metal floor of the *Singularity*'s corridors, a warning to those who would follow. He guessed he might owe his life to her, for if he and Gravely had not come upon her body when they had, they might have been the mad captain's next victims.

He almost left the room behind, not wanting to desecrate this, her final memorial. But something, something inside urged him to go forward. Not as a voyeur of the dead. No, there was something here that he needed to see. Something he was meant to find.

He stepped inside and jumped a little as the door slid closed behind him. He shone his light around the room, from pictures, to computer pads, to an old-fashioned bound book, *Physical Geography of the Sea* by Matthew Fontaine Maury. "She must have been the navigator," he thought.

This book had probably come from him, on her first commission. He picked up the book, rubbing his hands across the leather cover, brought it to his nose and breathed in the musty aroma of three hundred years. Of something real, something not plastic or prefabricated. But when he opened his eyes, he saw the technology of the present age—the blinking red light of a holorecorder sitting next to where the book had been.

He set the book down on the table and picked up the tiny device. Probably her last personal log, he thought. The red light flashed angrily at him, demanding that he press it, urging him to see what was contained therein. Whether out of curiosity or some preternatural sense that this was the thing he sought, he pressed the button.

An image appeared in front of him. The same girl, dressed in the uniform of a naval officer. The compass and sexton emblazoned on her shoulder confirmed his suspicions; she was the navigator on this ship. She had seen better days. There was blood on her face, dried for the most part, the wound from which it sprang having been closed by what looked to be a temporary suture. But this was a respite at best from battle. That much, her eyes told him.

She was gasping for breath, as if she had just run full sprint from something or someone, endured some horrible physical struggle. She'd also been crying. She wasn't crying now. No, she was determined. Determined to share whatever she must.

"My name is Lieutenant Samantha Erickson," she said. She paused and glanced off camera in the direction of a distant scream that echoed its way down the halls of the ship.

"I don't have much time," she said, looking back at the camera. "If you are watching this message, I have either managed to launch it in an escape pod or you have found the *Singularity* yourself. In either event," she said, glancing once again toward the door as what sounded like rifle fire boomed somewhere off screen, "I don't intend to ever leave this ship. And that makes what I have to say all the more important."

She took a deep breath, involuntarily smoothing the sleeves of her uniform, a habit left over from basic training, no doubt. Then she continued.

"An hour ago, the *Singularity*, under the command of Captain Alexander Gravely, entered the black hole, Sigma-1. Our objective was to discover a new means of travel, one that did not require stasis, and therefore did not result in the dreams. We made this effort with the best of intentions. We had hoped that perhaps we would save lives. In reality, it appears we have only lost our own and possibly endangered many more."

Her voice cracked and Ridley wondered whether she could continue, but continue she did.

"That was an hour ago. The jump itself lasted less than thirty seconds. We entered the black hole, but then something happened. We saw things. Things I cannot explain. Things that will seem mad to anyone who hears this message. It was as though we were transported across the whole of the galaxy all in one moment, some galaxy at least.

"In that moment, we saw vistas and worlds unimagined. Black stars that seemed to give no light, but rather cast gloom upon the empty, dark seas of dead worlds below, planets unlike any I know. Or any that can be. The beings that lived upon them were shadows from my darkest nightmares, from the dreams themselves. And then, what we saw was no longer a vision of distant planets, but the ship itself.

"In the instant that followed, the lights went out. Before they did, I saw them, the things from the dreams, lurking in the shadows. Those beings, those creatures from other worlds, from one quite the opposite of our own. They are everywhere on this ship. They are wherever the light fails. They stand in the darkness, watching. They watch me even now, here. I do not think they are strong enough yet to do anything. Not of their own accord, at least. I have no reason to believe this, but I think they grow stronger on fear. And there is much to feed them now.

"After the lights failed, several of the crew went mad. Curling. Jacobs. Frier. Even the captain. I do not know who is left. I ran. The last thing I saw was Captain Gravely rip out Dr. Isakson's throat with his bare hands."

Once again, her words failed her. Ridley even reached out to grab her, such was his certainty that she would faint. As his hands passed through empty air, there was another noise from off camera, one that he could not describe. Whatever it was steeled her and she looked back into the camera with renewed resolve.

"So I've decided on a course of action. My first step will be to disable the engines, if I can. It is my belief that whatever is on this ship must not leave it. Such a thing cannot be allowed to escape. More importantly, if I can I will launch a copy of this holo on one of the ship's evacuation pods so that others may know what happened here. So they will know what we did and never attempt it again.

"Then I will destroy the ship. I believe it has become a gateway, a passage of sorts. Just as I always thought the shadow walls were in the dreams. Doorways to the worlds I witnessed in that awful long instant in the heart of the black hole. I fear this ship has become to them what the shadow walls were to us. A portal by which they may pass through.

Hopefully destroying the ship will send them back from whence they came, close the gateway, and eliminate them forever."

Then she took a deep breath and paused, and Ridley knew this was the most important thing of all. When she spoke again, her voice was on the edge of control; whatever reserves she had tapped on the verge of exhaustion. "Tell William," she said, "that I did what I must. And that I love him. This is Lieutenant Samantha Erickson, signing off."

As quickly as she appeared, the girl standing in front of him melted away, back into the tiny device he held in his hand, the simple red light now blinking furiously again. While she had spoken, Ridley had stood in stunned silence, listening as all his worst fears were confirmed. He glanced from side to side, too aware of the darkness that now surrounded him and fearful of the things that must lurk therein.

"She could have been mad," he said to himself. But even as he did, he knew it was a lie. She had not been mad. She had been the sanest person he had seen in the last few days. For this was insanity, here on this ship on the cusp of a black hole. Let it go back, he thought. In fact, he knew it must.

He looked down at the holoplayer in his hand. The rest of them had to see this. They had to know what he knew. When they did, even Jack couldn't deny the obvious. They had to destroy the ship.

Ridley turned on his heel and rushed out the door. In his haste, he did not hesitate to step directly into his nightmare. When the door closed behind him, Ridley did not find himself in the darkened corridors of the *Singularity*. Instead, he stood on a broken cobblestone drive, one that lead under a canopy of dead and decaying trees to an ancient, antebellum mansion that had once housed the insane.

# CHAPTER
# 23

"Oh my God, no," Ridley whispered.

He spun around, hoping against hope to see the door through whence he had just come. But it was gone; his eyes met only the shadow wall. The one he now loathed and feared even more than he had before. The cold wind blew through dead trees and in its clutches carried a whisper, "David."

He stood there, locked in fear and doubt until what seemed like hours had passed. Even though he had no choice. The blowing wind called to him, beckoned him to walk the path he had trod a hundred times before. To come within the copse of dead trees. To stand in the skeletal shadow of their embrace.

Dr. Ridley walked. He didn't bother to question what had happened. Whatever rules pertained to the world outside of this ship did not hold here. He could trust nothing. Expect nothing. There was only his hope that at the end of this road, at the end of the dream, the one he had never reached, he would find his way back to reality.

He came to the statue that stood in the midst of the ancient fountain, the one he doubted had ever held water. No sooner had that thought left his mind than he heard a gurgling from deep within. A thin stream of liquid came from a hidden opening, weak at first, and then stronger, until the water coursed down the statue of the woman, over the bronze coal that she held in her hands and down the face of the boy, moistening the tears once only carved in stone.

Ridley looked down at the broken pavement beneath his feet. There was a trembling, slight at first, and then unmistakable as the ground began to shake. A wave seemed to pass over him and shattered cobblestones turned smooth and perfectly even, like the day they were first laid. The wave passed on, and ragged trees suddenly stood tall and true, sprouting, over newly rejuvenated grass, great green leaves that in an instant turned bright golds and oranges and reds, raining down on him like an autumn shower.

A whirlwind seemed to roar up the road, passing through the shaking trees and striking the building with such fury that Ridley thought it might collapse down upon him. He held up his hands and closed his eyes, but no sooner had the winds come than they were gone. When he opened his eyes again, the asylum was pristine, a shining beacon on a hill. Patients in white gowns milled about the grounds and when Ridley looked down at himself, he realized he was clothed in the dress of 200 years prior, back when such places were more than just dreams.

"Ah, Dr. Ridley," a voice from behind said. Ridley whirled around, but the specter that stood smiling at him did not seem to notice either his behavior or the wild look in his eyes. "We were beginning to wonder if you were coming. You found your accommodations satisfactory, I hope?"

"Accommodations?"

"Yes. On your trip down from Atlanta. I take it the train was comfortable?"

Ridley gawked at the little round man in his brown pants, held up by suspenders that peeked out from underneath his white coat. He had an almost unrestrainable desire to hit the man, to punch him squarely in the middle of what he could swear was a smug and sinister smile and then flee. But though the world had changed, he could still see the shadow wall pulsating in the distance, its black tendrils reaching up to the sky.

"Of course," he murmured, almost choking on the dryness of his mouth. "Of course, the accommodations were fine."

"Excellent," the man said. He slapped Ridley on the back and chuckled as if they were old friends. "I can't tell you how thrilled we are to have you here," he said, his hand still on Ridley's shoulder. He started to walk, and in doing so, carried Ridley along with him. "Frankly, without your help, I'm not sure this is a case we could crack, but I have no doubt that you will work miracles. This is, after all, your area of expertise."

"My area of expertise," Ridley repeated. He felt numb, like he'd taken too many pain killers.

"Right. We deal mainly with men here. Hysterics are a bit of an undiscovered country for us. Your history with the disturbed minds of females is well documented."

"Yes . . ."

"In any event, this particular patient," he said, stopping to open the door, "has been extraordinarily difficult."

Ridley barely heard him. He stared up at the mighty chandelier in the center of the ornate foyer, the only part of the facility most visitors would ever see. He was shocked at its grandeur, particularly compared to the ruin he normally witnessed.

"What are her symptoms?" Ridley mumbled. Absentmindedly almost. Stupidly perhaps, given the circumstances.

"Oh, the usual." They came to a door. The doctor removed a set of keys and unlocked it. "Abusive to herself. Others. The child mostly."

"There's a child?"

"Isn't there always in these cases? Apparently, she suffered severe blood loss while giving birth. Her husband says she hasn't been the same since."

"It can't be," Ridley thought to himself. Everything here was wrong. The place was too old. The story similar, yes. But not the same.

"She has an obsession," the small man continued, "not unlike most with her affliction."

"And what is that?"

"Fire, it appears. She seems to believe that only fire can purify the soul." The man chuckled heartily. "Utterly bizarre, what the insane can conjure. Don't you agree, Doctor?"

"What did she do with it?"

"Do with it? Do with what?"

"The fire, Doctor. The fire."

"Oh, well, nothing directly I suppose. It was more hot coals, you see. She burned her son something horrible, with one."

Ridley stopped walking as he gazed down a corridor that he had traveled before, albeit in days where the paint was chipped and peeled, the windows shattered.

"That will be all, Doctor. I believe I can take it from here."

"But, Dr. Ridley," the man said, his fat face instantly turning a flustered red, "you don't even know where we've housed the patient."

"I know, Doctor. Trust me. I'm the expert here, remember? Now, I have a job to do."

He continued down the hallway, leaving the other man standing behind him in confusion. Because he didn't look back, Ridley missed it when the befuddled stare melted away, replaced by something colder, crueler.

Ridley didn't know the room number she was in, not for sure. But he had seen her walk into that room a hundred times and he could simply feel when he reached it, when his steps had taken him far enough that he could be nowhere else. He peered through the tiny, barred opening in the center of the door. She stood there, his mother. In a white dress that flowed all the way down her body, one entirely inappropriate for this place.

Before Ridley could even try the handle, the door creaked open. Ridley looked around and he realized that everyone else had vanished. The doctors, the patients. No one remained but Ridley and the woman in the room. He pushed the door gently and it swung open the rest of the way. He stood in the threshold, between freedom and imprisonment, between her and him. He watched as she turned, spinning in place, until she faced him.

"David. You came, finally. I always knew you would. Eventually. I knew you'd never leave me here."

She walked over to where he stood, running her hands along the cold concrete of the wall as she did. "It's so lonely here, David. I wish you would come see me more often. I'm sorry, you know, for what I did."

"Stop it," Ridley murmured. "Just stop it."

"Stop what?"

Ridley stood in the doorway, glaring at the thing that masqueraded as his mother. "They feed on fear, they feed on fear," he repeated to himself in his mind. If it was fear she sought, he would not give it.

Slowly, deliberately, enunciating each syllable, emphasizing each word. "You are not my mother," he said. "I know what you are and I'm not afraid of you. I know that I am still aboard the ship and that this is all an illusion. The time for games is over. I know the truth, and soon, the rest will as well."

Ridley watched the look on the demon's face change, as the façade, the lie, dropped away. As the look of caring, of longing, of maternal love, disappeared into what he thought was confusion. What he hoped was perhaps even concern. But despite his mantra, despite his promise to himself that he would show no fear, he felt it creep back into his heart as the beast lowered its gaze and looked up at him under hooded eyes. It grinned and that horrid smirk, Ridley feared, was proof that he was undone.

"So be it," the beast uttered, no longer the sound of a woman, no longer the voice of his mother. "We gave you a chance," it said, in its own deep growl, "to reconcile with one lost, long ago, to make things right before your own end. Yet you denied it. No matter. We will give you truth instead."

At that instant, Ridley felt a rumble in the floor. He turned, glancing out a window in the hallway beyond. Before his eyes, the scene changed. The whirlwind returned. The living trees died a second death, polished cobblestones cracked and shattered. Paint peeled off the walls and rained down around him. Then the whirlwind reached her as well.

Her face began to roil, to split along the edges, becoming the black, empty mouth of the creatures from his dreams. Her eyes sunk into her skull, but the rest of her face remained. Her back arched, arms and legs cracking into impossible angles. She became an image of a demon from man's oldest nightmares, one made all the worse by the human form it still bore.

The thing took one step toward him and Ridley could stand no more. He ran, ran through broken doors and twisting corridors. He ran through a maze of hallways, ones he had never known to exist in the asylum before. Behind him always was the beast. He could see it in the corner of his eye. See its disfigured body jerking behind him at impossible speeds. Felt its hot breath on his neck.

He knew that if he could escape, if he could just get outside the building, then he would be free. He wasn't sure why he knew that. Perhaps it was simply a lie he told himself, one that made his legs move faster. Something to give him hope when it seemed that all hope was lost. He saw it, a doorway at the end of the corridor. He ran faster, but so did the beast, braying at him like a pack of wild dogs.

The darkness seemed to reach him. Tendrils of blackness grabbed at him, smoke-like appendages surrounded him. So close. Ten more feet he thought, even though he wasn't sure he would make it, not with the demon's cold hands upon him. With five feet left, he ran as hard as he ever had, leaping free of the shadow's reach, throwing himself at the door, almost laughing with joy as it sprang open. Then the shock. "Oh no!" he thought. And that was the last truly coherent thought that Dr. Malcolm Ridley ever had.

When he opened the emergency airlock, the computer system on the *Singularity* automatically sealed the corridor behind him to prevent an explosive breech. But it didn't stop Ridley from being sucked into the cold vacuum of space. Ridley screamed silently. For almost a minute, until his brain finally, mercifully, lost the battle with unconsciousness,

      Ridley stared back at the *Singularity* as it floated away from him, while the moisture in his eyes and mouth boiled away. The last thing he saw before death took him was the image of his mother, standing in the open airlock of the ship, smiling. Meanwhile, the little light on the holorecorder, the one that Ridley clutched in his hands even in death, continued to flash an angry red.

# CHAPTER
# 24

Gravely, Aidan and Rebecca walked down the dark corridors of the *Singularity*, trying to retrace Rebecca's steps. Aidan thought they should look for Dr. Ridley first, but the captain had been insistent. She was afraid they might need the rifle.

"We had split up," Gravely said, "a mistake I don't intend to make again. We were each covering one corridor of the crew's quarters. There was nothing worth finding. Personal logs, data recorders, that's about it. Nothing that I think will be of much help to you or Mr. Crawford."

"Then what happened?" Aidan asked.

"Then," she said, stopping and looking at both of them, "I had a very long conversation with a man who I believe was supposed to be my grandfather. Great, great, great grandfather."

Neither Rebecca nor Aidan looked surprised. Gravely had expected their reaction.

"What did he say?"

"He was very clear. 'Save this ship.' He reminded me that as long as our family has been in the Navy, we've never lost one."

"Save the ship," Aidan whispered.

"I've seen him in my dreams, every mission the last twenty years. This is the first time he has spoken to me."

"Then what?"

"Then he disappeared. After, I went to get Ridley. He was nowhere to be found. I checked the rooms, the corridors. Nothing."

"He can't have just vanished. Once we hit the bridge, we can run a scan, something. We'll figure it out."

"That's my intention."

A glint of metal flashed from the floor. Gravely reached down and picked up a rifle. "Yours, I presume," she said, handing it back to

Rebecca. "Try not to lose it again."

Rebecca couldn't fight back a shiver as they walked to where the bridge should be. She thought back to her last attempt to reach it, the one that had led her to walk in circles. Where she saw something that should not be. She was shocked, then, when they turned a corner and there it was. Jack was waiting for them, and so was Austin Crawford.

He'd appeared again, only a few minutes prior.

"They're coming," he said. "They are going to try and make you leave the ship. You mustn't let them."

Jack set his jaw, never looking at his father.

"I won't," he said.

"Good, son, good. I'll be here with you. You'll be able to see me, but they won't. Remember. Above all things, you must protect the ship."

He was standing, leaned against the forward console, when the three of them entered.

"Expecting something, Captain?" he said to Gravely, glancing down at the way she held her weapon, poised and ready to shoot.

"I don't know what to expect anymore, Mr. Crawford. Not on this ship. And that is why we need to leave."

"Leave?" He laughed. "We've just arrived."

"You know the situation," Aidan said. "We're getting close to that black hole. Besides, we've got everything we need."

"That's not true. Our primary objective is to save this ship."

"No," Rebecca interrupted, sounding confused, "that's not our objective at all. The data is what we came for, not the ship. We are only to save the ship if we can."

"Dr. Kensington, I am in charge of this operation. I decide what our objectives are. And I say saving the *Singularity* is imperative."

"What are you talking about, Jack? This is my command."

Jack chuckled darkly. "Oh come now, Rebecca. Do you really think that they would leave you in charge of something like this? No, ISS wanted this to be a civilian operation. Officially, in case there were any problems. But make no mistake, I am in command."

His father leaned over and whispered in his ear. "Good, son, good. Let them know you mean business."

"Well it doesn't matter anyway, Jack," Rebecca said. "The ship can't be saved. The engines are damaged. We can't move her."

"Damaged?" Jack said, a hint of desperation creeping into his voice.

"Yes," Aidan answered. "The standard drive's gone. Warp drive is intact, but this close to a black hole, we try to warp out and the ship goes boom."

"They're lying to you," his father said. "They can fix the damage."

"And you can't fix it?" Jack shrieked.

"Weeell. . ." Rebecca stuttered. She had never seen Jack like this, and it scared her. "Maybe if we had an engineer, someone who was more familiar with the basic mechanical aspects of the standard drive . . ."

"But that's Cyrus," Aidan interjected, "and as you know, he's in no condition. You just need to relax, Jack. This is not a tough call. We've got no choice."

"There has to be a way! You people are useless to me. Useless! Why do you think I brought you along, Rebecca? This is supposed to be your area of expertise!"

Rebecca started to respond, but Gravely put a hand on her shoulder. "Why are you so concerned about saving this ship, Mr. Crawford? Is there something you want to tell us? Is there something we need to know?"

Jack's father whispered in his ear. "Calm down, son. You are losing them."

"I believe this ship is invaluable, Captain Gravely. This ship has been places, seen things that we can hardly imagine. I am not about to let it slip into a black hole, not if we can save it."

"The other ship's engine," his father said, circling around Gravely, who felt something, even if she couldn't see it. "We can use it."

"What about the engine of the *Chronos*?"

"What?"

"Wait," Aidan said, "you're insane. Do you even know what you're talking about? That's not even under consideration."

"Why not? We need an engine. It has one."

"You're not taking my engine!" Gravely shouted.

"If you remember correctly, Captain, as far as the computers are concerned, it's *my* engine. The *Chronos* isn't going anywhere without my authorization." Jack looked around at the others, letting the impact of his reminder wash over them. He was back in control. "Look, it's very simple. The *Chronos* has the capability to transfer the engine to the *Singularity*. Installation is not difficult. What I am proposing is very possible. Isn't that right, Dr. Kensington?"

"Jack . . . no . . . Yes, we could move the engine from the *Chronos*, and we might even get it installed. But it would take hours. And more importantly, with a ship this size, chances are we'd run up the engine and the whole thing would overload. Then we'd have two dead engines and two dead ships. We just can't take that chance."

"What you describe is a worst case scenario . . ."

"A not unlikely worst case scenario, Jack."

"Well, that's a risk I am willing to accept."

"This is madness," Aidan said. "You're as crazy as Cyrus."

Before Jack could say anymore, Rebecca noticed something. Something outside the ship that was approaching the great, glass dome of the bridge at high speed. Jack watched as her eyes fluttered upward, as they then grew wide with shock and fear. The scream came next. All of them followed her gaze upward just in time to see Ridley's body smack into the glass dome above them.

It hung for a second, the cold, frozen eyes seeming to lock on Captain Gravely. She wouldn't say she considered Dr. Ridley a friend, but he had been a man she'd known for a very long time. One that she trusted. A valued member of her crew. Someone under her command and therefore her responsibility. She did not know how he had come to this, whether by his own hand or that of another. She could conjure a thousand different explanations, each of them stranger, more bizarre than the last, but none of them would probably cover what had happened.

She removed a computer pad from her pocket, unfolded it, and issued one of the few commands left to her, despite Jack's control of the *Chronos*'s systems. From the ship floating above came two flashes. Two metal balls spun downward toward them, the Charlottes landing with a thud on the bridge ceiling. They grabbed on to Ridley's body. Their thrusters fired, pushing them away from the *Singularity*, back to the *Chronos* from whence they came.

"We'll take him home," Gravely said. "It's the least we can do." She turned to Jack. "Mr. Crawford, we're not giving you the engine from the *Chronos*, and we're not staying on this ship any longer. This mission is complete."

"Captain Gravely, I think you've forgotten that I am the one that controls the *Chronos*, not you."

"Well, I think you've forgotten something else as well. In a few hours, this ship is going to fall into a black hole. Now, if you want to be on it when it does, feel free. But I would rather die on my ship, my way, than to have whatever happened to Dr. Ridley happen to us. Now if you will excuse us, we'll be going back to the *Chronos*. You know where to find us when you come to your senses. Otherwise, enjoy the descent."

"Come on, Jack, please," Rebecca pleaded.

"Leave him be," said Aidan. "He'll come around eventually."

Jack watched as Aidan and Captain Gravely turned their backs on him and walked toward the door of the bridge. Rebecca stayed, her eyes pleading, but he didn't see it. He didn't hear her either. All he heard was the voice of his father.

"You can't let them go," he said. "You can't let them leave. They are betraying you! They want you to fail! They want the mission to fail! If they go, you'll never escape. If this ship is lost, the nightmares will follow you all the days of your life. They will haunt you into the grave. Are you going to let that happen? Are you?"

Jack reached back and pulled his gun, aiming it at Gravely's head. He squeezed the trigger, and the sound of thunder echoed throughout the room Aidan spun around, his eyes moving from Gravely to Jack Crawford who still stood, arm outstretched, gun raised. Then he looked at Rebecca. She was holding her rifle, pointed up awkwardly. The end was smoking.

For another moment Jack stood, the dark red circle on his chest growing larger with every second. He was confused. His mind was telling his hand to pull the trigger, but something was wrong. Somehow, the message wasn't getting through. Then he realized that he had been shot.

The pain didn't come until the realization struck him. The gun dropped from his hand, clattering along the ground. He looked over to where his father still stood. The man was staring at him, his head cocked to the side. Then he turned his palms up in the air and shrugged, vanishing.

Jack's knees buckled and he fell to them. The pain that shot up through his legs was overshadowed by the throbbing in his chest. He collapsed onto his back, his eyes staring up at the glass dome to the dark heavens above. His breathing slowed, each breath shallower than the last.

The next few moments, Jack's thoughts divided in two. Half of his dying brain merely experienced, while the other half, the half that still remembered his training, the half that was still filled with the cold rationality that even death could not replace, questioned whether what he saw was real or merely a figment of his imagination in its death throes. A random firing of neurons as they flashed to life and then fell cold.

What did he see? A light, but not a warm one. Not the kind that welcomed him, but one he knew he would enter nonetheless. In that light were figures, men and women, old and young. One of them was his father, the man he had killed with his bare hands. That was what they all had in common. He had murdered them all and they had come for him in death.

Jack had one last moment of horrifying clarity before he died. The ones he had seen before? The spirits that had come to him in his dream? The ones that had stood on the bridge? They had been impostors. Liars who wore masks to confuse and coerce him, to make him do their bidding. No, these phantoms, these ghosts from beyond, they were real. And the light was their burning hatred, the raging fire of their passion for revenge.

"What do we do now?" Aidan asked as he put his arm around Rebecca, lowering the gun that sat frozen in her hands in the same position she had fired it.

"Let's get back to the *Chronos*," Gravely said. "Leave him. He wanted to stay with the ship. At least now we can grant him that wish."

* * *

The shadow returned to the *Chronos*. It walked with a purpose, seeking. It came to the infirmary, passing through the doorway and standing before the vessel.

"Your time has come," it said. "You are our final hope."

The shadow melted into smoke, the vapor entering the console beside the holding cell. It sparked once, flashed twice, and the gentle hum of the force field died away. The shadow was gone, but the thing that was Cyrus remained. It took one step forward, passed through where the force field had been, and was free.

# CHAPTER
# 25

The *Chronos* had left orbit with a crew of four and two passengers. Now the three who remained sat on the bridge. Rebecca hadn't spoken since she'd killed Jack. It was necessary, she told herself. He had lost it, and if she hadn't acted, they might all be dead. But rationalizations, even true ones, were no comfort. A man was dead, a life was lost, and she had taken it.

Captain Gravely and Aidan did not mourn Jack. Their concerns were far more pressing.

"So Jack's dead," Gravely said finally. "And that leaves us with a problem."

"The computers are locked down." Aidan never could help voicing the obvious.

"Can you unlock the computers, Dr. Kensington?"

Rebecca looked at Gravely, unsure if the question was directed at her, even though her name was mentioned. Gravely and Aidan merely watched her, letting her answer in her own good time.

"Unlock them?" she said, the question starting to break through the fog in her mind. "No," she muttered. "It takes both of us. Both Jack and me. Now that he's dead . . . no, they can't be unlocked."

"So we're dead in the water then," Gravely said.

"It's worse than that, Captain," Aidan said. "We aren't dead in the water. We're moving."

"Toward the black hole," Rebecca finished his thought, and Aidan sighed.

"Yes, exactly. We've been locked on to the *Singularity* for almost a full day. It's been dragging us toward the black hole since the beginning. Not a problem with our engines, but without them . . ." Aidan held out an upturned hand. There was no need to say anything else.

Aidan stood up and paced around the bridge. He had an idea, but he wasn't happy with it, and he hoped he could come up with something else, something less risky. The others watched him, aware that he was sorting out his thoughts. Finally he spoke. "I hate to say it, Captain, but I think we have to engage the warp jump on the *Singularity*."

"I thought you said that was impossible."

"No, not impossible. I said it was risky. Very risky. I'd say there's an 80% chance we lose the ship if we do it. But, given the circumstances, I'd say it's our only option."

"Could we move the *Chronos*'s standard drive? Like Jack wanted to?"

Aidan shook his head. "No, the computer locks are hardwired. Wouldn't work. It would still be locked down."

Gravely slumped down in a chair in front of the forward console. "So we abandon the ship," she said. "That's not a result I am prepared to accept, Mr. Connor. Especially if it means going back to the *Singularity*."

"I don't think we have a choice, Captain."

Gravely looked around the bridge, absorbing every inch of it, burning it into her mind. She wanted to always remember it. She had hoped for so much more time.

"Her maiden voyage," she said. Then she smiled at the others. "I guess the great ones always go down like that, huh?"

"Wait," Rebecca said, holding up a finger. Aidan and Gravely turned their attention to her, though the look on her face told them her brain was still churning. "Aidan, do you remember, before we left solar orbit, when we talked? Here?"

"Yeah," Aidan said. "Of course."

"You explained something to me then. About why a ship needs a navigator."

Gravely leaned forward in her chair, clarity coming into her eyes. "Because the computers shut down."

"Yes," Aidan murmured, understanding. "When they shut down, we have to reboot them."

"And that's a hard shutdown, right?" Rebecca asked.

"You've outdone yourself, Dr. Kensington," Gravely said, delighted. "There's a problem, though. How do we engage the warp drive? Jack had that locked down as well."

"We don't have to engage the one on the *Chronos*," Aidan said as Rebecca nodded vigorously. "We can use the *Singularity*. Since the two ships are connected, the warp bubble will automatically flow around both ships. We engage the warp bubble, launch the warp drive. Then all we have to do is cause an emergency drop. When we do, I'd say there's a 90, 95% chance the computer system has a hard shut down. When it boots back up, Jack's locks should be broken."

"But we still have the problem of going to warp near a black hole."

"True, but we won't have to go far," Aidan said. "Not far at all. We just have to get to warp and then drop out. I think the chance we lose the ship is negligible. Even if we do, the sudden loss of warp containment should be enough to reengage our systems. Worst case, I go over there and get blown up."

"That's a pretty bad worst case," Rebecca said.

Aidan smiled. "For me, certainly."

"And what if we don't get a hard reboot?" Gravely asked.

"One worst case at a time, Captain."

There was a sudden skittering sound at the door to the bridge that told them they were not alone. They watched as it slid open, their eyes falling down to the floor as the Charlotte marched into the room.

"It must have finished Ridley's autopsy," Rebecca said, "but I can't imagine that it found anything unusual."

Aidan bent down as the Charlotte propped itself on its back legs, holding up two arms like a puppy that wanted to play.

"What do you have old girl?" Aidan asked.

A panel slid open on the Charlotte's back. With one of its legs, it reached inside and produced a small square of plastic, one with a light that pulsated red, almost angrily.

"What's this?"

"Ridley must have had it," Rebecca offered.

Aidan pressed the flashing red button, and the recording of a person appeared, one they all recognized as the woman Ridley and Gravely had found on the *Singularity* what seemed ages ago. They watched, as Ridley had watched before them, learned the horrible truth about what had happened on that accursed ship, what fate had befallen the crew.

"God in Heaven," Gravely whispered. "What did you people do?"

"Something terrible," was all Rebecca could say.

"They couldn't have known," Aidan turned to them, an ashen mask having fallen over his face. "You asked us once, Rebecca," he said, as the image of the girl disappeared back into the holorecorder and the red light resumed its furious pulsing, "why we endure the dreams.

"I think you have your answer now. That story? The one about the first ship to go to warp, the *Hypnos*? The one that everybody says is just an old legend? We know now it's true. And the men on that ship, they saw truth. No wonder they killed themselves."

"You think they saw the same thing on the *Singularity*, don't you?"

Aidan shrugged his shoulders. "Sounds crazy, doesn't it? At this point, maybe not so crazy. I think that the warp jumps offer a window into another world and the sleep merely masks it. Just not all of it. They say in dreams are truth and in these, that can't be doubted. Not anymore."

"What do you mean, Aidan?" Gravely asked.

"We've all seen them," he said, shaking his head. "Heard them. Even if we never talked about it. Even if we never could. Afraid that somebody would think we were crazy. Too stupid to realize that we all saw the same thing. The shadows? The ones that are always there? Watching us? Whispering to us? The ones that your father saw on the cliffs of the valley he walked through every time his ship left Earth orbit?

"Turns out they weren't just figments of our imagination. The dreams *are* a window into another world, if I guess correctly. And let me tell you, if the dreams are a window, then the black hole is a doorway, a portal. When the *Singularity* went through it, it brought something back out. Maybe now the ship's also become a gateway of sorts. The shadows, the others, whatever you want to call them, they needed a vessel to escape before. The sickness? The sleep madness? Braddock's Syndrome? It's not a disease. It's a possession."

"You mean like Lieutenant Felix?" Gravely said.

"No," Aidan answered. "No I understand something now that I never could figure before. Lieutenant Felix wasn't the danger to your ship. It was Ensign Kelly. It was the man he killed. He killed Ensign Kelly because somehow Felix knew the truth. He knew that Kelly wasn't Kelly anymore. That he had become something else.

"But he also knew that you would never believe him, knew that no one would. So Lieutenant Felix killed the thing that had been the ensign. I think when he did, whatever was inside of him got out, and there was just enough fear on that ship that it was able to gain strength and seek its revenge."

"All along," Rebecca said. "All along they've been using us."

"That's why they wanted us to save that ship. There's a reason. It's their gateway into this world, their path out of whatever lies beyond. With it, they don't need the dreams anymore. They don't need us. They'll be free."

"So that's why Ridley is dead," Gravely said, "Because he found this. He found it and was going to tell us, so they killed him."

Aidan merely nodded.

"Then why don't they kill us now?" Rebecca asked.

"Maybe they can't," Aidan said. "Maybe they don't have that kind of power here. Not yet at least. But on that ship," he said, gesturing to the image of the *Singularity* on a console screen, "there they can do anything."

"Then you can't go back," Gravely said. "If you go back now, knowing what you know . . ."

"It can't be helped. Besides, I think I have an advantage they don't expect. Anyway, I don't think the plan has changed. I go back," said Aidan. "One of us has to. Engage the warp drive. Get us out of here. The only difference now is I think we need to destroy the *Singularity*. Finish what she started," he said, pointing to the holorecorder.

"There's one thing," said Rebecca, "if you're right about the dreams and if you're right about Braddock's, then Cyrus . . ."

She was cut off by a chime from the computer. Gravely walked over to the console. "Scan complete?"

"It's been scanning the *Singularity* since we arrived," Aidan said, peering over her shoulder at the screen. "It must have completed . . . wait. That can't be right."

Gravely saw it, too. Power had been restored to the *Singularity*.

"But that would mean the engines were fixed," Gravely said. "Who could . . ." She didn't finish the question before she answered it. "Cyrus. But he's in lockdown."

"No," Aidan said, "something tells me he's not. Computer, give me a display of the infirmary."

An empty room reached their eyes.

"That's impossible," Gravely said. "He couldn't escape on his own."

Aidan glanced at her and she met his eyes. The message was clear. Nothing was impossible, not out here. And Cyrus wasn't on his own.

"Computer," Aidan continued, "give me the airlock."

The screen flashed and changed, now showing an external view of the *Chronos*. It was as Aidan feared. The connecting cables between the two ships were cut away. Cyrus had used them to enter the *Singularity* and then ensured that no one would use them to follow.

"It's fine," Aidan said, seeing the desperation in Rebecca's eyes. "I'll just free jump between the two ships."

Gravely shook her head. "Free jump? Are you crazy? What if you miss?"

"I won't miss, Captain."

"It won't matter," Rebecca said. "Even if you get there, if the ships aren't connected, the warp bubble won't work."

"The *Singularity* has grappling hooks too," Aidan said. "I'm willing to bet he didn't sabotage those. He was worried about being followed, not this."

Aidan looked at Rebecca. He could see in her eyes that she wanted to object. But there was nothing for it. His plan was the only one that made any sense.

"We have to go fast," he said. "If the power is back on, he's not far from fixing the engine altogether. When he does, he'll be gone, and all we'll be able to do is wait for the inevitable."

"Alright," Gravely said. "Let's do it."

"There's one more thing, Captain. We can't do this unless we take the ship to warp. And that means . . ."

"The dreams," Rebecca whispered.

"Yeah," Aidan answered. "The dreams. This time, they will be the worst they've ever been. They know what's at stake and they will do anything they can to stop us."

Gravely looked at Rebecca. For a moment she hesitated.

"Let's go."

# CHAPTER
# 26

Aidan stood in the white glare of the airlock, pulling his gloves tight onto his hands. The sleeves of his suit met the edge of the gloves and the material melded together, forming a vacuum-tight seal. He glanced at the image on his computer pad. The *Singularity* had not moved yet, though he wondered how much longer they had before Cyrus finished his repairs. A chime sounded behind him. He turned as the door opened. Rebecca and Gravely entered.

"You two should be getting ready for stasis," he said.

"Well, we didn't want to let you leave without seeing you off," Gravely said. "Besides, if you miss, there won't be much point, will there?"

Aidan smiled. "I guess that's true."

"Good luck," she said, handing Aidan a rifle. "Come back soon."

She offered her his hand and he took it.

"Knew I shouldn't have taken this job."

Gravely chuckled and turned to Rebecca. "I'll be waiting on you."

The door closed behind her and Rebecca and Aidan were alone. She had told herself that she wouldn't make this difficult on him, but she had one request that she simply couldn't keep quiet.

"Aidan," she said, "you'll need help."

"Can't do it, Rebecca," he said, shouldering the rifle and pulling the strap tight so that it wouldn't move once he was in zero gravity.

"Aidan, now's not the time for macho bullshit."

"Not being macho, Rebecca. You and I both know that when we go to warp, I'll have to be awake. You won't be able to handle that."

"And what makes you think you will? If you're going to take that chance, you can't tell me I can't."

"I've seen it, Rebecca," he said as he picked up his helmet. "Last time, before what happened to the *Vespa*. I went beyond the wall. I didn't remember it, not until recently."

"But no one ever . . ." she whispered, torn between concern and an almost overwhelming curiosity.

"I know. But I did and I'm fine, more or less. I figure that staying awake for the warp isn't all that different. I'm the only one that can do this, Rebecca, and I have to do it alone."

She hesitated for a moment, but then she slumped in defeat. He was right, of course. There was no other choice. She reached up and pulled him close, hugging him tight. They had not known each other long and now she had a sinking feeling they never would. When she let him go, it seemed like it was for the last time.

"I'm staying till you make it across," she said.

"Deal."

He pulled the helmet down over his head. The suit pressurized itself and a light on Aidan's right hand turned green. He stepped into the airlock and hit a panel on the side. A force field ignited. Aidan waved at Rebecca. She held her hand up to return it.

It was time. Aidan turned toward the outer door. He kicked his feet against the floor as the magnetic locks engaged. He reached up with one hand and grabbed a metal loop that hung down from the ceiling. With the other hand, he tapped a panel and the airlock door opened.

He felt the rush of air as it escaped into outer space. When the roar subsided, he turned and looked at Rebecca one last time. Then he kicked his feet to the side, breaking the magnetic lock, and stepped to the edge of the *Chronos*. The *Singularity* floated below.

Aidan knelt down and grasped the sides of the ship. He engaged his heads-up display, and the computer calculated the proper trajectory that would lead to the *Singularity's* airlock. What it couldn't tell him was how hard to push off. Aidan took a deep breath, said a silent prayer, and threw himself into the emptiness beyond.

The airlock door slid closed, and Rebecca ran to the portal, slamming her hand against the console and lowering the force field. She peered out the small window in the airlock door, watching as Aidan disappeared below, toward the *Singularity*.

"Let him make it," she murmured. "Let him make it."

Aidan felt his stomach drop into his feet as he leaped from the platform. He floated toward the ship below, moving at no great speed, but nevertheless feeling completely out of control. The image on the heads-up display flashed red as his trajectory carried him away from the *Singularity's* airlock, a target that seemed far too small for his exceedingly imprecise effort.

He tapped the console on his arm, firing the compressed air thrusters strapped to his back, moving him left and right, up and down. The HUD flashed green for but a second before turning red again; he was overcompensating. The ship seemed to race toward him. He was too high, then too low. Then the HUD turned green again, and he let the thrusters go full blast. The only problem was he had no breaks. He slammed into the floor of the airlock, rolling with a painful thud into the doorway.

He almost floated away again, but at the last moment, he kicked his right foot hard against the door, locking him in place. Floating there upside down—one foot planted firmly on the outside of the ship, his heart beating and his breath racing like he'd just sprinted a hundred meters—he had the almost overwhelming desire to cry out in celebration.

He pulled himself up, locking himself in place, and finally standing on both feet. He looked up at the *Chronos*, and even though he couldn't see her, he knew Rebecca was watching. He held up his hand and waved and then turned back to the airlock doorway.

Unlike Aidan, Rebecca *had* cried out when he smashed into the *Singularity*. She didn't start breathing again until he stood up and waved. She watched him attach a computer to the console terminal of the ship. The door slid open. He turned around and looked back at her one last time and then disappeared inside. A moment later, grappling hooks fired from the *Singularity*, clanking against the *Chronos* and locking on. Rebecca smiled. One objective down. Now it was her turn. Gravely was waiting on her.

"I won't ask you if you're ready," she said, "mostly because I know I'm not."

The two women climbed into their stasis chambers. There would be no countdown this time. Instead, they would slip away into a normal, if chemically induced, sleep. The only way they would know that Aidan had begun his mission would be when the dreams started. And the only way they would know he had succeeded would be when those same dreams ended.

Otherwise, the experience was how she remembered it. The glass domes closed above them, the sweet-smelling breeze surrounded her. She didn't panic this time. Instead, she let the sleep take her. And then, Rebecca and Gravely floated away into an empty darkness, one far more pleasant than the dreams to come.

# CHAPTER
## 27

When Aidan stepped onto the *Singularity*, the first thing he noticed was the lights. Before, the ship had been bathed in darkness. Now the metal walls sparkled in the dawning glow. Aidan shivered. Somehow, this was worse.

Aidan jumped as the door slid open in one silent whoosh. Everything was too normal now, too ordered. And quiet. The lights were on, but the engines were still dead. He stepped into the hallway and shivered. At least in the darkness, it had not looked like the ship he remembered, the one from his dreams. Now he couldn't deny it, even if he wanted to. Every hallway he knew intimately, every curve, every turn. But there was one difference.

Shadows remained, even though the light shone down upon him brilliantly and completely. Upon those blank spaces, where the darkness seemed to reign over the light, Aidan wondered. Saw and heard things that no longer surprised him, even if they did still frighten him. He walked through those hallways, just as he had in his dreams. Except this time, he carried a rifle with him that he held at the ready, jammed against his right shoulder.

He took his time, creeping down the hallways, peeking around corners, knowing that Cyrus could appear at any moment.

He stopped when he heard a rumble, felt a deep vibration rolling through the infrastructure of the ship, shaking him to his core. He started running then, knowing that he had no more time—Cyrus had fixed the engines.

As he ran, he stopped worrying about the whispers, about what walked around him. He didn't feel the burning in his legs or his lungs. He simply made a decision to go for the bridge. If Cyrus were waiting for him in one of these hallways, so be it. He would deal with that when it happened. But it was an empty fear. Aidan didn't see Cyrus, not until the great doors of the bridge sprang open.

He stood bent over the front of the control console, his back turned toward the door. Aidan raised his weapon and pointed it at Cyrus. As his finger tightened around the trigger, as he considered shooting him right then and right there, Cyrus raised his head.

"Hello, Aidan," he said without turning. "Would you shoot an old friend?"

Aidan hadn't noticed at first, his attention had been so fixated on Cyrus, but this room was darker than others. The shadows seemed thicker here, much of the floor covered by inky puddles of night made manifest.

"You're not Cyrus," Aidan said, "and we're not friends. Now, step away from the console or I will put you down."

Cyrus turned and faced Aidan, the black, empty holes where his eyes should have been appraising him. Cyrus chuckled and Aidan shivered.

"Come now, Aidan. Don't you want to save the ship? Don't you want to redeem yourself? For what you did?"

A tremor ran down Aidan's spine, and the gun started to shake in his hands. He gripped it tighter, steadying himself lest his voice shake as well.

"It's just a ship, Cyrus. If I did what you say I did, then nothing will make up for that. It's the people that died that matter. Not the ship."

The grin on Cyrus's face melted away and when he spoke, his voice had changed.

"So be it," he said.

He outstretched his arms, bringing his hands together in a great clap. As he did, pure darkness erupted from the sides of the bridge, slamming together in front of where Cyrus stood, cloaking him behind it. The shadow wall from the dreams had appeared and now stood between Cyrus and Aidan, as thick and impenetrable as ever.

Aidan looked from side to side, but there was no opening. He raised his gun to his shoulder and fired. The bullets slammed into the wall like pebbles on the surface of a lake, little waves rippling along it, up to the ceiling and down to the floor, left and right to the walls, finally reverberating back on themselves. They did not rip the fabric of that black curtain and Aidan knew that the bullets, wherever they may have gone, did not pass through to Cyrus. There was only one way to stop him. He would have to pass through the wall, one more time.

"I guess he's forgotten," Aidan thought to himself, lowering the rifle, "I've already done this once."

Aidan took two long, leaping strides and threw himself into the wall. He passed through in only a moment. He did not find himself in some other world, did not travel to a mirror world were darkness held sway over the light. Apparently, he was free of that now. Instead, he slammed bodily into Cyrus, shocking them both.

Cyrus flipped over the back of the console, landing with a thud on the ground below. Aidan could have finished him then. But when he looked up, he froze. The room had changed. Or at least, what he could see in it had. No longer were there splashes of opaque shadow standing out against the light. The blinders from Aidan's eyes were gone, revealing the truth of what moved in the night.

The shadows were there, glaring down at Aidan, smoke-like tendrils rising from their thin, tall bodies. They roared at him, cursed him in words he could not understand. He felt their hatred, saw the rage in their empty eyes. They were the things he had feared all these years.

Aidan pulled himself to his feet and tapped the computer console. As the warp control appeared, the creatures around him howled. Aidan ignored them and engaged the warp bubble. The last thing he did before Cyrus grabbed him from behind and threw him to the ground was fire the warp engines.

* * *

Rebecca awoke on a cobblestone street that was more like a corridor—one that ran through a ruined town that she had only seen once before, in a dream not unlike this one. The only thing different was that Gravely was there with her.

"Thank God," Rebecca said. "I don't know that I could have done this by myself." Then confusion. "Wait, what are you doing here?"

Gravely glanced at the broken streets, the dead leaves blowing across the shattered cobblestones and wondered the same thing.

"I don't know," she said. "But I think they want to scare us now, and that's never how my dream worked. They were always trying to coax me into something, to lull me into a sense of false comfort. Maybe they figured their strategy should change."

"Yeah," Rebecca said, "Maybe."

The wind blew down the narrow streets, roaring through the tight corridor of the stores, just as it had the first time Rebecca had been there. Rebecca, dressed in her loose white dress and no shoes, shivered.

"I guess the cold and discomfort add to the fear," Gravely said, thankful that she was wearing the same uniform as when she fell asleep. "Just try and remember. It's not real. It's all in your head. All of it."

Rebecca rubbed her arms and nodded and both women wondered who Gravely was really trying to convince.

"Maybe we should just stay here," Rebecca said, looking over her shoulder at the wall of darkness behind her. "Stay here and wait for Aidan to finish."

"Maybe. I assume whatever is up there is not something we want to see."

"No. No, not at all."

Gravely peered at the diner to their left, split in half by the great black wall. She might have failed to notice the change were it not for the sign that read "Bottomless Coffee," the price of which was hidden behind the wall. She watched as the last 'e' on coffee was swallowed up, followed by the other one and then the first f.

"Waiting's not an option," she said. Gravely grabbed Rebecca's arm and pointed at the advance of the shadow wall. "Let's go."

The two women started walking, the barrier moving slowly but inexorably down the street behind them.

"What's next?" Gravely asked. "I hate surprises." And that was the truth, if only half so. Any conversation was better than the silence, the one broken only by the cool breeze and the whispered words that floated upon it, all of which sounded to Gravely like the calling of her name.

Rebecca answered, "The girl."

Like clockwork, the *ting ting* of a ringing bell met their ears. The girl rode by on her pink bike with the white streamers, pulled to the middle of the street and looked back. "Hurry up, silly!" she said, "You're gonna miss the festival!"

"The festival?" Gravely asked as the girl peddled away. For the first time, Rebecca noticed she cast no shadow.

"I don't know," she said. "I didn't quite make it there last time."

They followed her, passing broken-down storefronts and the collapsed stoops of abandoned apartment buildings.

"Do you recognize this place?" Gravely asked. "Have you ever been here before? Or did they create it themselves?"

"Fiddler's Green, or the image of it," answered Rebecca. She whispered, as if they might be listening. As if they didn't already know. "The Exclusionary Zone. I spent some time there, when I was finishing my doctorate. They make us all go, so we always know what can happen if we aren't careful. If things go wrong."

Gravely couldn't help but laugh. "I've gotta say, seems as though we didn't learn our lesson, did we?"

"No, I guess not. Anyway," Rebecca continued as a half-broken bottle skittered across the ground, "I could never get this place out of my mind. Everything just abandoned. It gave me nightmares for a really long time. They never went away."

"That explains it then."

They continued on, up the curving path, Gravely beginning to wonder if the road would ever end. Then she noticed something, a scent carried on the breeze.

"Do you smell that?"

"Yeah," Rebecca said as they turned the corner and emerged in the great open courtyard in which sat the abandoned fairgrounds. "It's a fire. A big one, it seems."

"I think you're right." Columns of black smoke came into view, rising in the distance beyond the amusement park. The little girl sat on her bike in front of the gates, grinning back at them. She giggled before climbing aboard the bicycle and disappearing into the park.

As the two women passed through the gates, Rebecca heard the click of a turnstile that was no longer there, and the hum of carnival music filtered down from the abandoned bandstand. Gravely followed Rebecca and she could almost see the lights glowing up the stretch of the abandoned arcade. They came to the carousel, dead leaves and painted, screaming horses. Rebecca stopped and watched it as it turned, the hint of the calliope in her ears.

"Come on," Gravely said, unnerved by the way Rebecca stood and stared at the ancient, creeping carousel. "I think the fires are just up here."

Gravely's voice broke Rebecca from her trance. She breathed deep and the smell of burning wood stung her nostrils. There was something else there too, a scent she couldn't quite place. Something almost sweet, almost enticing. Almost. Something was off. Something important.

The two women continued on, leaving the wooden menagerie behind. Then they came to the end of the fairgrounds, and the square opened up again into a great plaza.

"Oh my God," Gravely whispered, the taste of bile rising in her. Rebecca said nothing. It was all she could do not to scream.

* * *

As Aidan's left shoulder smashed into the ground, he wished that he had just shot Cyrus when he had the chance. Now his rifle went bouncing away from him, sliding to the feet of one of the shadow creatures. Aidan was just thankful the thing either was unable to use the gun or didn't know how. It scowled at him, a guttural roar pouring forth from the blank space where its mouth should be.

It struck Aidan then. Not a change, but the absence thereof. He was alive and awake and the ship was in warp. He looked around at the demons that surrounded him, gibbering profane and unknown curses. At Cyrus, who stood glaring at him, ready to strike him down, perhaps even in the next moment.

But Aidan was not mad, at least no more so than he had been when he engaged the drive. He looked back at the oily wall behind him, as it pulsated and flowed, dividing the darkness and the light, and suddenly it made sense.

What lay behind the wall was the thing that those on the *Hypnos* had seen when they faced the warp jump with their eyes wide open. But Aidan had walked that path before, the day he decided to pass through the wall for the first time. For him, there were no more mysteries to reveal, no more veils to be sundered. He had seen the truth and it could not harm him any longer.

"Why have you come?" the thing that had been Cyrus asked.

Aidan pushed himself up into a sitting position, and as he did, he felt a shooting pain in his arm. It confirmed what he had feared when he landed and heard a cracking sound; something was broken.

"I came," he said, looking longingly at the rifle sitting fifteen feet from him, a space that might as well have been eternal, "to stop you."

Cyrus grinned widely and as he did, the dried blood and puss on his face cracked like the grease paint on some demon clown from Aidan's childhood nightmares.

"You came to stop us?" he said in a thousand voices, the words twisting and circling around each other, echoing in and out upon themselves. "As if any of your kind ever could."

Aidan had told himself he would show no fear. He had promised himself that, in fact, he would feel none, either. Now, as he lay crippled, the swelling in his arm growing commensurate with the pain, he began to wonder, for the first time really, just what these things were.

"Do you know," it asked, "how long we have waited? How long we have dwelt in darkness? Beneath night-black suns? Cursed and forgotten? Banished from the world of the light to wait for our coming redemption? Do you know?"

Aidan said nothing. He was more concerned with where Cyrus was standing than what he was saying. For his part, Cyrus did not wait for an answer.

"For unnumbered millennia, for untold ages of time and epochs of man. We, who once ruled over all things, who once walked among the stars. Condemned to foul and lonely places, to the black spaces between space, to whisper in the darkness. Only to see the glory of the morning through your imperfect eyes, escaping only clothed in your flesh. No, Aidan Connor, you never would have stopped us, not when we are so very close to our return."

Aidan held his breath as Cyrus took a step toward him. But it was only a step. Cyrus turned and looked down at the warp console. It would have to be enough, Aidan thought.

"Now," Cyrus thundered, "we shall leave this place of darkness and retake those worlds you and your kind infest. Your time has ended."

It was the only second he needed. Aidan tapped his arm once, bringing up the program he had added just before he'd come aboard the *Singularity*. Cyrus turned back to Aidan, prepared to deliver the final blow, but then, somewhere beyond the shadow wall, the door to the bridge slid open.

Aidan grinned and a look of confusion spread across Cyrus's face. There was a sound of metal joints clicking into place. Before Cyrus knew what hit him, a robotic monster emerged from the middle of the shadow wall. It flew through the air, eight metal legs spread wide.

As the Charlotte dug the ends of those legs into Cyrus's face, Aidan dove for the rifle the sat at the feet of one of the shadows. His left hand slid through it and Aidan nearly lost his focus as a crushing cold embraced him. When he jerked his hand free, he almost expected to see it frozen solid. The shadow bent down low over Aidan's face and wailed like some ancient Irish banshee.

Aidan was distracted only for a moment. He grabbed up the rifle, jamming it against his shoulder despite the pain of his broken arm, just as Cyrus ripped the mechanical spider from his face, throwing it across the room. The Charlotte landed on its back, flipping itself over and prepared for another attack. There was no need. Aidan took aim and fired. The bullet vanished into the black cavity of Cyrus's left eye. He stood for a moment longer. Then, in a final fall, Cyrus's body collapsed into a great lump.

The shadows roared, their voices forming a discordant chorus of awful howls. Aidan ignored them, pulling himself up to his knees.

Using his rifle as a cane, Aidan stood, nearly crumpling against the console as he did. He limped to the warp controls, sliding back the manual cover. He hoped they had been in warp long enough to fry the computers and cause a manual reset. The plan was simple—he would disengage the warp while at the same time triggering an overload. If he was lucky, he'd be back on the *Chronos* long before the core breached and lost containment.

Aidan realized something, though, as his hand hovered over the panel that would send the warp drive into collapse. It hit him quickly but not with the force he would have expected. Maybe because he had known the truth for a while, even if he didn't want to remember it.

Standing there, surrounded by the wailing, living embodiment of shadow, he realized that he had done this before. That he had triggered a core collapse one other time in his life, that day on the *Vespa*, when, in his own madness, he had sent his friends to their deaths. Aidan shook his head quickly from side to side to clear his mind. He would face that later, when this job was done. But before he could act, before he could end the warp jump and destroy the *Singularity*, a familiar voice met his ears.

"Are you sure you want to do that?"

\* \* \*

Gravely and Rebecca stood with the fairgrounds behind them and stared up at a vision from the darkest of dreams. That they were in the ruined city of Fiddler's Green or an image of it, at least, could not be denied. But the ritual they witnessed was not of this world; its rites were never howled beneath the gibbous moon of Earth. Or so they hoped.

The shadows had come to that place and they no longer hid. They had massed in a full semi-circle around one who appeared to be their leader. Their bodies were bent and crooked and they wore black cloaks that seemed to meld with their beings. All except the one.

His cloak was red, like an abomination of something holy, the high priest of a heathen religion. He held the girl, smoky tendrils acting as hands. "Rebecca!" she shouted. Rebecca took a step forward, but Gravely grabbed her arm. Rebecca looked at her, eyes pleading. Gravely shook her head.

The demon's blood-red cloak fluttered in the breeze. It seemed to shimmer in the light of the fires that burned behind them. Great, wooden pyres that towered in the air. They burned, but were not consumed. What made them so hideous, however, was the people. The men, women and children lashed to their beams, from the very bottom to the top where they were crowned with a wreath of a dozen people, all tied together.

They burned too, and Rebecca watched as their skin seemed to melt, to turn red and then black in the heat. The fire did not quench their pain with death, though their screams put the lie to any notion that they did not feel its heat. As Rebecca saw the image of Cyrus in one of their faces, she turned away and vomited, though nothing came from her stomach but bile.

"You have come, Rebecca," the one in the crimson cloak said, "as we always knew you would. We have waited for you for so very long. You have known this was your destiny, and although there were those who tried to prevent it, fate cannot be deterred. How fortunate that you join us now on this auspicious day."

"How does he know my name?" Rebecca whispered to Gravely.

"Because he knows everything about you. Somehow they know everything about us all."

"And you, Caroline Gravely," the beast continued, "you who are so pure of heart. How we have longed to reunite you with your ancestors, your family. To give you back what you lost. Yet you resisted us. Until now, on the day of this festival, when we shall gain our release from the bonds that have enslaved us these many, many years.

"Join us now freely. This is not a request, but you do have a choice. Join us or burn forever in the funeral pyres of your race, as those of your kind who came before you and rejected our most generous offer."

"We know your lies!" Gravely shouted. "Our eyes are open. Those aren't the ones who resisted," she said, pointing at the writhing figures behind, pointing at Cyrus. "They're the ones you tricked into passing through the wall."

Though the creature's face was more like roiling fog than skin, Rebecca knew that he was smiling. The game was over and she had a feeling he didn't need them anyway.

"So be it," he said. "Then you will die, as this one dies. No great purpose, no life beyond, no eternal rest. Only the shade."

The tendrils of one hand move to the girl's face, pulling back her head. At the same time, the other hand transformed itself into a glowing, black blade.

"No!" Rebecca screamed, and had Gravely not held her around the waist, she would have run to the child's aid.

"She's one of them," Gravely whispered, "she's one of them."

But even Gravely doubted when the girl let out a high-pitched scream of terror and desperation. Cut short from a wail to a gurgling cough as the demon ran the black blade across her throat. Blood the color of his robe spewed forth, covering her blue jumper and turning her white sneakers a sickening pink. The hand released her and her body collapsed to the dirty, broken cobblestones below.

"You let him kill her," Rebecca sobbed, "you let her die."

"Honey, she's not real. Look."

At that moment, the girl's body began to quiver. Her arms moved again, pushing herself up and onto her knees. She looked up at Rebecca and Gravely, blood still oozing from the wound. The image of the girl melted away, and in its place, among discarded clothes and melted flesh, stood one of the shadows.

The damned wailed anew and the scent of burning flesh surrounded the two women. Gravely didn't know where to go, but they could not stay here. The shadows advanced, steadily gaining on them, even if they looked as though they might fall at any moment.

"Let's go, Rebecca. Let's go now!"

The two women turned and ran, back into the amusement park. As they passed, it was as if some switch was flipped and power returned to circuits that had been dead for untold decades. The lights came on. The rides began to turn. It was no longer the ghost of music that they heard, but full-throated reality. The neon sign on the House of Ghouls beckoned them. The prerecorded voices of carnies begged them to try their luck just one time. Then they came to the carousel.

It no longer spun lazily, but at full gallop, the sound of the calliope blaring maniacally. Crazed horses and their wild, painted faces now thundered around the circle. Mad elephants and demon lions joined them. Up and down, up and down. Dancing and jumping. Rabid beasts, locked forever in a circle, chasing each other's tails.

Rebecca and Gravely could go no further. The shadow wall had come to the park. It climbed now, all the way to the stars that had peeked through the coming dusk. Stars set in a mad sky unlike any

Gravely or Rebecca had ever seen. They turned back, seeking shelter, but they found none. The shadows surrounded them on one side. The black wall of sleep crept toward the carousel on the other.

The red-cloaked creature advanced. Rebecca stared up into his cold, vacant eyes, determined that if she were to die, she would not let him see the fear in her heart, even though she had a feeling he knew all of her thoughts. The beast held out his arm, forming the same gleaming obsidian blade as before. He raised it in the air, prepared to make the killing blow. Gravely took Rebecca's hand and squeezed it. A scream split the silence.

* * *

Aidan knew the voice. He would have recognized it anywhere. Perhaps if it had been any other he would have simply ignored it, cutting the warp, overriding the engine and running. Instead, he turned. The shadow wall was gone as were the wraiths that had lurked there only seconds before. There was only one other staring down its nose at Aidan. He would have been disconcerted if he were experiencing for the first time that feeling of looking into a mirror. After so many visits, he was almost used to it.

"So you've come again. One last chance. One last try to stop me. Your last gambit. Right? After all, we've killed the captain. We've killed Jack. And now Cyrus. So I guess all you've got left is me."

"It's not that," he said, circling Aidan slowly, staring at him all the while. "It's not that at all. I know what you're going to do. You're going to destroy the ship, aren't you? But before you do, I want you to consider what I've told you."

"If this is all in my head, if this ship's not real, then what difference does it make to you?"

"Because," he said, "I am you. I'm all the sanity you've got left. If you blow up this ship, it will mean you turned your back on me. It means you will have decided that I'm the enemy. You will have chosen the irrational. You will have picked a fantasy over reality.

"There's no coming back from that, Aidan. If by some miracle they do find you—if they do find us—out here in the nothing, it won't make any difference. You'll never wake up, not really. You'll just keep on living this fantasy. Until real life ends and this dream goes with it.

Think about that. Think about the dreams. How real they were. So real you couldn't tell the difference. And the only way you knew they were an illusion is because you knew it going in. This seems real to you, too? Doesn't it? So what?"

"I'm done with your lies," Aidan said. "I'm done with all of this."

"Lies? Has everything I told you been a lie? Can you say that for sure? What about the *Vespa*, Aidan? You know I spoke the truth about that, even when you lied to yourself. You know what really happened on that ship. You destroyed it. Out of fear and uncertainty, you killed the other men. Your shipmates, your captain, your friends. And now, you are faced with a choice.

"You can embrace that same fear, that same uncertainty and you can destroy this ship. Or, you can do what you failed to do before. You can be brave. You can do your duty. Think how close you are. The engine's repaired. The warp drive's intact. All you have to do is move the ship away from the black hole. And then you can take the *Chronos* and the *Singularity* home. I promise you, the world won't end. Not for you especially. For you, it will be a whole new beginning."

Aidan glanced down at the control panel, at the schematic of the warp bubble that covered two ships. The *Singularity* and the *Chronos*, connected by the thin cables of the grappling hooks. He looked up at the other Aidan, the one who appeared so much younger than he. The one from before he made his fateful choice, his most terrible decision. The weakest moment of his life. He saw Lieutenant Felix in his mind's eye.

"A time will come where you will be called upon," he had said. "In your hands will rest the fate of many. Perhaps then you can redeem your lost soul."

That time was now, he thought. This time, he would be strong.

"So," he said, "if I destroy the ship, I'll go crazy. Is that right?"

"You're already crazy," said the other, "but this is your opportunity to get it all back."

"Well, then I guess I better not destroy the ship, huh?"

Relief passed over the other's face. "No, Aidan. No you shouldn't. You've made the right decision."

Aidan grinned. "I know."

It happened so fast that Aidan's doppelgänger, the shadow that wore his face, didn't even realize it till it was too late. Then the mask slipped; he lost his composure, howling "No!" in a voice that was not Aidan's.

Aidan reached down and, with a flick of his finger across the computer screen, set the warp drive for maximum. Another half second and Aidan had changed the destination as well, adjusted it from the minuscule distance he had intended to travel—just enough to fry the *Chronos's* circuits and cause a hard reboot—to someplace much different. Somewhere near, but impossibly far at the same time.

To the heart of the black hole, the one he had almost forgotten about till the shadow mentioned it. The one that was oh-so-close. Then, as the beast howled impotently, Aidan Connor punched the engine.

* * *

The demon in red raised his blade high above his head. Gravely took Rebecca's hand and squeezed it. Then, in that instant, something changed. Above the wail of the calliope, slashing through the canned carnival music, there was a screech that could only come from one of the shadows, and yet sounded entirely unlike any they had heard before. A scream that cut across time and space.

"No!"

The shadows had no faces, not really. But if they had, Rebecca imagined the waves of emotion that would be passing over them. Shock, confusion, maybe even fear. In the end nothing but pure, helpless, hatred.

Rebecca and Gravely felt themselves lifted from that place. Bodily, as if the hands of God Himself snatched them up. They sailed through the air, leaving the dead town and the ghost carnival and the horrible fires behind. Up, up, up they went, until they were so high that even the shadow wall could not reach them. And as they flew upwards, terror washed away and joy replaced it. They awoke back on the *Chronos*, away from the darkness and shadow.

# CHAPTER 28

They weren't sure exactly what had happened until they stood on the bridge, staring out into empty space. The computers had shut down, just as Aidan had expected. And, as he had predicted, upon reboot Jack's lockdown was erased and forgotten.

The soft female voice—for it was always female—asking for Captain Gravely's command had returned. She had backed the ship slowly away from the black hole, the one that the computer suggested had been frighteningly close, the event horizon perhaps only an hour away. As she did, they watched on the screens above them the video of what had happened.

The ships had been together, floating there in the warp bubble, moving almost imperceptibly lest the gravitational pull of the black hole tear them apart. Then, in one sudden movement, the direction of the *Singularity* changed.

Immediately after, Gravely and Rebecca watched as the warp engines fired in their full glory. What had happened next was precisely what Aidan had expected. The sudden change of direction and dramatic increase in speed had snapped the thin lines of the grappling hooks, shattering the warp bubble that surrounded the *Chronos*, leaving it behind as the *Singularity* vanished.

Like most people, Rebecca and Gravely had witnessed a warp signature before. Seen the telltale distortions in space, like the contrails of airplanes of old. But this one was different. For as the *Singularity* and the space around it moved into the distance, there came a point where they simply vanished. As if they and everything with them had passed behind a great cloak, one perhaps even thicker and all concealing than the shadow walls.

"So he's gone then," Rebecca said.

Even though Gravely knew it was not a question, she felt compelled to answer. "Yes," she said. "Yes, I think he's gone. He was a good man."

"He was the best."

For a long time, they simply stood staring out into that infinite darkness. Looking into the abyss. There was much left to say, but not on this subject. Not when there was already so much left unsaid. But there were decisions to be made. Hard ones at that.

"Seems to me," Gravely said finally, "that we have a choice to make."

"I know."

"Well, what do you think?"

After everything she had seen, there was little that Dr. Rebecca Kensington could say with certainty anymore, but there was one thing. She would never have the dreams again, which meant she would never go to warp again. It was a decision one might make with ease on Earth, where the limitations thereof were relatively insignificant. Here, in the farthest reaches of space, she knew exactly what it meant.

"We can't do the sleep again. We don't know if we would make it out alive even if we did. And we can't stay awake during warp either."

"No," Gravely said, "not after everything we know."

"They would come for us then and all that he did," she said, pointing out toward empty space, "the sacrifice he made, would be for nothing."

Gravely nodded. "The engines on this ship can take us to 90% of light speed. We're two light years from Anubis, four from Riley."

"Then Riley it is, I guess," Rebecca said, "I hear they don't like strangers on Anubis."

"No," said Gravely, "and from what I know of that place, I wouldn't want to go anyway."

An hour later, Gravely and Rebecca returned to the stasis chamber. Rebecca had sent a hyperspace communiqué that contained the entirety of their story. All that they had discovered. What had happened to the *Singularity*. That Jack had gone crazy and how they had discovered the truth about the warp.

"Do you think they'll believe it?"

"I don't think it will matter," said Rebecca. "Whether they believe it or not, they need the warp jumps. They'll just cover it up, until they figure out something else. But at least they'll know. I think we can be certain of one thing—what we tried with the *Singularity* will never be tried again."

So there they were, lying down once more. This time, to sleep for years. Four and change, at least as they counted time. To everyone else, it would be more like eighty. The women had not discussed it, for they shared at least one common bond. Everyone they knew, everyone they loved, was dead. They had nothing to lose and nothing to leave behind. Rebecca only hoped that in eighty years the colony of Riley would still exist.

She buried deep her greatest fear. That they would arrive to find that the shadows had returned. That they had finally found a way to cross over, the way that she knew Aidan had denied them when he took the *Singularity* back into the black hole.

No, she forgot that fear. As she laid her head on the pillow and the capsule closed around her, as the air filled with fragrant scents and she felt herself drift away, just as she had on the porch in Pensacola all those years before, she knew. Whatever dreams might come, they would be happy. Somewhere within them, he would be waiting.

# EPILOGUE

Aidan Connor awoke to darkness. When his vision cleared and his mind with it, he realized he was staring up at the black void above the glass dome of the *Singularity*. The computers hummed gently, the glow of their screens the only light in the room. He pulled himself to his feet, running his finger along the console screen.

"Command, Aidan Connor?" it asked. Aidan felt a shiver ripple across his skin. He had expected this, somehow, even as he prayed he was wrong.

"Location?" he asked.

The answer didn't come instantly, even though he knew it should. He bowed his head, interrupting the calculations before they came to their inevitable conclusion.

"Computer," he said, "locate the nearest gravity wells. Maximum zoom."

The screen changed, the image stretching and expanding. He had seen the image before, but never in waking life. The thousands of black holes that appeared confirmed it, the hand that fate had dealt him. How long had he slept, drifting in that infinite shade, that impossible vista where time and space meant nothing? Millions, billions of years perhaps, until everything—people, stars, nebulae, galaxies—had died. Leaving nothing but the darkness, nothing but the empty, cold, void. Only shadows. Aidan slumped down in a chair and waited.

They came for him. Creeping in the unlit corners of the ship. Rising up from where they had spent untold thousands of years. Seeking their revenge. They formed one entity, one wave of black death and hatred. In an instant, they would crash down on him with all the fury of a billion years of hate.

But then it happened, as Aidan stared up into the great void above. Something appeared. Something that had not been in the dream of before. A single, solitary, point of light.

It grew in strength and luminosity, until it formed a powerful beam that burst forth into the bridge and struck the shadows, splitting the wave asunder. They fled before the might of that morning glory, wailing as they fell back to their hiding places, to the dark holes from whence they came.

Aidan rose and gazed at that aurora, watched as it massed and expanded itself into a mighty wall of brilliance that shone from one side of the bridge to the next. Aidan stood before this great, radiant wall, felt its warmth on his face, and heard the call that came from beyond. Not in some alien tongue, but in words he understood.

THE END.

# THE DEVIL OF ECHO LAKE

### DOUGLAS WYNNE

Billy Moon would have given his life for rock 'n' roll stardom, but the Devil doesn't come that cheap.

Goth rock idol Billy Moon has it all: money, fame, and a different girl in every city. But he also has a secret, one that goes all the way back to the night he almost took his own life. The night Trevor Rail, a shadowy record producer with a flair for the dark and esoteric, agreed to make him a star. . . for a price.

Now Billy has come to Echo Lake Studios to create the record that will make him a legend. A dark masterpiece like only Trevor Rail can fashion. But the woods of Echo Lake have a dark past, a past that might explain the mysterious happenings in the haunted church that serves as Rail's main studio. As the pressure mounts on Billy to fulfill Rail's vision, it becomes clear that not everyone will survive the project.

It's time the Devil of Echo Lake had his due, and someone will have to pay.

"The work is as tidy as the town and as pat as a familiar horror film." -

Publishers Weekly

Diagnosed with a brain tumor, Geoffrey returns to his hometown for a reunion of the Jokers Club (his childhood gang) with the hopes of unearthing the imagination he held in his youth.

Unfortunately Geoffrey's tumor quickly worsens, bringing on blackouts and hallucinations where he encounters the spectral figure of a court jester who had been his muse as a child. The jester inspires Geoffrey's work on his manuscript, fueling his writing at a ferocious pace. The dead and the living co-exist in the pages of Geoffrey's story, in a town where time seems to be frozen in a past that still haunts the present.

Will the pounding growth in Geoffrey's head be held at bay long enough for him to discover who is targeting his friends, or will the pages in his unfinished novel rewrite history?

"This is a novel full of visceral, intense moments. It will keep you holding on until the brilliant end." - Richard Godwin, author of *Mr. Glamour* and *Apostle Rising*.

An evil force is at work at the Hospital where Nathan is recovering from injuries he received at the hands of his Mom's abusive ex-boyfriend. Demonic looking men with pale faces and glowing eyes lurk in the shadows. Someone is harvesting skin and organs from living donors against their will.

In his dreams, Nathan can see these demons in their true form -- evil creatures who feed on the fear and hatred they create in their victims. Nathan's only ally is the Doctor who cares for him. Bound together by their common legacy, they alone seem to share the ability to see the demons for what they truly are.

Together they must find a way to stop these creatures before they, and their loved ones, become the next victims.

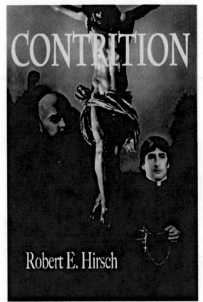

In a tiny community on the Mississippi Gulf Coast, Brother Placidus finds little Amanda LeFleur sacrificed below a crucifix, in the attic of The Brothers of the Holy Cross. It is not the first body he's found there.

Assigned to the investigation is detective Peter Toche whose last case was that of a murdered child, a child that has been haunting his dreams, forcing him to face his worst fears and the evil that has targeted his town.

As additional victims are discovered, Tristan St. Germain, a mysterious man who was rescued by a parish priest from the waters near his home, may hold the key to the safety of all mankind.

Little Amanda was only the beginning...

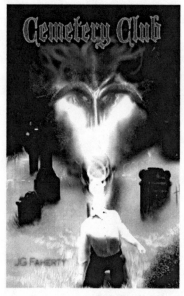

"Faherty's latest novel provides readers with as much fun in a graveyard as the law will allow." -Hank Schwaeble, Bram Stoker Award-winning author of DAMNABLE and DIABOLICAL.

Rocky Point is a small town with a violent history - mass graves, illegal medical experiments and brutal murders dating back centuries. Of course, when Cory, Marisol, John and Todd form the Cemetery Club, they know none of this. They've found the coolest place to party after school - an old crypt. But then things start to go bad. People get killed and the Cemetery Club knows the cause: malevolent creatures that turn people into zombies. When no one believes them, they descend into the infested tunnels below the town and somehow manage to stop the cannibalistic deaths.

It's a race against time to find the true source of evil infesting Rocky Point, as the Cemetery Club ventures into the cryptic maze, to face their demons in a final showdown.